Rekindling Trust

Rekindling Trust

Widow's Might
Book Two

Sandra Ardoin

Corner Room Books

SANDRA ARDOIN

ISBN: 978-1-7334630-4-1 (Print); 978-1-7334630-5-8 (E-book)
Library of Congress Control Number: 2021905117
Cover design by Evelyne Labelle, Carpe Librum Book Design.
Edited by Lynne Tagawa

REKINDLING TRUST

Get *Unwrapping Hope*, the novella that kicked off the Widow's Might series, as my thank you when you sign up to receive updates and special offers at www.sandraardoin.com/newsletter.
If you prefer to purchase the novella, you'll find it at
https://books2read.com/u/47EWlg

There is no fear in love; but perfect love casteth out fear: because
fear hath torment.
He that feareth is not made perfect in love.
1 John 4:18

Chapter One

"Don't do this, Barrett. It isn't what you want. We both know it."

Barrett Seaton wrestled with the temptation to obey his brother's plea and turn the carriage around. Wynn was right. He didn't want to do this. But Barrett's wants had nothing to do with the matter.

The carriage horse stomped the ground, impatient for Barrett to tell him which direction to go—left, right, straight. Etched on the wooden sign planted at the crossroads an arrow pointed east to Riverport, two miles down the road. A few feet beyond it, another sign read *Oakcrest Sanitarium*. Its arrow pointed west.

Wynn shifted on the seat and turned away from Barrett. Away from the possibility of infecting him? "You should have left me where you found me."

Never.

"If you won't listen, then take me and leave. Go back to your practice in La Porte. You didn't need to uproot your life to hold my hand in my last days."

His last days? The words bruised like a fist to the gut.

Barrett tried to ease both of their minds with a grin, but Wynn's back remained turned. "Who else would I uproot it for but a brother?"

His hold on the leather reins tightened. He stared east, at the road that ran straight as a ribbon, bordered by cornfields on each side. The stalks rose a good six feet high, with creamy silks sprouting from the ends of the ears like blonde tresses falling over a woman's shoulders. It would be a good season for farmers. But what did the season hold for the brothers?

"We Seatons stick together, remember?" They were supposed to, anyway.

Wynn hunched down on the seat. "You're bound to see her...and *him*."

"Danby no longer sits on the bench and Edythe..." Edy forgot about Barrett long ago. She'd pledged her life to Lamar Westin in front of God, her father, and the best of Riverport society. He laughed, a hollow sound that grated on his ears. "She's probably content and herding a dozen children by now. I'm sure I will see her at some time, but for me, she's in the past."

"Keep telling yourself that, little brother. Maybe one day you'll believe it." Wynn turned his head away and coughed into his handkerchief, a wracking, phlegm-filled cough that shook his body and the body of the carriage. He tucked the cloth in the pocket of the suit coat Barrett had bought him, but not quickly enough to hide the patch of blood.

Judge Danby had done this to Wynn. If Barrett believed in retribution—an eye for an eye—he would soon have the opportunity to exact that retribution on Edy's father. If he were a vengeful man.

But he was not Danby. Unlike the judge, Barrett believed in justice, not in destroying the lives of innocent people simply because he could.

What he failed to understand was why God allowed the innocent to be persecuted and the righteous to suffer under the actions of tyrants.

Barrett clicked his tongue at the carriage horse and guided the animal to the west—toward Wynn's new home. Would his brother ever leave Oakcrest alive?

Too soon, the sanitarium came into view, set in the midst of a well-landscaped yard and surrounded by three acres. It was a cheery-looking place if not for the reason for its existence.

Barrett stopped the carriage and set the brake. The facility was known as the best of its kind within hundreds of miles, the only sanitarium Barrett considered for his brother. How ironic that the location brought them back to an area that held unwelcome memories for both men.

The door opened and Dr. Ellis walked out, followed by a woman in a blue-striped dress, a crisp white apron, and a starched cap.

"Good afternoon, Mr. Seaton." Smiling at Wynn, the doctor said, "You must be Mr. Flannigan. We've been expecting you." He stepped forward and helped Wynn from the carriage.

Barrett had argued with his brother, disliking deception, but Wynn had insisted he be placed in the sanitarium under the fictitious name of Ned Flannigan. He'd said he preferred no one know of his return. As far as the staff was concerned, Barrett's relationship to the new patient was that of attorney and friend.

Dr. Ellis handed Wynn off to the nurse. "Nurse Hammond will get you settled in your room, and I'll be in to examine you shortly."

Wynn glanced over his shoulder at Barrett, the wide eyes and childlike anxiety on his older brother's face prompting a flashback to the day Wynn went to prison.

Barrett held his gaze and dipped his chin in a silent reassurance that everything would be fine. He'd lied to his brother twelve years ago, and he lied to him today. There would be no "fine" for Wynn Seaton. Not in the long run. Even if he regained his strength and left the sanitarium, tuberculosis was incurable.

"Please come in, Mr. Seaton." Dr. Ellis started for the door. "There are papers to be signed."

And a payment to make.

As a private hospital, Oakcrest Sanitarium was about to cost Barrett a tidy sum each month—a sum he'd made through his work as an attorney and multiplied through conservative and well-placed investments during the time of a crippled stock market. Still, it was a far cry from the Danby fortune.

As long as he could afford it, Barrett would not begrudge his brother a comfortable place to live. And if he pleaded long and hard enough with God, that would be for years in the future. In the meantime, he would see that his brother received the best care his money could buy.

Barrett followed the doctor into the large two-story Georgian building. A number of ferns and other potted greenery as well as colorful carpets and cheerful paintings bolstered the home-like appearance inside. Only the smell of soap and disinfectant and the faint coughs sounding from upstairs spoiled the building's homey appeal.

Nevertheless, this place was quite an improvement over the stark, cold atmosphere of the shack where he'd found Wynn. Even now, Barrett didn't understand how his brother could bear his suffering with such courage and composure.

He ambled to a painting on the wall of a sailboat on a placid lake, its sails billowing as it cut through the water on a sunny day. Just the kind of scene to cheer a soul who likely would never experience such freedom again. "I'm impressed by the surroundings, Dr. Ellis."

"I'm glad it meets with your approval. We receive our main support from the generous donations of caring citizens throughout the state of Indiana." The doctor joined him at the painting. "We have Riverport's Judge Hayden Danby to thank for this particular piece."

Barrett's stomach tumbled. Wynn would be treated in a facility supported by the man who put him in prison.

Since when did you begin to dabble in practical jokes, God?

8

HIGH-PITCHED GIGGLES drew Edythe Westin's attention away from the pillowcase she'd spent the past hour embroidering in the drawing room. She smiled at the laughter, a rarity in her father's house, and set aside the handwork to step into the expansive foyer. She must see for herself what provoked the carefree glee in her children.

More merry giggles nearly overcame the clack of her heels on the marble. When her mind registered the scene before her, she froze, skeptical of her vision. Her eight-year-old son was sliding backward down the curved banister of the staircase. He flew off the end and hit the hard floor on his derriere.

"Timothy!" She reached out to help him to his feet, his face still lit with the exuberance of his action—one he knew full well was forbidden by both her and her father.

If only she could see that pleasure on a regular basis, though. To see it on the face of Andrew, her oldest, would bring her particular joy.

She bent over to brush imaginary dust from Timothy's short pants. "What were you thinking?"

"But it was fun, Mother."

"Fun?" Secretly, she wished she'd had the courage to do such a thing at his age, but she couldn't tell him that. "You know what your grandfather would say if he caught you."

The mild scolding had barely left Edythe's mouth when she heard a shriek. Unable to stop, Sarah Jane plowed into Edythe's side, nearly knocking her to the floor. At least Timothy's twin hadn't landed in a heap next to her brother.

"Sarah Jane."

Wide-eyed, her daughter threw her leg over the banister and dismounted as if she'd ridden the wooden rail like a horse. "Sorry, Mother."

"Where did you two get the idea to do something so dangerous?" The twins gazed upward at the top of the stairs where the oldest of her brood stared down at her. She might have known.

"Andrew dared us," said Timothy.

Of course he did. What was she to do with the eleven-year-old who persisted in rebelling against and resenting everything his elders said and did? Not that she completely blamed him. Still, she couldn't allow him to endanger his siblings. "That was foolishness, Andrew. Dares are foolish."

"Sometimes, they take courage, Ma."

Ma? He often goaded her with the term when his grandfather wasn't around to correct him. If her father heard him call her Ma, he'd receive a harsh lecture.

When they were younger, her children called her Mama, but the judge had put a stop to the informal title when her family moved in with him after her husband's death. He insisted they call her "Mother." She hated it.

"Please watch your tone, Andrew." Even as she said the words, Edythe heard no bite in them.

At times like this, she especially missed Lamar's presence in all of their lives. Her husband had a way with their children that kept them in line without provoking anger and resentment, especially from Andrew. On her own, she was a failure at discipline.

Her rebellious son swung a leg over the banister and pushed off, skating backwards down the slick wood as his siblings had done.

"What in the name of Sam Hill is going on here?"

Edythe and her two youngest children jumped at the familiar bellow. Andrew lost his balance and tumbled sideways onto the stairs, rolling down the last three steps to the marble. He lay still, eyes shut.

With her heart in her throat, Edythe dropped to her knees beside him. "Andrew, are you hurt?" Had he broken anything?

Knocked himself unconscious? She smoothed his hair—straight and a rich dark brown, like hers. She cupped the side of his face, and his breath warmed her hand. "Talk to me, son. Can you get up?"

"Andrew got the wind knocked out of him. Serves him right for acting like a buffoon."

At his grandfather's insult, Andrew's eyes opened and his mouth stretched into a tight line.

Edythe prayed her son wouldn't say something they would all regret. She tugged his arm. "Can you stand up?"

"Leave him alone. He's fine and doesn't need your mollycoddling. Do you?" Her father stared at Andrew, beating him with a silent challenge.

Her son struggled to his feet and ducked his head. "No, sir." His voice held more respect than it had when he'd spoken to her. Because the judge demanded respect.

"You're fortunate you didn't break something, boy."

If it hadn't been for her father's roar, Edythe had no doubt Andrew would have landed safely. He was a nimble and athletic child, tall for his age, yet too young for his attitude.

Her father's glare shifted to each child in turn, with a near imperceptible softening when it rested on Sarah Jane. They all stood in meek anticipation. "Go to your rooms and do not let me see or hear you before you are called for supper." When the children hesitated, probably too cowed to move, he pointed up the stairs and yelled, "Now!"

All three broke into a run, unable to escape fast enough. Their little feet stomped up the stairway.

Upstairs, doors slammed, leaving Edythe and her father alone in a space where long-ago images intruded and sounds escalated, as loud as a memory.

The slamming of a door.

Dirt clinging to tears that rushed down the soft cheeks of childhood, becoming streaks of mud on lips, a gritty taste on the tongue.

Mustiness reaching out with choking hands.

Drowning in darkness—so black and ever so lonely.

A throat raw from screams echoing underground.

Then light—glorious daylight and fresh air. The face of her father staring down from a place of safety, anger disfiguring his features.

The incident belonged to and had remained in her early childhood...until her father used it to coerce her into doing his will. Barely eighteen and brokenhearted, she hadn't had the backbone to fight the threat to send her to her grandfather. She'd only known she'd agree to almost anything to keep from seeing that ancient fiend again.

Edythe drew in deep breaths until her heart stopped racing but clasped her hands in a tight hold. "The children meant no harm, Father."

He walked to the banister and ran a hand over the finish of the mahogany wood. "They could have scratched it."

"They didn't." She hoped.

He picked up a stack of envelopes from the hall table. "If you don't gain control over them, Edythe, they'll turn into a bunch of hooligans."

Like *he* controlled them? Like he'd always controlled her?

Is it so difficult to grant us one day of peace in this house, God?

As soon as the thought formed, she asked forgiveness for her disrespect. She had enough trouble with her earthly father's judgment. She didn't need more with the one who sat in judgment on her from His throne in heaven.

Edythe returned to the drawing room, unclipped the top from the phonograph case, and rotated the crank. She stood at the side of the instrument while it played, letting the soothing music on the cylinder wash over her and calm her until she could think.

Ages ago, prior to her marriage, Barrett Seaton had wheedled laughter from her on dark days. In his presence, she found the joy missing in her home and achieved a measure of self-confidence. Barrett gave her the freedom to be the best of herself. Though she never publicly disrespected her father, she'd gained the courage to defy him and meet with the teen boy with whom she'd fallen in love, whose persuasive personality was so different than hers.

In the end, though, he turned his back on her. He abandoned her in the same way her mother had done when she was a child.

Foolish as it seemed, she missed him. She missed both of them.

The music ended and Edythe walked out of the drawing room. Somehow, she must leave this house, for the good of her children and her sanity. But with no income other than that which her father allowed, how was she to support herself and them? Remarriage?

She'd been fortunate with Lamar. It didn't mean she'd be as fortunate with someone else. Was marrying another man she didn't love the right answer to removing her children from beneath the authority of her father?

Chapter Two

Edythe led the way into Ogilvie's Grocers. She held Sarah Jane's hand while Timothy and Andrew followed behind. Every few seconds, she glanced over her shoulder to be sure the boys were close and not lagging to wander off on their own. Perhaps she shouldn't have brought them with her this morning, but despite their bent for trouble at times, she enjoyed being with her children—all three of them.

If she had come here with only the twins, she wouldn't worry so much. Timothy was normally a good boy when not under the influence of his older brother. However, Andrew rarely let a moment go by if it presented an occasion to cause trouble.

She despised thinking of her child—her oldest baby—in that way. She detested thinking of herself as a failure when it came to motherhood. Unfortunately, she couldn't deny the fact that both were true. She'd heard it often enough from her father and those who complained about the turmoil Andrew caused.

Mark my words, Edythe, one day that boy will end up in prison.

Not if she could help it, even though she wouldn't put it past Judge Danby to volunteer to sentence him if given the opportunity. Fortunately for Andrew, his grandfather had retired from the bench.

Edythe never understood why her father held Andrew in such low esteem...his own grandson. It was an attitude that began the moment Andrew was born, long before the boy was capable of being a troublemaker. It wasn't right, and it wasn't fair. Then again, no one had ever accused her father of sprinkling fairness around like spring showers.

"Mother, don't forget to buy carrots for Shadow."

"I won't, Sarah Jane."

"If you do, I will remind you."

Yes, she would.

Edythe squeezed Sarah Jane's hand, her contented smile eclipsing her concerns. Nothing was more important to her daughter than that rabbit and the rest of her menagerie—a goose, a pregnant cat, two turtles, a hen, and a monstrous and intimidating dog. The latter wasn't satisfied until he'd spread an ample supply of saliva on everyone in sight.

That was this week. Who knew what they would feed next week. Apparently, word had spread through the animal community that those seeking refuge need only step onto Danby property where they would find themselves wrapped in the cocoon of a little girl's care.

"Good morning, Mrs. Westin." Mr. Ogilvie smiled at Edythe, Timothy, and Sarah Jane. The smile fell when it landed on Andrew.

Edythe couldn't blame him. Three months ago, he had caught her son shoving another boy near a stack of canned goods, toppling them over. The household ate beans and tomatoes from dented cans for months.

"Good morning, Mr. Ogilvie. I need paprika and three onions, please."

Sarah Jane tugged on her hand. "And carrots, Mother."

"And carrots, Mr. Ogilvie."

"Yes, ma'am."

He was in the midst of gathering her items when a shout erupted from outside the store. "Give it back, you scamp."

Edythe turned in a circle, taking a head count of her children. As expected, she was missing one. "Oh, Andrew," she muttered. She couldn't let that boy out of her sight without risking shouts and angry voices.

She let go of the twins and hurried out the door. A clerk had Andrew pinned to the brick wall with one hand. With the other he tried to tear off her son's cap, but Andrew held on to it with both hands, as if his life depended on keeping it on his head.

The livid clerk caught sight of Edythe. "The boy took two potatoes from the bin and hid them in his cap, Mrs. Westin."

Closing her eyes, she counted to three, then opened them. Andrew's nostrils flared and he lifted his chin. Something other than anger beamed from his brown eyes. Hope? Anticipation? She couldn't quite read it. "Did you take the potatoes, Andrew?" She'd asked a silly question. It was obvious he hadn't been born with a head so high his cap didn't reach his ears. "Give them back. Right now."

He stared at her. "They're rotten, anyway."

Mr. Ogilvie joined them. "Mrs. Westin, I value your business but must ask you to leave your children home from now on. They are a disruption to the shopping experience of my other customers."

Andrew narrowed his eyes to little more than slits. "My ma can do what she wants."

Edythe couldn't let her son speak to others that way. "That's enough out of you, young man. I'm sorry, Mr. Ogilvie. This won't happen again. Will it, Andrew?"

For a moment her son's eyes lit with something akin to respect. It lifted her spirit...until the light vanished and he spit on the sidewalk. "I figured you'd take somebody else's side over mine, just like at home."

Her inclination was to hide from the gathering crowd, but it occurred to her that he tested the depth of her resolve. If that were the case, she couldn't afford to fail. She straightened and stared him in the eyes. "Andrew Westin, you will apol—"

"You don't talk to your mother like that." Mr. Ogilvie stepped up to Andrew and ripped off the cap. Two small potatoes rolled off her son's head and hit the sidewalk with successive thuds.

At the grocer's interruption, the heat of an angry flush burned Edythe's face. She reached for her son. He slid from her grasp and marched down the sidewalk. "Come back here, young man."

He picked up his pace, heading in the opposite direction of her father's house. She lowered her arm and turned to the twins. "Let's go home, children."

"Mother, you didn't get the carrots."

"I'll have everything delivered to your home, Mrs. Westin." Mr. Ogilvie grinned at Sarah Jane. "Even the carrots."

"I'm terribly sorry, Mr. Ogilvie. Thank you." Edythe herded her youngest children down the sidewalk.

No doubt rumors regarding the incident would fly around town, sullying further her son's reputation and hers.

BARRETT CLENCHED HIS hands at his sides. It was all he could do to remain where he stood a couple of doors down from the grocer. The child was clearly guilty of both theft and disrespect. Barrett had choked the inclination to march up to the defiant boy and demand he apologize to his mother, then to the man from whom he stole.

Now that he'd seen Edythe for the first time since his return, the old protectiveness betrayed his alleged indifference. While he might no longer wish to acknowledge her on the street, he knew Edy well enough to know how severely her son's harsh words cut her.

On the other hand, he wanted to demand she take the young man in hand and not allow her son to run over her as thoroughly as her father used to do. Had she not learned anything in the years since Barrett last saw her? Did she continue to hide the passion and strength he knew, deep down, she possessed but feared exercising, or was this simply a bad day for her?

With her son's attitude, he would guess Edy's husband also held little sway with the boy.

Her choice to marry Lamar Westin all those years ago had caught Barrett by surprise. One day he thought her love was his, the next he'd found it belonged to someone else.

Why must she be more beautiful now than in his memories? Why wasn't she fat and haggard, instead of tall and lithe? She possessed a form that belied the birth of the children she now escorted in the opposite direction down the sidewalk.

Three children. Three children that were not his.

He turned away and walked into the barbershop, leaving behind thoughts of Edythe Westin—trying to, anyway. He had more than his share of issues to deal with, like setting up his practice and seeing that Wynn had everything he needed at the sanitarium.

But first, an overdue haircut.

Barrett took a seat in a chair along the wall to await his turn in the busy shop. With a subtle study of the men around him, he strove to identify anyone he remembered from his years growing up in Riverport.

Mr. Ferris, the barber, of course. A fixture in town since before Barrett was born, though he'd never given a Seaton male a haircut. That was done at home.

Was that Mr. Reinwald two seats down? If so, he'd aged greatly.

Maybe it had been a mistake to return to a place where its good citizens remembered the name of Seaton and the unjustified shame brought upon it. He may have erred in thinking he could establish a law firm here and attract clients.

He was Wynn's only remaining family—his support. Letting his brother die in the tumbledown shack he had found him in almost two months ago was out of the question.

Barrett glanced out the front windowpane at the busy street. The place had changed over the years. He almost hadn't recognized it when he first arrived. New businesses. New people. He'd never have imagined electricity, a department store, a brewery, or the number of other three- and four-story buildings up and down Commerce Street. The town boasted three bridges that spanned the river instead the one he'd crossed for the last time at eighteen. Maybe, with the influx of new residents, his practice would do well enough.

A middle-aged man with arms and legs as thick as tree limbs filled the doorway to the barbershop. His form darkened the room. "Did you folks see that spectacle down the street? Ol' Danby's grandkid got caught up in trouble again."

Ferris stopped in the midst of clipping an elderly man's hair, the scissors pointed in a dangerous angle toward the customer's head. "What'd he do this time?"

The man laughed. "Stole a couple of spuds from Ogilvie and stuffed 'em inside his cap."

The barber huffed. "If his ma don't get hold of him, that boy's gonna wind up behind bars one day."

"That's what Ogilvie's clerk said."

"I'm sure Mrs. Westin wishes that man of hers was still around. Westin seemed to keep some control over the young'uns."

Barrett absorbed every word. Lamar Westin was dead? Or had he up and left?

"I ain't sure Danby does the boy any good." The customer in the chair spun in the seat, oblivious of the scissors that nearly took out an eye. Barrett recognized the owner of the feed store. What was his name? He waited for the man to elaborate on his statement. "Ever since his wife skedaddled with that lawyer, the judge has been as hard as flint. I always felt sorry for his daughter. She was a sweet child. Still is far as I can see."

Ferris scanned his shop, his glance a tad nervous, as though he expected to find Danby sitting in one of his chairs. The judge's harsh ways stoked that anxiety in people. The barber's gaze landed on Barrett and narrowed a bit like he tried to place him but couldn't.

When it was his turn in the chair, Barrett dusted hair off it and settled in the seat. The smell of witch hazel lingered from the shave given to the previous customer.

The barber placed a towel around him. "Trim for you today?"

"Yes, please."

Ferris picked up the scissors and a comb. "New in town?"

"Yes."

"You look familiar. Gotta name?"

"Yes."

Before Barrett could say more, a man behind him snorted. "Maybe he doesn't speak English, Zeke. Probably all he knows are the words yes and please."

Ferris leaned close, smelling of coffee and tobacco. "You speak English?"

There was no dodging the truth, not if he wanted to practice law in Riverport. "Yes, I speak English. Yes, I want a trim only, and yes, I have a name, Mr. Ferris. It's Seaton."

"Seaton?" Proof of his name registered with the widening of the barber's eyes. "You the one that went to prison?"

"No, sir. I'm Barrett."

A gaze in the mirror showed him an older farmer laying down his newspaper. A moment later, he shuffled out the door.

Barrett had just provided the occupants of the shop fodder for several days of gossip while they regurgitated the events of the past. He anticipated quite a flapping of gums when it came to the story of Wynn's arrest and conviction, Barrett's claim that Danby's personal bias influenced his brother's trial, and Edy's ultimate choice.

How long before she learned he was back in town, and would it matter to her?

I'll write, Edy.

Not that his letters prevented her from marrying someone else within two months of his leaving.

Ferris clipped a few hairs from the top of Barrett's head. "Your brother still in prison?"

"No."

"You in town on a visit?"

"I'm opening an office here. I'm an attorney."

"You don't say." The barber wiped his sleeve over the area on the top of his bald head. "Guess you heard me mention that Mrs. Westin's a widow."

So *death* had taken Westin away.

Barrett strived to make sense of why hearing the barber's words shook him. He never rejoiced in anyone's demise, but something burgeoned inside him. With four words, emotions he'd cut out years ago rose to afflict him once more. *Mrs. Westin's a widow.*

"Were you around when that scene took place at Ogilvie's?"

Snickers tainted the air inside the barbershop, reminding Barrett of another visit to Riverport to learn that Edy had married Lamar Westin. He'd felt like the butt of a joke that day, too.

The men here could gossip all they wanted after Barrett left, but he'd not contribute to it. "All I really want is a haircut, Mr. Ferris."

The man sniffed. "Whatever you say, but I wouldn't go lookin' for no trouble if I was you. Best I recall, that didn't work out so good last time."

The trouble began with Edy's father. It ended with Wynn's prison sentence, Edy's faithlessness, and Barrett's regret.

Maybe Wynn was right in saying Barrett had made a mistake moving back here. Maybe he should return to La Porte.

No. He couldn't deny his brother the companionship of family, especially if these were Wynn's last days. If need be, he wouldn't deny himself the opportunity to say goodbye and, if God allowed, hold Wynn's hand as he took his last strained breath.

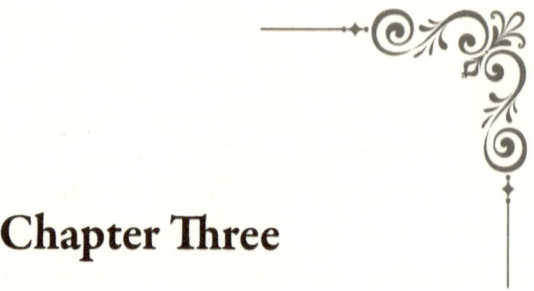

Chapter Three

Inhaling the scent of pot roast, her favorite dish, Edythe walked into the dining room and saw her children already sitting around the table. Normally, she must call them multiple times in order to lure them away from whatever activity entertained them.

Sarah Jane wore one of her best dresses. A large blue bow tamed her tawny hair and sat straight on her head for once. The boys wore Sunday suits, their hair combed, parted, and slick with oil.

"My, you all look lovely and handsome. What is the occasion?"

Her father sat at the head of the table, his attire no less formal than on any other day. "Are you being coy, Edythe?"

"Coy? No, sir. It looks like a special occasion, but I don't—"

"It's your birthday, Mother." Timothy nearly bounced in his seat.

Sarah Jane grinned. "We made you presents."

Her birthday? Edythe recalled the date. "Yes, it is my birthday. I'd forgotten."

Andrew sat slumped and quiet in his chair. For the most part, he'd behaved himself since the fiasco at the grocer's.

She took her seat at the table. "Do I smell roast?"

"Grandfather asked Mrs. Cameron to make it. She made a cake, too."

Pleased by his thoughtfulness, Edythe glanced toward the other end of the table. "Thank you, Father."

He cleared his throat. "That's enough chatter, Sarah Jane."

Their cook and housekeeper, Mrs. Cameron, must have heard

her name, because she carried in a platter and set it in front of the judge.

Edythe eyed the meat, potatoes, and onions. "It looks delicious, Mrs. Cameron."

"Thank you, ma'am."

On occasions when her father ate with friends or associates, Edythe took advantage of his absence to invade the kitchen and prepare a light supper for herself and the children. While not a superb cook, she enjoyed doing something she rarely had opportunity to do. It reminded her of what it was like to be the mistress of her own home.

At the end of the meal, the judge gave the children permission to leave the table and retrieve their gifts. The twins bounced from their seats and out of the room. Andrew followed behind them with sedate steps and a bored manner. In a few minutes they all returned with paper-wrapped packages tied with ribbon and set them on the table before her.

"Happy birthday, Mother." Sarah Jane kissed her cheek.

"Happy birthday, Mother." Timothy's wet kiss dampened the other cheek.

Andrew returned to his chair.

"Well, boy, what do you have to say?"

Her oldest glanced at Edythe and mumbled, "Happy birthday."

She fingered the paper on her daughter's gift. "Well, let me open these, shall I?" She pulled an end of the white ribbon bow and laid aside the paper. It took her a moment to understand what she was seeing. Once she did, her breath caught. "Did you do this by yourself?"

"Yes, ma'am. Well, Mrs. Cameron helped me find the box. Do you like it?"

"It's...It's lovely, Sarah Jane." Edythe held up the small, box-style frame for the others to see. Inside the girl had pasted an artistic collection of some of her favorite things in nature: a blue jay's feather, a maple leaf, a daisy from the flower garden. All in all, she'd squeezed about ten objects into an eight-inch by five-inch box. Objects that defined her daughter's interests and delighted her, which in turn delighted Edythe. "Thank you, darling."

"Open mine next." Timothy craned his neck to see over the table as she pulled the red ribbon from his package—another wooden box, this one with a lid.

Opening it, she pulled out a small windmill made of a folded sheet of paper attached to a thin stick with a tack. He had drawn a large shape on each "blade"—star, circle, square, diamond. "This is a lovely little toy. Thank you, Timothy."

"It's not a toy, Mother." Disappointment filled his voice.

"I'm sorry." She should have realized it held greater scientific purpose for him. Timothy's toys always became a means to an end. She studied the colorful contraption. Though she knew the answer, it would please her son to explain. "How does it work?"

"Blow on it." He leaned over the table and blew, but the gust of air wasn't strong enough to do more than flutter the ends of the paper. "See? Distance affects the amount of wind it receives and its ability to turn. Now, you try it."

Edythe blew on the paper and grinned as it spun. "So, the closer one is to the windmill, the easier it turns?"

"Yes, ma'am. But don't get too close. You can use it to study wind speed and direction. Did you see how the shapes blend the faster it turns?"

"That's a silly gift for a mother."

Timothy glared at his sister. "It is not, Sarah Jane."

"Is too."

"Enough." The judge's growl quieted the twins.

Edythe blew once again and considered the windmill with more intent, so much so, her eyes almost crossed. "That's very clever,

Timothy. You'll make a fine inventor."

A smile covered his face. "Like Thomas Edison."

"Better."

One more package rested on the table in front of Edythe—thin, flat, and bendable. She guessed it to be a sheet of drawing paper. Andrew was a fine artist, and she couldn't wait to see what he'd drawn for her. Sliding it closer, she untied the green ribbon and pushed aside the wrapping paper. The smile on her face wilted. She recognized their old home, barely. Rather than an artistic endeavor of quality, something she knew him to be capable of, this looked like something a five-year-old would draw.

When she looked at him, he sat with his shoulders slumped, eyes on the edge of the table in front of him.

"Let's see it." Her father motioned with his hand for her to hold it up.

Please, don't say anything.

Edythe held the drawing for him to see. He snorted. "Is that what you call an appropriate gift for your mother?"

Her lips sealed in the words she wanted to say, she should say. But she had never learned how to win an argument with the judge. "It's very nice, Andrew."

"Here is my gift." Her father pulled a small jeweler's box from inside his coat pocket and gave it to Sarah Jane to pass to her.

Edythe startled. When was the last time he had given her an actual gift rather than a handful of bills and the order to buy herself something worthy of a Danby? She took the box from her daughter and stared at it.

"Well? Aren't you going to open it?"

"Yes." She opened the lid. On a bed of red satin sat a ring of white gold. Her breath caught. She picked it up and examined the large ruby in the center, surrounded by tiny seed pearls. "It's beautiful."

"It was your mother's. I assume you've reached an age to wear it without losing it."

Edythe restrained a soft snort. She was twenty-nine...no, thirty today, and he only now believed her mature enough to be given her mother's ring?

Sarah Jane's eyes widened, revealing that her daughter did possess a bit of young lady hidden inside that tomboy personality.

"It's beautiful. I don't remember seeing it before." Then again, after Edythe's mother left, he had locked away everything she hadn't taken with her—including her daughter.

He stood up and tossed his napkin on his plate. "Your mother had excellent taste...in most things. Excuse me."

Once he left, Edythe smiled at her children. "Thank you. All of you. This has been a wonderful birthday celebration."

Later, in her bedroom, Edythe laid all her presents out on the bed. Her gaze locked onto the box with the ring, a valuable ring.

If only she could remember her mother wearing it. She remembered so little of the woman who abandoned her husband and daughter. A woman who ran off with another man and left behind her small child to be raised by someone who was not physically abusive, but whose thirst for control over her had much the same effect.

Edythe might not be so careless as to lose the ring, but what if she sold it? What if it brought enough money to move herself and her children into a place of their own?

The idea of selling it left a sour taste in her mouth. Besides, what would she do afterward? She'd need some type of work to continue living in freedom.

Carrying the box to her dresser, she dropped it in a drawer. She'd decide what to do with the ring another day.

FISHING POLE IN HAND and a creel hanging off his shoulder,

Barrett tromped through the grass and brush to the bank of the river. He and Wynn had fished from this spot dozens of times while growing up in Riverport. If he was going back in time by being here, he might as well go back to the location of some of his better memories.

He sat in the grass at the edge of the bank where it sloped into the river, ready for a lazy Sunday afternoon. Nearby, a fallen hickory tree, its skeletal branches dallying with the low water level of summer, created an ideal place for fish to gather.

Barrett prepared his hook and tossed the line into the water, close to the limbs but not so close as to risk getting it tangled. After half an hour of a few bites and one bass in the creel, he leaned back and tipped his slouch hat over his closed eyes, feeling more relaxed than since his arrival in town.

While the sun beat down on his body, his mind slipped back to days of coming to the river with his brother—whom he admired more than anyone other than his grandfather—and skimming stones across the surface. The two brothers talked of plans and dreams. Some came true for Barrett, like his wish to be an attorney. Wynn's desire to open a furniture store never had a chance to come to fruition.

Before he could stop it, Barrett's memories transformed into a full-blown scene of the first day he talked to Edy. He eyed the spot mere yards from where he now sat and let the past take over the present.

He saw himself as he approached the river, prepared to catch supper to take back to the farm. Edythe Danby sat on the riverbank, arms wrapped around the knees drawn to her chin. He'd known her from school but had paid little attention to her beyond noticing that glossy hair as dark as her eyes. Though one of the prettiest girls in school, she'd lacked the gregarious spirit of the females who normally attracted his notice. But that day, something forlorn in the way in which she stared across the river drew him toward her.

"Mind if I sit?"

Seemingly lost in thought, she jumped at his voice. She studied him for a few seconds, and then, like a queen permitting the advancement of a subject to her throne, gestured to the ground near her.

He left a couple of feet of grass between them. "I come here often to fish."

Those velvet eyes enlarged. "I'm sorry. I didn't mean to intrude on your spot."

"If anyone is intruding, it's me. You were here first." He prepared his line and tossed it in the water. "I don't remember seeing you outside of school."

"I don't get out much." She had the quietest voice.

"Why not?"

"I prefer being home." Edythe frowned, then her chin quivered. "That's a lie. I hate being at home."

With a little encouragement from him, words poured out of her. Words that made Barrett uncomfortable. Words that left him angry. Words that touched his heart—his soul—in a way he'd never experienced.

Over the next months, they met here whenever they could get away. He'd begun to call her Edy, giving her a nickname that didn't remind her of what her father called her. At first, he considered it a challenge to make Edy laugh and laughed himself when he succeeded.

Soon, the desire to be together drove them to meet almost daily. He wanted to call on her at her home, but she'd refused, afraid her father would object. Sometimes, he took her to the farm, but they avoided town where the judge had too many friends that would happily report that his daughter was seen in the company of a male—and a farm boy, at that.

Was that why he returned here today? To relive those days?

The swish of the grass behind him ended his reminiscences.

"Catch anything, mister?"

Barrett raised his head. Two boys stood by his side—Edy's boys, the troublemaker and the younger one. It was all he could do not to run them off. He wanted to. He should. Call it curiosity or a simple matter of being a glutton for punishment, he propped himself on his elbows. "Got one bass."

The boys dropped down on the grassy patch next to him and readied their fishing poles. Had they never been taught the etiquette of waiting to be asked to join someone?

"You come here a lot, mister?"

The younger one dug into a can of dirt and pulled out a worm. "I don't think he does, Andy. I haven't seen him."

"It's been several years."

"Years? How come?" The little one frowned. "Don't you like fishing?"

"I like it, but I just moved back to town." Barrett sat up and added a worm to his own hook.

"I'm Andy Westin. This is my brother, Timmy. What's your name?"

If he hadn't already, their grandfather would discover Barrett's return to town soon enough. Unlike Wynn, he'd never intended to keep his presence a secret. But knowing the judge's attitude and his temper, it might be best for the boys that they not mention him by name. "You can call me B. J." A number of people he'd dealt with in his business referred to him by his initials, because that was how the sign on his previous office door read.

"Well, Mr. B. J., this time of year the river's low around here. But we still catch bass, some carp, and blue gill."

"Sounds like you two are experienced fishermen."

"Andy says our papa brought us fishing." The boy hung his head.

"I don't remember it."

"You weren't even six when he died, so of course, you don't remember." Andy's expression turned wistful. "But I do."

Already knowing the man was dead, Barrett made up his mind not to ask about Edy's husband.

"Anyway, it's up to me to teach Timmy how to fish."

"You don't have an uncle or..." Barrett couldn't help it. He dug for clues with the same determination that Timmy dug in the can for worms.

"Nah. We live with our grandfather and he wouldn't recognize a fish unless it was gutted and cooked in butter."

Although the comment was comical, the angry tone kept Barrett from laughing. He was getting quite a picture of the Danby household. Over a decade had passed, and not much had changed.

"He stole our house."

"Stole your house?"

"Andy, if he stole the house, he would be in jail."

The warning from the younger boy made no impression on the older one. "He did. He stole it and Ma did nothing about it."

The words were too similar to the boy's indictment against Edy the day he was caught stealing the potatoes. Often, Barrett had been called upon to defend adults with the same bitter attitude. Some committed crimes as retribution against others. Some as a way to make themselves feel powerful. It was unusual for him to see such defiance in one so young.

If he continued in his present direction, Barrett feared the boy trod a dangerous path—a path that led to ruin. Edy might have betrayed their relationship—their future—years ago, but that didn't mean he'd rejoice to see her son end up like Wynn.

"It wasn't Mother's fault." Timmy pushed his brother with little result.

Andy pushed back, knocking the younger boy to the ground.

Fishing poles fell, and the two brothers began wrestling, rolling on the ground and grunting.

"That's enough, boys."

Andy sat up and yanked Timmy up with him.

In a softer voice, Barrett said, "Brothers shouldn't fight, and children should respect their parents, even if they don't agree with all they do."

Andy stiffened, staring across the river. He slapped Timmy's arm and hopped to his feet. "Let's go."

Timmy frowned. "What's the matter?"

"Nothing. I said we gotta go."

The boys gathered their fishing poles and creel and trudged back through the grass. Every few seconds, Andy peered over his shoulder.

Barrett's gaze skimmed the area across the river. Two boys, one who looked to be thirteen or so and the other nearer Andy's age, stood on the bank, watching. Once Andy and Timmy disappeared from view, the boys moved on, vanishing among the trees.

What about seeing those boys made Edy's son so jumpy?

Chapter Four

Sanctuary.

The word best described Verbenia Jensen's home. A quiet, peace-instilling sanctuary from the turmoil that often defined Edythe's life.

Even with a parlor full of ladies talking at the same time—a constant clamor—she sank back in the upholstered armchair and took in the scene with a contented smile. These seven women had become her closest friends over the last couple of years.

Edythe looked forward to these Sunday afternoon Widow's Might meetings. Women from various walks of life accepted her without expectation, without demand, and without criticism. It was exhilarating and uplifting.

"Ladies, shall we discuss our next endeavor?" Verbenia stood in front of the fireplace, her back as straight and expression as firm as a schoolmarm. The older widow had taken Edythe and her young friends—fellow widows—under her wing to support their struggles with spiritual guidance and her own experiences. "Would anyone like to suggest a project that is dear to your heart?"

Ruby Kelly raised her hand. "I've prayed about this already."

Claire Kingsley turned to the woman. "And?"

Only moments ago, Claire had announced that she would marry the architect with whom she worked and leave their group. Phoebe Crain recently left them when she became engaged to her beau, Spence Newland, and they replaced her with Louisa Gruhn, a sweet young woman with a four-year-old daughter. Both Claire and Phoebe planned October weddings.

Edythe didn't begrudge any of the women in the room an opportunity for happiness with another man, though she saw herself as a Widow's Might member for life.

Ruby said, "I don't believe we've done anything lately to provide some respite for the patients at the Oakcrest Sanitarium. Perhaps there's something they need to ease their suffering."

"I will take part in whatever is decided, but don't ask me to go to that place." Mavis Lipp's husband had succumbed to consumption five years ago. Edythe didn't blame her for her decision.

Louisa, still feeling her way in the group, ventured a question. "What did you have in mind, Ruby?"

"I'm not sure." Ruby glanced around the room. "Has anyone a different idea?"

Edythe normally remained silent, happy to go along with whatever the other ladies chose to do. Still, a suggestion came to her that refused to be suppressed. "My father considers Dr. Ellis a friend and has supported the sanitarium over the years. Not long ago, he mentioned that the patients often lack interesting things to keep them busy and their minds off their illnesses. They could use some forms of entertainment. What if we collected used books from the community and provided the residents with a small library?" The more she'd talked, the faster the words poured out. Now, she shut her mouth, satisfied to revert to silence once more.

The others stared, lips parted. Evidently, she participated verbally even less than she'd imagined.

"I think that's a splendid idea, Edythe." Verbenia winked at her. "What do the rest of you think?"

Slowly, they each recovered from their surprise and voiced their agreement.

"Then it's settled." Verbenia turned to her, and every hair on

Edythe's neck rose to attention, wary of the glow on the woman's face—the glow of victory. "Why don't you take charge of this one, dear, since you're familiar with the place and, I presume, the staff?"

"I..." Edythe found her tongue tied, her thinking also in knots. *Hiding behind a refusal is weakness.*

"I'll visit Oakcrest tomorrow and talk to Dr. Ellis about it."

"Good. Now, our refreshments await, ladies. Please help yourselves." As Edythe rose to follow the others, Verbenia stepped in front of her. "How is Andrew?"

"Andrew?"

"Yes, I understand there was some trouble at Ogilvie's last week. I don't mean to interfere, and I'm no gossip, but if you ever need an ear to listen, I'm here."

"Thank you, Verbenia." Based on the birthday gift from her son, Edythe's family was anything but fine, and she was tempted to seek out this wise woman's counsel. But not today. "I'll keep your offer in mind."

EDYTHE REINED IN HER horse, Jester, near the entrance to the Oakcrest Sanitarium, stopping her two-wheeled gig behind a larger carriage. The main wing of the large white building resembled a Southern plantation house more than a hospital to treat persistent illnesses—mostly consumption, or what doctors called tuberculosis.

Her father's sister had perished from the disease over two decades ago, which was one reason he dedicated his charitable dollars to Oakcrest. She marveled at the thought that he once cared for someone enough to honor her memory with his money.

These places based their treatments on healthy diets and fresh air. It wasn't the first time she had entered the sanitarium, but each time it left her both hopeful for the patients who occupied the rooms and saddened by their plight.

Inside, she caught herself before wrinkling her nose at the strong scent of disinfectants. Dr. Ellis once told her he took pride in the spotlessness of the sanitarium and had established a strict schedule of scrubbing every corner, as dust was a prime contributor to the spread of the disease. With that cleanliness in mind, she wasn't afraid of contracting tuberculosis through a simple visit.

"May I help you?"

She turned to see the matron standing beside her, a woman of authority and control, as intimidating as her father. "Good afternoon, Matron McGill. I'm Edythe Westin."

"Yes, I'm sorry. I didn't recognize you at first, Mrs. Westin. How are you?"

"Fine, thank you." Her fingers curled into a tight ball around the handle of her purse. "May I speak with Dr. Ellis?"

"He's with a patient at the moment. If you'd like, I'll take you to his office where you'll be comfortable waiting."

Being her father's daughter did have its advantages at times.

Edythe followed the woman, the sound of their footsteps echoing down the spotless hallway. The matron stopped in front of a closed door, fingered the keys hanging from her chatelaine, and slid one into the lock.

Three additional doors on each side lined the hallway, some open, some closed. Edythe assumed they were patient rooms, though she'd never ventured beyond the doctor's office.

A tall, well-built man backed out of a room near the end of the hall. Judging by his suit and the hat in his hand, he wasn't a patient. At his sudden deep laughter, Edythe held her breath. It couldn't be.

He turned in her direction, and she ducked into the doctor's office. With her heart about to jump out of her chest, she eased the door shut and pressed her back against it, his image prominent in her mind.

His hair was the reddish-brown of a ripe acorn, the same color as the neatly-trimmed beard that did little to disguise his facial features. If she were right in her identification, the last time she'd seen him, he'd been on the cusp of manhood. Now, he was a full-grown man.

"If you'll have a seat, Mrs. Westin, I'll let Dr. Ellis know you're here."

After the matron left, Edythe waited until she heard a firm, masculine stride pass the office. She opened the door and peeked into the hall, glimpsing his retreating form before he disappeared around a corner. The straight shoulders were broader than she remembered and his gait more controlled. Even so, she'd seen Barrett Seaton. She was certain of it.

What brought him back to Riverport, and why the Oakcrest Sanitarium? She peered in the other direction and down the hall to the room where she'd first seen him. Who had he visited?

The safest thing was to wait in the office for the doctor, discuss the reason for her visit, and leave. What did it matter who Barrett had come to see or why he'd returned to Riverport?

But she had to know.

She crept down the hallway, looking over her shoulder several times. Once she reached the room, she drew in a deep breath and knocked on the door.

"You back already, Barrett? You know you don't need to knock."

The faint voice tickled her memory but the identity of the man inside the room evaded her. What would she say to him? *Hello, I recognized Barrett Seaton and wanted to see who made him laugh?*

"Who's there?"

Edythe pushed on the door and stepped across the threshold. Her gaze landed on a man seated in a chair by the open window. She exhaled his name. "Wynn."

His eyes widened, then his chin dropped. "Hello, Edy."

Wynn Seaton had aged to the point he looked more like Barrett's father than his brother. His clothes hung on him, and his shoulders

36

sagged. A wry smile tilted his lips. "The ol' consumption thinks it can beat me down."

"I'm sorry." She moved farther into the room but kept a discreet distance. "Is there anything I can do for you, Wynn?"

His brow shot higher, and he no longer looked at her, but at something behind her.

"You have no business here, Mrs. Westin."

Too late, she recalled Wynn's words. He'd thought she was Barrett. He had expected his brother to return.

Inch by torturous inch, Edythe turned. Barrett's gaze latched onto hers, a gaze that once exhibited a love for her—or so she'd thought. Now, that gaze could freeze a campfire.

FIRST HER BOYS. NOW Edy. Was there no end to the way God planned to play with Barrett's emotions?

With stiff, sluggish movements, she'd rotated and faced him. Her complexion appeared ashen when compared to the well-coiffed hair that framed it. The paleness of her skin accentuated eyes as dark and sparkling as jet beads. Those eyes dipped to focus on the floor tiles.

Her slumped bearing brought to his mind the day her father caught them in one another's company. Given the man's nature, he'd assumed the worst. Her body had trembled throughout his harangue, and Barrett felt helpless to protect her.

He was no longer helpless, nor was he obligated to provide her protection.

"I...I wasn't aware you were back in town, Barrett."

He tried to wipe the scowl from his face but failed with the reminder of all the Danbys had done to the Seatons. "Understandable. I sent you no calling card."

Watch your tone, Barrett.

But he couldn't allow her reticence and vulnerability to pull him under, to charm him again.

He'd imagined speaking with Edy face-to-face numerous times since arriving in Riverport. Each time, he saw himself as reflecting a calm and indifferent manner—not friendly but not antagonistic.

What he hadn't imagined was this tight ball sitting in his stomach, the damp palms, and a rush of tenderness he hadn't experienced in years. Not even seeing her last week in front of the grocer's had fully enlightened him as to how beautifully she had matured into a woman—a graceful and elegant woman. Up close he could see that her eyes retained the richness of strong coffee. Her hair still shone with a dark softness similar to a mink's coat. And that face...as smooth and innocent as a babe's.

He'd once considered himself fortunate that such a lovely girl from a wealthy family even spoke to him, much less agreed to spend time with him. Now, he wanted her gone. He wanted this lure urging him toward her gone.

Barrett walked into the room and stopped when she took a step back. "How did you know about Wynn?"

"I saw you standing outside the door a few minutes ago."

"So you thought you'd satisfy your curiosity by bursting in here?"

She backed another step. Maybe he should regret his sharp tone, but he figured he was entitled to it. When a woman claimed to love you one day and up and married another man the next... Well, he was entitled.

"She hardly burst in, Barrett. She knocked, and I invited her."

Wynn remained in the chair, looking worn and old, a reminder to Barrett of the judge's vengeance.

"Why?" From the corner of his eye, Barrett noticed Edythe's gaze bounce between them, as though she watched a game of lawn tennis.

"I thought you'd come back, though I couldn't understand why you knocked." Wynn eyed Edythe. "Maybe this is a good thing. You figured you'd see her at some point. Her being here gives you two a chance to talk...get things settled."

He wasn't ready to settle anything, especially when this melting rock inside told him he might fail to stand his ground.

She made the first move with the appearance of a wobbling smile. "Dr. Ellis is expecting me."

The doctor? Barrett studied her. She appeared healthy, but...

He bit his tongue to keep from asking if she was ill, yet the idea that she suffered from the same disease as Wynn finished the work of softening that rock into a ball of moldable clay.

He sidestepped to let her pass. "Mrs. Westin." She turned, and he lowered his voice so it wouldn't travel down the hallway. "You asked Wynn if there was something you could do."

She waited.

"You can forget you saw him. He's here under the name of Ned Flannigan and doesn't want the good people of Riverport to know he's returned."

She glanced at Wynn and back to Barrett. After a simple nod of agreement, she slipped out the door.

Wynn struggled to rise from the chair. "I understand she hurt you, Barrett. I hurt you. Why is it you can forgive me but not Edy?"

"You did nothing to require my forgiveness." He helped his brother to the bed. "It's the other way around. If I hadn't stolen away to see her that night, I could have provided you with an alibi."

Wynn's chin plunged to his chest. "And you think the judge would have believed you?"

Probably not, but that wasn't the point. The point was that Edythe Danby had beguiled him. Because of it, he went back on his promise to be with his brother that night, setting Wynn up to fall into Danby's trap. To be accused of robbing the drugstore of over fifty dollars and injuring the druggist.

No, Wynn had done nothing wrong. Barrett should have been

the one imprisoned for the betrayal of his brother.

Chapter Five

Edythe didn't remember the drive home. She barely recalled Dr. Ellis agreeing to allow the Widow's Might women to donate books and establish a small library in the facility. By the time she walked out of the building, the carriage parked in front of hers had gone.

Now, she stood in the tiny stable at the back of her father's property, mindlessly grooming Jester's sweat-soaked, dappled coat. Short gray hairs clung to the cotton fabric of her plum-colored dress, but the mindless action of brushing the animal as he stood calm and drowsy in his stall soothed her. The gelding was one of the few possessions of Lamar's she had insisted they keep. Perhaps she had passed on an affection for animals to her daughter.

For the first time, it occurred to her that her father had acquiesced to one of her requests...and over a horse. What would he do if she actually stood up to him in other matters?

Outside the building, a chicken squawked and a dog barked. Edythe walked to the door. Sarah Jane scooped up the chicken as it ran past. She scolded Mr. Peters, the giant dog who probably owed his pedigree to just about every identifiable breed. Once the dog obeyed and sat like a gentleman, Sarah Jane wrapped the canine in a hug. The hen she'd named Harriet squawked her panic at being shoved so near Mr. Peters' mouth.

A few yards away, Timothy knelt on the ground, bent over his latest experiment, whatever he called it. As long as it didn't involve fire or gunpowder, she gave him the freedom to stretch his mind. He had inherited his father's best traits—intelligence and persistence. Who knew where they might lead him one day.

And what about Andrew? Brave and outspoken since a toddler, he didn't take after either of his parents. Although, there was a time when he'd adored both of them. How he missed his father.

Edythe had not loved Lamar in the way a wife should love her husband, in the way he had loved her. Somehow, though, they had formed a satisfactory marriage based on friendship and respect. Many couples coexisted on much less.

Lamar had been a good man, though somewhat inadequate in his dealings with her father...a failing she had no business finding fault with. Overall, they'd had a congenial but short life together, and unlike her mother, she would never have traded her children for a moment with Barrett Seaton.

Edy. No one had called her by that name since she was eighteen, and only the Seaton brothers had used it. Hearing it again brought back memories of both the best and worst times of her life. It didn't slide past her that only Wynn had used it today. Barrett couldn't get past "Mrs. Westin."

While her heart went out to Wynn in his illness, she wished he had chosen somewhere else for his treatment, somewhere far from requiring her to be ever on the lookout for Barrett. How would she walk through town without looking over her shoulder, expecting to see him at every turn?

How would she calm her racing heart whenever his image entered her mind?

Why should it race when he'd proved he didn't love her? When he, like her mother, had abandoned her? When he'd treated her with contempt today? What right had he to feel contempt toward her when he'd left her? When he'd broken his promise to write. Not one letter arrived after he left Riverport. Not one.

The more she thought of the way he had spoken to her today, the more her anger simmered.

Oh...horsefeathers! Forget the man.

She looked around the yard but saw no sign of Andrew. "Sarah Jane, where is your brother?"

The girl pointed to Timothy.

"I mean Andrew. Where is he?"

"I don't know, Mother."

"Timothy, have you seen Andrew?"

"No, ma'am."

Where had that child gone this time? His habit of sneaking off generally meant trouble.

"Here I am." Andrew walked around the corner of the stable in one piece and, for once, without an angry adult chasing after him. He coughed several times and appeared pale.

"You aren't coming down with something?" Edythe reached out and felt his forehead. Cool. He coughed again. She sniffed and wrinkled her nose, the source of his cough all too clear. "Have you been smoking?"

Andrew pulled away. "What does it matter?"

"It matters. You are a child. Children shouldn't smoke."

"I'm half grown."

She crossed her arms, already shaken from her confrontation with Barrett. Dealing with Andrew wiped away any effort she might have made toward tranquility since returning home. "Half is not whole."

Her father was right about one thing. Her lack of control over her children, especially this one, portended heartache for everyone. If she didn't rein in his behavior while he was still young, how would she when he outgrew her?

"Go to your bedroom and stay there, young man. I'll send Mrs. Cameron up later with your supper."

He glared at her.

"You had better move before I grab a switch from the nearest tree."

His eyebrows arched. "You wouldn't."

Could she really punish her child in that way? At this moment, yes. "Don't test me, son." She pointed to the house. "I've had enough of your shenanigans, and they will stop. Do you hear me?"

He stared at her. His eyes narrowed into a display of bewilderment more than hostility. At the same time, his lips winked as though he fought a smile.

"Go *now*."

He stuffed his hands in the pockets of his dirty trousers and ambled to the back door of the house, seemingly unruffled by the order.

It worked. Edythe's hands shook, and she almost dropped Jester's brush. Andrew obeyed her.

BARRETT TOSSED HIS line into the shallow water and let the earthworm wriggle on the hook, disturbing the school of minnows nearby. Like last week, he leaned back against the sloped bank, ready to pretend nothing in the world affected him. Ready to pretend speaking with Edy hadn't shaken him.

His pragmatic side assured him Monday wasn't the last time their paths would cross, so the sooner he took those encounters in stride, the better for his peace of mind.

After a week of hotel living, he'd purchased a house. Even if the worst happened—if Wynn passed on—and Barrett decided to leave town again, it was a better investment than paying hotel charges indefinitely.

With his bank account, he could afford a larger residence, but what difference did it make? Nothing compelled him to impress people, especially, certain people. And its location a block from the downtown district made it ideal to house his office.

Barrett frowned at the fishing pole. If he didn't get back to business, that bank account wouldn't afford him a cup of coffee at the cheapest restaurant, and he'd be surviving on what he caught in the Wabash River.

A tug on his line set him upright again.

"You got one!"

Barrett peered over his shoulder. Andy Westin. Would he never get away from the family?

"Reel him in." The boy dropped his pole, grabbed Barrett's net, and bounced to the water's edge to scoop up the bass writhing on the hook, half-in and half-out of the river. "Come on, I got the net."

Cranking the reel handle, Barrett raised the fish and Andy scooped it in the net. The boy reached in and pried the hook from the bass' mouth, not skittish about doing so—a true fisherman.

Barrett figured Andy wasn't one to be skittish about much of anything. He must have gotten his boldness from his father. It certainly wasn't passed on by his mother.

On second thought, something about the boys standing across the river last week had spooked Edy's son. What hold did they have on him?

"He's a good one." Andy dumped the fish into Barrett's creel, then stared at it, practically licking his lips. "He'll make a fine supper."

"I suppose he's big enough for two." What was he doing? He'd come here prepared to make a campfire and cook his catch...alone. The less time he spent with Andy, the better.

The boy's gaze whipped to Barrett, hope flashing as powerful as a lighthouse beacon. "You mean it? We can cook him together?"

Barrett cast aside his objections. "Why not?"

"We can build a fire and eat here, like we're making camp. Me and Papa used to set up a tent and spend the night at the river."

Was Andy that desperate for a male's attention? "Do you ever do things of interest with Judge Danby?"

A scowl bit a hole in the boy's enthusiasm. "You know my grandfather's name?"

"Everybody knows Judge Danby."

"Bet nobody likes him," Andy muttered. He picked up a small rock and pitched it sidearm into the river. "Look, I got it almost to the middle. I can throw a rock a long ways."

Barrett respected Andy's wish to change the subject. "That's quite an arm. Do you play baseball?"

"Naw. Well, not too much. I like to fish." He held out a hand. "You got a knife? I'll get this bass gutted and scaled."

Barrett paused to decide if he trusted Andy with a knife, then handed over the one he kept in his tackle box. "Here. Make sure you leave enough for us to eat."

Andy scoffed. "I know what I'm doing."

Barrett ran a hand over his beard, hiding a smile. "I can tell by that scar on your thumb."

The boy looked at the pad of his thumb and shrugged. "This isn't from fishing. I got caught on a barbed wire fence last year."

A few minutes later, Barrett had to admit the boy knew his business when it came to cleaning fish. He started a campfire and heated the oil in the fry pan he'd brought. When it was hot, he added the filleted fish.

While the bass cooked, Andy dropped his line in the water. "I've never seen you before last week, Mr. B. J."

"I grew up here and recently returned." As Andy had dodged the question about his grandfather, Barrett hoped he wouldn't ask about the past.

Edy's son pulled in a small carp. "Papa ran a real estate office. What do you do?"

"I'm a lawyer."

"Grandfather doesn't like lawyers."

How well Barrett knew. "That's a shame. We're generally nice fellas." Barrett liked to think he was nice, anyway...when he wasn't being hostile to the boy's mother.

Andy snickered, made quick work of the latest catch, and added it to the frying pan. He broke off a piece of the fried bass, and popped it into his mouth.

As they sat on the riverbank and ate, Barrett threw out a question with the same nonchalance with which he approached fishing. "Who were those boys on the other side of the river last week? Friends of yours?"

"Sort of." Andy concentrated on devouring the fish with no further clarification.

Realizing he'd get nothing else and not choosing to push for it, Barrett ate his share of the fish, then doused the fire, and packed up his things. "I'm done for today."

"Me, too." Andy gathered his pole and followed Barrett into town.

They walked down Riverside Street and waited for an oncoming buggy to pass before attempting to cross Commerce. The man in the buggy yanked on the reins. He jumped to the ground and marched toward them, his glare fixed on Andy. "There you are, you hooligan!"

On instinct, Barrett stepped in front of the boy. He recognized the man as the grocer, Mr. Ogilvie, the one whose potatoes Andy tried to swipe. "Mind telling me what's wrong, sir?"

Ogilvie halted and pointed to Edy's son. "This ruffian threw a rock and broke my store window."

Barrett frowned at Andy, who shook his head. "It wasn't me."

"When did this happen?"

The man continued to glower at Andy. "About twenty minutes ago. I was doing some bookkeeping in my office when I heard the plate glass shatter. Pieces covered the displays and the floor. It's a mess."

Barrett breathed easier. "You're accusing the wrong boy."

"How do you know?"

"Andy has been with me for the past two hours." Barrett held up his fishing pole. "We've been at the river."

Andy held his pole up like a sword pointing to heaven. "Yeah. Don't go accusing me of somethin' I didn't do."

"Quiet." Barrett laid a hand on his shoulder. "The man was mistaken. It could happen to anyone." And the boy's reputation didn't help him. "Can you describe the boy you saw?"

"It happened so fast." The grocer studied Andy. "Well, I didn't actually see his face, and now that I look, the shirt color was different."

He'd simply assumed the culprit was Andy Westin, as the police had mistakenly assumed Wynn—who hadn't possessed a sparkling reputation himself—had robbed the drugstore.

"Have you reported the incident to the police?"

"Not yet." Ogilvie eyed Barrett this time. "I don't believe we've met."

"The name is Seaton."

The man's brows rose. "Seaton? I remember." He climbed back into the buggy. "I guess like travels with like." The grocer turned his horse and drove off.

Andy looked up. "What'd he mean by 'like travels with like'?"

"Nothing. Let's go."

If everyone in town held Barrett in as high esteem as Judge Danby and Mr. Ogilvie, his law practice in Riverport was doomed to fail before it ever began.

Chapter Six

In contrast to Edythe's more reticent personality, Claire Kingsley was no shrinking violet. She marched up the walk to each home they visited and asked boldly for a book donation for the sanitarium. Edythe hung back and smiled, holding out a box to collect whatever the homeowner had to give.

As they approached a modest one-story home on a quiet street, Edythe shifted the weighty box in her arms. "I wish I knew how you do it."

Claire glanced at her. "Do what?"

"Talk to total strangers and convince them to donate their unwanted belongings."

"Oh, that." Her friend waved a hand. "It probably comes from spending two years as a sales clerk at Newland's. I wouldn't have had a job at the department store for long if I couldn't talk the customers into buying from me." Claire chuckled. "If you really want to learn how to talk to people, I'll introduce you to Roslyn Malone. That woman can talk up a storm and teach you a few things in the process. But she has a heart of gold."

"She's the one who works at the store's perfume counter?" The one whose husband embezzled money from Newland's—from Spence Newland, his employer and friend. "You live with Mrs. Malone, don't you?"

"For now. When Mark and I marry, she'll probably look for someone else to move in with her." Claire's steps slowed. "I hope she does. I'm worried about her. A couple of times, she's seen a man prowling around her backyard. The last time was a week ago."

"How odd. Did you see him?"

"No. I was already in bed. By the time she woke me, he'd gone. Mark is so concerned he's threatened to move our wedding up." Claire grinned. "Not that I mind all that much. It's funny. I fought against remarriage, but now, October can't get here soon enough for me."

A couple of weeks ago, Claire shared with their Widow's Might circle how God had helped her deal with her fear over an inability to have children. She spoke of Mark Gregory's love and support, which had encouraged her to accept his proposal.

Edythe couldn't imagine the heartache of the miscarriages her friend had experienced. Her children were her joy. Her life.

Claire knocked on the door. "Why don't we make this the last stop? We've almost filled the box. It must be heavy. Are you sure you don't want me to carry it?"

Edythe's arms did ache but she shrugged it off. "You talk. I'll tote. I should return home to check on the children, anyway."

The screen door opened to reveal the woman of the house, whose haughty chin rose at seeing Edythe. "It is a mother's job to supervise her children or they become uncivilized."

Edythe shrank back. "Good afternoon, Mrs. Ogilvie."

"Good afternoon, Mrs. Westin." The biddy glanced at and dismissed Claire, then turned back to Edythe. "My husband says the police are still looking for the boy who broke his store window yesterday afternoon."

Edythe's stomach sank. Someone had broken the grocer's window? *Please, not Andrew.* According to her son, he'd gone fishing.

"Mr. Ogilvie confronted your oldest about it."

What a shame Edythe and Claire hadn't quit collecting with the last house.

"Fortunately for young Andrew, he'd been at the river. At least, that's what the man said who was with him."

"Andrew was with a man? Who?"

"You mean he didn't tell you?" Mrs. Ogilvie sniffed her disapproval of a mother who appeared ignorant of her son's companions. "Mr. Ogilvie said he was with one of those Seaton boys." She barked a laugh. "Guess we can't call them boys anymore. If Andrew is keeping company with the one your pa sent to prison..."

The woman left the sentence hanging for full effect, but Edythe finished it in her mind. If Andrew were keeping company with a criminal, it was no wonder he found himself in trouble.

With Wynn in the sanitarium—something Mrs. Ogilvie didn't know—Edythe realized beyond a shadow of doubt that Barrett had accompanied Andrew. How had her son met him? At the river? Was Sunday the first occasion in which they had spent time together? Given Barrett's treatment of her at the sanitarium, why would he choose to be around her son?

Barrett had fished the river many an hour as a youth. He'd told her that nothing taught a person patience better than tossing a line in the water and waiting for a fish to clamp on to the bait.

As though a day hadn't passed, she relived the first time they ever talked. Needing to get away after one of her father's overbearing demands, she'd gone to the river. A short while later, Barrett arrived for an afternoon of fishing. His merry grin had coaxed a shy smile from her.

She spent the next two hours—and the next six months—sharing that place on the riverbank with Barrett, laughing and talking more than she had ever remembered doing. All without her father's knowledge...until they were caught.

Mrs. Ogilvie's grin was less than merry. "Listen to me go on. I'm sure you ladies aren't here to talk about hooligans of any age."

Evidently, she'd accomplished her purpose and was ready to get down to the business of their visit.

Claire glanced at Edythe, and then explained why they had knocked on the Ogilvies' door. They left a few minutes later with three battered books and an old seed catalog. Fortunately, Claire didn't ask about the undercurrents in the conversation with the grocer's wife, and Edythe didn't volunteer any information.

"Hand me the box, Edythe. I'll carry it back to the carriage."

She handed her friend the box of books, her mind still reeling with the revelation that Barrett and Andrew had not only met but spent time together. Had Barrett sought out her son? If so, for what purpose? It didn't make sense when he'd all but thrown her out of Wynn's room last week.

The two Seaton brothers had always been close. Had Barrett formed some reprisal plan for Andrew, because he laid the blame for Wynn's conviction at the feet of her father? Despite Barrett's claim at the time, Judge Danby was a lot of things, but he wasn't corrupt. From all she'd heard through the gossip grapevine, the evidence against Wynn was too powerful for her father or a jury to ignore.

Besides, that wasn't the Barrett she had known. But then, that Barrett had gone back on his word to her.

Another thought slowed Edythe's steps. What would her father do if he learned that Andrew and Barrett were seen together?

He'd been furious when he found her with him the week before Wynn was arrested, berating her for sneaking around with a boy behind his back, one who he'd claimed wasn't fit to open a door for her. Afterward, he rarely let her out of the house except for church and outings with Lamar, the man he'd chosen for her to marry.

It didn't take much intellect to realize the foundation of the judge's complaint against Barrett rested on his desire to study the law. Though her father had refused to tell her what happened when she was little, she had heard the rumors that her mother ran off with an attorney in a neighboring town. There was no reason to doubt the story, since it was well known that from that day on her father held most lawyers in contempt—out of the courtroom and whenever possible, in it.

Edythe hurried toward the carriage. She must warn Andrew not to say anything about his fishing companion in front of his grandfather. Then, she'd plead with him to avoid any further contact with Barrett...for everyone's sake.

EDYTHE STOOD AT THE end of the walk to Barrett's house and read the freshly planted sign in the yard. *B. J. Seaton, Attorney-at-Law.* Her heart pounded harder than Mrs. Cameron's mallet on a slab of cut-rate beef.

She could do this. She must do it. Andrew had left her no option.

Her knuckles tapped the door with unintended softness, and she waited, not sure if he would hear the knock or, peering through the glass, choose not to answer.

When confronting Andrew about the time spent with Barrett, her son had planted his feet and crossed his arms in defiance. Yes, he had fished with Mr. Seaton. Yes, they ate their catch together. No, he did not break the grocer's window, and no, he would not promise to stay away from Barrett.

B. J. likes me and doesn't treat me like I'm some little kid sitting on a street corner and begging to shine his shoes.

Edythe respected her son too much to deny the depiction of his grandfather's attitude toward him. The judge treated Andrew poorly for no fathomable reason. Once she'd asked him why, but he merely glared at her and said, "Don't play at being simple-minded, Edythe. It's unbecoming." She still didn't understand.

The door opened, interrupting her thoughts. Barrett stood on the other side. With the lack of surprise in his expression, he'd either seen her on the porch or expected her visit. "Come in, Mrs. Westin."

Edythe had passed this house numerous times and admired the charming exterior with its bay windows and scrollwork. Her first look at the inside didn't disappoint. The room to her right appeared empty, with the exception of a small table and lamp next to an armchair, but she adored the carved fireplace mantel and floral wallpapers. "You have a lovely home."

"It will do." He escorted her into the room across the hall.

Empty crates were scattered over the floor. Every vacant surface contained stacks of books, a multitude spread across the desk, piled on the floor, and a few on a small table near the front window. Two large bookcases along the wall held even more, all legal tomes.

He didn't offer her a seat in the chair in front of the desk, nor did he sit in the large one behind it. Edythe remained near the entrance to the room, leaving plenty of space between them.

"I don't remember sending out announcements with my address."

"When you take out a notice in the newspaper, it ruins the secret." He'd caught her by surprise at the sanitarium, but with several days to relive the past, her response came out sharper than normal. Years ago, he had been the one person able to draw out the brasher side of her nature. Apparently, time hadn't changed some things.

His lips ticked up as though she amused him. At least, they gave that impression. He propped a hip on the corner of his desk and clasped his hands in front of him. "Are you in need of an attorney, Mrs. Westin?"

Edythe cringed each time he called her Mrs. Westin with that undisguised note of disdain. Why he thought he had right to treat her so was beyond her. "This is a personal matter, Mr. Seaton."

"I'm afraid you've wasted your time in coming here. There is nothing personal between us."

His comment hit her like a slap to the face. Nothing personal between them? Whose fault was that? "It is personal when you keep company with my son against my wishes."

"I'm not sure what you mean. We've each chosen to fish at our favorite place on the river at the same time, so we shared the spot. That's all. It's happened twice, and there were no premeditated arrangements for the outings. If you'll remember, I like to fish. Evidently, it's something your son enjoys too. There's no harm in it."

If she were truthful, he might understand. "No harm? My son and his grandfather have a...a difficult relationship, Barrett. You should understand how that is, since you and my father—"

"Butted heads?"

Despite an attempt to restrain it, her own tiny smile slipped out. "Like two rams doing battle."

His expression softened. A moment later, it hardened again, as though he'd caught himself relenting in the anger he aimed her way—an unjust anger. "From what I saw the day Andy tried to steal the potatoes from the grocer, the judge isn't the only person he has difficulty with."

Edythe's skin warmed at the knowledge that he'd witnessed her failure as a mother.

No less rigid, he said, "I'm sorry. That was uncalled for."

Almost everything he'd said to her was uncalled for. "I'm asking you to leave my son alone."

His head shifted slightly, then his gaze reverted back to her. "I appreciate your concern for Andy, but I like the boy and don't intend to shoo him off if we find ourselves at the river at the same time. Now, if you don't mind, I'm busy."

What right did he have to treat her with such hostility? "Barrett, I don't understand. I see no reason why you should—"

"What are you doing here, Ma?"

Edythe closed her eyes. *Father in heaven, why now? Why here?*

Chapter Seven

A ndy Westin stood at the door of Barrett's office. Judging by his reddened face and heaving shoulders, his mood was dark. Barrett considered telling him to grow up. Then again, he was only eleven. How mature should he act?

And who was Barrett to criticize Andy's childish reactions when Barrett's own level of maturity dwindled whenever he was around Edy? On a scale of one to ten, it fell to near zero knowing he'd withheld the fact that her son stood behind her, listening to their conversation.

There is that speaketh like the piercings of a sword: but the tongue of the wise is health.

The verse from Proverbs 12—the chapter he'd read that morning—had stuck with him, the wisdom convicting him. *Lord, I've allowed a lack of forgiveness toward her to become so ingrained in me that I can't even see her without becoming the type of man I despise, one whose words pierce like a sword.*

Such actions were no better than those of her father.

Andy marched into the room, a malevolent expression aimed at his mother. No matter his displeasure with her actions in the past, Barrett was tempted to come to her aid. But the boy was her son not his. He was her responsibility. A small grunt left his throat. Nothing would change the fact that Andy's father was the late Lamar Westin.

"Andrew, you shouldn't be here."

"You're the one whose got no right to be here, Ma. You got no right to tell me or Mr. B. J. who we can be friends with. Right, Mr. B. J.?"

Edythe turned, her tight expression wordlessly seeking Barrett's help. When the cavalry failed to arrive, she took her son's arm and tried to lead him to the door. "Let's go home, Andrew."

The boy planted his feet, his knees locked. "I came to see if Mr. B. J. wanted to go fishing next Sunday."

"I'm sure he's busy. Aren't you, Mr. Seaton?"

Andy yanked his arm from Edy's grasp. Pain flashed across her face and she rubbed her shoulder.

That did it. No matter his feelings toward her, Barrett refused to stand by and see her injured. "You hurt your mother, Andy. Apologize."

"But she—"

"I said apologize."

Andy's jaw worked back and forth. His eyes shot fire—at Barrett this time, even as they pooled with a little boy's tears. "Sorry, Ma. I'm sorry for being born into your family." He bolted out the front door, slamming it behind him.

Edy dashed to the door after him and threw it open. "Andy!" She stopped and hung her head, her back to Barrett.

"Give him some time."

"Time won't do any good. He resents me. He resents his grandfather."

Barrett had represented a number of bitter people in court. Their spiral into defiant and criminal behavior usually began with some incident that scarred them as a youth. "How long has he been like this?"

She shut the front door and turned around. "After Lamar died, we moved in with my father. It started not long after that. For some reason, the judge has always disparaged Andrew, but it became more evident after we began living under the same roof."

SANDRA ARDOIN

It couldn't be easy being caught in the middle of the issues involving her father and her son. "Maybe you should take the upper hand with both of them. Try standing up for your son on occasion."

She stared at him in that way he remembered. The one that said she tried to think of something sharp or witty or argumentative to say to put him in his place and exhort him to mind his own business.

But she was right. He had no place in her family's affairs. Yet, he couldn't stop from asking, "Why move in with your father? Why stay?"

"When was the last time you were a widow with children, no home, and no means of support?"

Pain seared Barrett's clenched jaw. Westin had failed to provide for his family in the event of his death?

He picked up a stack of books from the floor and stood them on a bookcase shelf. Unlike some penniless widows, Edythe had her well-to-do father to rely on. No need to pity her, and the sooner she left his office, the sooner he could return to his work without feeling as though she watched his every move.

"B. J.?"

His hand jerked at the soft voice in his ear, closer than he'd like. The end book fell over, slapping the wood of the shelf. "That's what the sign out front says." He held his tongue between his teeth until the pain left him wondering if he'd bite the tip of it off.

He set the book upright. Donovan's *Tact in Court*. Naturally.

She picked up another book, turning it to the spine. "*Criminal Law*. You represent clients in criminal cases?"

"Yes." He took the book from her and added it to the shelf, not caring that none of them were in the order he'd planned. He'd fix them later. After she left and when he could think without her standing there, her height putting her nearly eye-to-eye with him.

Her proximity dared him to raise his hand and touch the smooth curve of her cheek.

"It makes sense."

He frowned. "What does that mean?"

"I remember how important it was to you to see that...that people received fairness in their trials."

That Wynn received a fair trial? Was that what she meant? "Everyone is entitled to justice. Sometimes it runs in short supply."

"So does trustworthiness." She crossed the room toward the foyer. "I'm sorry for disturbing your afternoon. Please consider what I said about Andrew. He may act tough and independent, but he's a sensitive little boy."

Having found her tongue, she walked out of the house without giving him a chance to find his.

Barrett moseyed over to the front window and pulled the sheer curtain aside to watch her climb into the buggy at the curb. She'd aimed that cryptic remark about trustworthiness at him. How had he been untrustworthy?

He recalled it being the other way around.

BARRETT WALKED OUT of the post office after sending a telegram to a friend in La Porte. He'd asked him to hire someone to deliver the rest of his belongings to the train station and ship them to Riverport. Once the few possessions he'd kept from his previous home arrived, the move here would be real—for however long he stayed.

He entered the general store, passed the scents of cinnamon and other spices, and approached the clerk stacking tins on a shelf. Newland's Department Store would be a better, faster choice for replacing the furnishings he'd sold when moving here, but he figured the employee of a smaller mercantile would be more likely to provide the information he sought. In addition, he preferred to support the Davids over the Goliaths.

"Good morning."

"Yes, sir, it is." The man's grin was infectious. He wiped his hands on the apron he wore. "What can I do you for?"

"I'm new in town and looking for a housekeeper, a woman to clean and do laundry a couple of days a week. Are you aware of anyone seeking such a position?"

"Let me think." The man rubbed his beard and frowned. "You might try Mary Quincy. Her husband lost his job at the brewery." As if a silent message didn't count as spreading gossip, he covered his mouth with the side of his fist and tipped his head back, gesturing that the man imbibed too frequently. "Can't say she'd be interested or that she'd agree to anything permanent, but I'm positive they can use the money."

Barrett pondered the wisdom of hiring someone who couldn't commit to a permanent position. On the other hand, that described him. "Where might I find Mrs. Quincy?"

The clerk gave him directions to the Quincy farm not far from town.

"Do you have a catalog?" Barrett asked.

He ordered a number of necessary items for his new house, thanked the clerk. and walked outside—right into the path of Judge Danby.

For the life of him, Barrett couldn't seem to avoid the family. They were everywhere he turned. He'd find it comical if these meetings weren't a constant reminder of heartbreak.

The two men sized each other up like pugilists in a boxing ring. No doubt, that would be the tenor of this meeting, because Barrett refused to walk on and let the judge believe he did so with his tail between his legs.

The man must be in his mid-fifties now—gray-headed and showing a few wrinkles around the beard on his face. With a straight back and squared shoulders, no paunch or sags, he wore his age well for someone with his sour disposition. "I'd heard you'd returned. Is your brother with you? He must be out of prison by now."

Danby didn't know about Wynn's stay in the sanitarium? That meant Edy hadn't said anything to her father. Barrett should be pleased she had kept her word. Instead, the realization piled more guilt on his head.

"He's a free man." As free as someone living a death sentence.

"Where is he?" The judge glanced around as though he expected to see Wynn hiding around the corner of a building or behind Barrett's back.

"He served his time, Judge. His location now is his business."

"But you came back to Riverport. Why?"

Barrett's neck muscles tensed. "I'm aware of no law that says a man can't return to the town where he grew up. And be assured, sir, I know the law."

The judge's nostrils flared. "Too bad you didn't teach your brother the finer points of the subject, such as the fact that robbery sends a man to prison."

"Oh, you can be sure Wynn learned a lesson from his experience. For one thing, he learned that reprisal has no business in a courtroom."

The man's eyes narrowed. "There was no reprisal involved, Mr. Seaton, only justice."

"Then you and I differ in our definition of justice, Judge Danby." Barrett took a step to pass him. "If you'll excuse me, I have a law office to open."

The judge blocked his ability to pass. "You plan to practice in Riverport?"

"Yes, sir, I do. I've made it my job to see that people like Wynn receive a fair shake in a court of law."

The man's arrogant smile turned cunning. "By all means, protect the downtrodden, but do not confuse guilt with injustice."

"No, sir, I leave that confusion to jurists like you."

Judge Danby said nothing, however, his gaze sharpened. He moved aside to let Barrett pass. "Mr. Seaton."

Barrett glanced over his shoulder.

"If you believe you'll burrow your way back into the lives of my daughter and grandson, you're mistaken. You gave up that right years ago."

It took nerve for the judge to assume he could manipulate Barrett in the way he'd always manipulated his daughter.

He sauntered on without dignifying Judge Danby's dictate with a response. If he had eyes in the back of his head, there was no question that he'd see Edy's father staring at him. He felt it with the prickling of his scalp.

Perhaps he had erred in riling the man. Not that Barrett cared for himself, even though the retired judge probably retained the contacts and the power to make his professional life miserable. No, against his better judgment, he liked Andy Westin and sympathized with him in the loss of a father he admired. Forcing Andy to suffer for Barrett's imprudent provocation was the last thing he wanted. He'd dedicated much of the past decade to achieving justice for those unable to achieve it for themselves. Where was the justice in making things harder for the boy?

Barrett's recollection of the judge's final comment stopped him. Contrary to the man's claim, he had no intention of resuming a relationship with Edy, and Andy had barged into Barrett's life, not the other way around. So why tell Barrett he'd given up the right to be part of their lives? Who said he wanted anything to do with anyone in the Danby household? Frankly, he was tired of fending off the lot of them.

At least the judge knew nothing of Wynn's location. Barrett found it interesting that Edy hadn't betrayed him in the matter, but what if her father interrogated her? How long would her silence last?

EDYTHE PACED THE DRAWING room floor, a grim weight in her chest. Every few minutes she stopped and glared at the mantel clock. Where was Andrew? She hadn't seen her son in hours, and it was growing dark outside.

"Stop wearing a hole in my floor, Edythe. The boy will be home when he's hungry."

His floor? Oh, how she wished for her own floors again.

"How can you sit there reading the newspaper without a care for your grandson's welfare?" Her voice rose in a way it rarely did when she addressed him.

"I worry more about those who might suffer the consequences of his activities."

"Why do you talk about your grandson that way?"

The judge folded the newspaper and slapped it on the seat of the sofa. "The truth can be difficult to face."

"Andrew is only a child."

"And old enough to begin to grow up."

Edythe strode to the foyer. "There is something wrong. I can feel it."

"Where are you going?"

"I'm going to find my son."

"Edythe, come back here and leave the boy alone." Her footsteps faltered at the bark in his voice. "Return to this room and sit down."

Try standing up for him on occasion. Didn't Barrett remember how hard it was for her to disobey? He of all people should understand the hold her father had on her. She'd been brought up to comply with his every order.

But she was coming to realize that was no excuse. She was Andrew's parent. As such, she was responsible for his care.

Edythe gathered the strength to ignore her father and march toward the front door.

SANDRA ARDOIN

"How long have you known Barrett Seaton was in town?"

His question stopped her, and a ball of anxiety rolled around in her stomach. She kept her back to her father. "You know Barrett is back?"

Did he also know of Wynn? She had promised to keep that news to herself and she wasn't in the habit of breaking a promise...unlike some people.

"Nothing gets by me for long, Edythe. Not in almost thirty years." Not since her mother left. "Clearly, you also knew but failed to mention it."

"There was no reason to say anything."

"No reason? I'm sure you know your son has been seeing him. *I* had to find out about it from a barber. Afterward, Mr. Seaton and I had a little talk."

She winced. Poor Barrett, attacked from all sides by her family. "You have nothing to worry about. That's in the past."

Could that be where she'd find Andrew? Was he with Barrett?

She took a deep breath and another defiant step forward, her intent halted by a knock on the door. A policeman stood on the porch. His hand gripped Andrew's arm and not in a pleasant way. "Andrew, I've been worried."

"Good evening, Mrs. Westin. I'm afraid we need to talk, ma'am."

She closed her eyes a moment, then reopened them, but the policeman remained. The situation must be bad. Very bad. She'd heard it in the officer's voice. She saw it in the way her son hung his head, and his body trembled. Gone was his normal scornful expression when caught doing wrong. "Are you all right, Andrew?"

"He's fine. Can't say as much for one of our town's residents."

Oh, what had her son done now?

"Come in, Officer Brennan. We don't need the neighbors gawking." The judge's cigar-smoke-laden breath passed over Edythe's cheek. "Shut the door before you tell us what he's done this time."

64

"Yes, sir." The officer treated Andrew to a look of sympathy, then hauled him into the foyer and closed the door. The two of them followed Edythe's father into the drawing room with Edythe bringing up the rear.

Her father stood near the fireplace, his hands in his trouser pockets, as he looked down on Andrew. Edythe stood next to her son. "Go ahead, Officer Brennan. Tell us what happened."

"Well, sir, we got a report of a fire on the Stark property at the edge of town. We arrived to find a shed near burned down and Mr. Stark unconscious on the ground. Someone had hit him on the back of the head with a board."

The judge's scowl deepened. "Is the man all right?"

"Doctor Jamison thinks he'll be fine, but Stark doesn't remember much."

Edythe placed a hand against her throat and said a quick, silent prayer for Mr. Stark's health. "What does that have to do with my son?"

"We caught him hiding in the bushes close to the burned shed."

She gasped. "Andrew, please tell me you had nothing to do with the fire and that man's injury." *Please, please, tell me.*

"I'm talking to no one but Mr. B. J. He's a lawyer and he'll believe me." The words were defiant but the voice that of a scared little boy.

"Mr. B. J.?" Her father straightened. His scorching glare was aimed at Andrew. "Are you talking about Barrett Seaton? Don't even imagine you'll see that man again."

Edythe knelt before her son and took his hands. "Did you have anything to do with what happened to Mr. Stark or his property?"

Despite his previous refusal to talk, he whispered, "No, ma'am."

"That's all I wanted to hear, Andrew." She rose. "My son is innocent. We'll let an attorney speak for him. Father, I need a recommendation for a good one."

"But I want—"

"Quiet, Andrew." She understood who he wanted and it was out of the question.

Her father shook his head. "Don't waste your time, Edythe. Lawyers rarely get involved in juvenile cases. It's up to a judge. Perhaps, it will do the boy good to see what happens when he breaks the law."

"I ain't going to prison when I didn't do nothing." Andrew wrapped his arms around her. "Don't let them take me, Mother."

Edythe had never heard her son so panic-stricken. Regardless of his presence at the Stark farm, she chose to believe him when he said he'd done nothing wrong.

Her father rolled his eyes. "Will you do something about the boy's atrocious grammar?"

Edythe's eyes widened. "You're worried about Andrew's grammar when his future is at stake?"

Her father turned to Officer Brennan. "Please tell my daughter and grandson what happens next."

Officer Brennan cleared his throat, his discomfort with the family tension showing in his face. "We'll investigate further, ma'am, but if the evidence shows he's responsible, he'll go before the judge. If he's found guilty as a delinquent, he'll be sent to Plainfield to the Indiana Reform School for Boys."

"A reform school? No." They couldn't send her child to such a place. She wouldn't let them.

"I understand it's run much like a military school, Edythe." Her father added a dash of compassion to his voice. "Andrew can use the discipline. He'll come out a better man."

A man? How long would he stay in that place? How could her father show this calm acceptance of her son's guilt? "Officer Brennan, you haven't the proof to charge him?"

"Not at the moment, ma'am. We'll wait to see if Mr. Stark recalls any details. So far, he doesn't remember much."

Edythe ran a hand over her son's head. "Go on up to bed."

Officer Brennan looked at her. "I'd advise you not to let him leave this house without an adult."

"Don't worry, Brennan, he won't." Her father's stare pierced Andrew. "Will you, boy?"

A spark of the old defiance flamed, then petered out. "No, sir."

After the officer left, her father ordered Andrew to his room, announcing her son wasn't to leave it until he'd given Andrew permission. Edythe hurried toward the door.

"Where are you going?"

"To find an attorney."

"At this time of night? I told you, it won't do any good, but if you must attempt it, wait until tomorrow. You won't find an attorney amiable if you disturb his evening."

Edythe stared up at the second floor. Perhaps her father was right. Andrew hadn't been charged with a crime...not yet.

"Where will you get the money to pay an attorney? Or are you forgetting that your husband left you with few resources?"

How could she forget when his death had trapped her in this house? But her father was wrong. She had one resource, and she wouldn't hesitate to use it.

Chapter Eight

Edythe had tossed and turned most of the night. Images of Andrew working long hours at a reform school, being bullied and mistreated by other boys, danced across the ceiling of her bedroom.

At dawn, she plodded down the curved staircase and into the dining room where her children already occupied their seats at the table. Breakfast was being eaten in somber silence. The twins looked up when she entered the room. Andrew stared at his oatmeal, empty spoon in hand. Evidently, a family crisis brought out the best behavior in her children, though it came at a high price.

"Good morning." Edythe took her seat as Mrs. Cameron laid a plate of fried eggs and ham in front of her. "Where is your grandfather?"

Sarah Jane swallowed the oatmeal she'd shoved in her mouth. "He left."

"Did he say where he was going or when he'd be back?"

"No, Mother."

Since he no longer worked regular hours, where had her father gone at seven thirty in the morning? It didn't matter. His absence made what she had to do easier.

"You won't let Grandfather send Andrew to that school, will you?" Timothy's glower reminded Edythe of the times she'd been on the receiving end of a similar expression of resentment from her eldest child. "He says that's where Andy's gonna go soon."

Her father said that to her children? Well, he was wrong.

The thought of her mother's ring lying in the box upstairs had tempted her to begin her search for a house of their own, away from his influence and out from under his thumb. But she couldn't. Not now. Last night's circumstances forced her to change her plans.

"Timothy, I'd like you and Sarah Jane to finish your oatmeal in the kitchen, please." Edythe waited until the twins left the room before she asked Andrew the questions that had haunted her during the night. "Do you know how that fire started?"

He shrugged his shoulders. What did that mean?

"Are you sure you didn't start it, even inadvertently? Were you smoking in the area? Did you drop a cigarette or matchstick and not realize until it was too late?" But that didn't explain the injury to Mr. Stark.

"I only smoked that one time. I told you, it wasn't me." He dropped the still-clean spoon on the tablecloth and leaned back in his seat, arms crossed. "You're taking Grandfather's side against me."

"No. I'm trying to understand. Why were you on the Stark property?"

"I didn't want to come home, so I walked around." Tears trickled down his face and dripped onto his pants. "I hate it here. I wish I could go back in time and stop Papa from dying. Then we wouldn't be here."

She tossed her napkin on the table and knelt by Andrew, sweeping him into her embrace as he cried on her shoulder. "It will be all right." *God, why must my babies suffer for their parents' failures?*

When his sniffles eased, she released him and stood. "Finish your breakfast, then run upstairs and dress in your Sunday suit. We're going out this morning."

"Where to?"

"I want to consult an attorney."

"But I didn't do it."

"I know, son, but it never hurts to be prepared." More prepared than she had been after Lamar's death.

WITH ANDREW AT HER side, Edythe stood outside the law office of R. C. Branfield, waiting for the attorney to open his door. He did so at nine o'clock on the dot.

"Mrs. Westin." He blocked her way inside.

"Good morning, Mr. Branfield. I realize I have no appointment but would you have a few minutes to talk with us?"

He aimed a frown at Andrew. "If this is about what happened last night, I'm afraid I can't help you."

He knew of the incident already? "At least hear us out."

"I'm sorry, ma'am. I truly am." He shut the door on them.

"What now, Mother?"

What now, indeed? "We try someone else."

"I think we should see Mr. B. J. He'll help us."

Barrett? No. "There's another lawyer up the street. Let's go."

Edythe prepared for an argument, but Andrew followed without a word. The second attorney was no more helpful than the first. However, he did provide an answer for his reluctance to see her. "Your father mentioned the situation. Unfortunately, there's nothing I can do."

No wonder the judge left before breakfast. She wasn't the only Danby to visit attorneys this morning.

She and Andrew plopped down on the stairs outside the man's office. It seemed her next move was all she had left, because she could only think of one attorney her father couldn't intimidate.

"Mr. B. J. won't let us down, Mother."

Edythe took her son's hand, bringing him to his feet with her. "Come along, Andrew. We'll see if your faith in your new friend is justified."

And if Barrett refused to help?

BARRETT ANSWERED A firm knock on his front door. Edythe stood on the porch, her reddened eyes underscored by shadows, as though she'd had little sleep. The sight twisted his gut, bringing back those days when she met him at the river after experiencing the judge's sharp tongue. Andy stood at her hip, for once meek and looking as though his world was about to end. "What's happened?"

Edy balled a handkerchief in her hand. "Please, Barrett, may we come in?"

At the desperation in her voice, he stepped aside and let them enter. Edythe strode to his office, her back like a steel rod, shoulders squared, and her purpose resolute. In contrast, Andy shuffled across the floor behind her, head ducked and posture slumped. Quite the reversal in character.

After gesturing for Edy to sit in the chair near his desk, Barrett slipped into his own chair across from her. Andy stood behind his mother.

"What is this about?"

"I'd like to hire you."

He stemmed the impulse to shout out a refusal of her business. "For what purpose?"

She twisted and glanced over her shoulder at her son. "Andrew might be in trouble."

"What happened this time?" His question earned him a pinched expression from her and a scowl from her son.

"Someone set fire to a shed on the property of a man named Stark."

Barrett had overheard a couple in the café where he'd eaten breakfast this morning as they'd talked about it. From the conversation, he'd assumed the incident was an accident, that Stark's building caught fire and he was injured while trying to put it out. No one mentioned Andy, but if he'd had anything to do with what happened, it was no wonder Edy and her son walked around with dark skin shading their eyes.

"From what I understand, Stark was injured."

Edy wound the handkerchief so tightly, her fingertips turned red beneath the lace of her glove. "Yes. The police think Andrew was involved." Her voice trembled. "They think he started the fire, then hit Mr. Stark on the head with a board and knocked him unconscious."

Barrett's gaze whipped to the boy and back to Edy. "Why Andy?"

"They found him nearby." She dipped her chin. "Hiding."

That didn't sound like the boy Barrett was getting to know. He would imagine Andy standing in the open and defiant or running off before being caught. "Did they find him with the board?"

"No."

Barrett leaned forward in his chair, curious to hear the boy's story. "Did you set that fire, Andy? Did you injure Mr. Stark?"

Edythe leaned forward in her seat. "He wouldn't—"

He held up a hand. "Let your son speak for himself."

Andy slid from behind the chair and approached the desk. "No, sir. It wasn't me. I had nothing to do with the fire and never touched that board."

"Then why were you there?"

"I...I didn't want to go home, so I walked around. I cut through the Stark place."

"What did you see?"

The boy's chin dropped, as though he feared looking Barrett in the eye. "I saw the shed on fire and Mr. Stark on the ground."

"Nothing else?"

Again, the hesitation. "No."

"Did you try to help him?"

"He wasn't moving. I thought he was dead."

The boy withheld something. "What happened next?"

"I started to run away, but I heard people coming, so I hid in the bushes."

"Why didn't you make yourself known?"

"I was scared." Andy wrapped his arms around his middle as a shudder moved through him, a grim understanding of the seriousness of the situation. He looked up, the normal brash rebellion absent.

Still, Barrett would lay odds the boy knew more than he said. "There's nothing I can do for him, Edythe."

She bolted from the chair. "Why not?"

For one thing, your son isn't telling the truth...the whole truth.

"Please, Barrett." She leaned forward, her hands propped on the desk. "We've been to two other attorneys. My father has convinced them not to help."

He overlooked the fact she hadn't come to him first. Why should she? "What do you expect from me?"

Her round-eyed stare said he should know what she expected. "I want you to represent Andrew should they charge him. I want his name cleared of suspicion."

The latter request might be asking more of him than he could manage, based on the fact that trouble was something her son excelled at. "In juvenile cases, the judge makes the decision." As far as he was concerned, it was a flaw in the system. Even children should have representation in court.

"At least, you can advise us." When he didn't give in, her lips flattened. She stood and clasped Andy's hand, defeat written in the lines dragging down her mouth. "Come, Andrew. We'll find someone else if we have to go to Indianapolis."

Andy broke free and gripped the edge of Barrett's desk. "I

thought you'd be the one person to believe me." His hurt appeal turned into an angry sneer. "I shoulda known you were no better than my grandfather. He'd like to see me at the reform school. He'd like to get me out of his house. I don't know why I thought you were different." He spun and stomped across the room toward the front hall.

Barrett had based his whole practice on taking the cases of people he believed were innocent but for one reason or another wouldn't receive the justice they deserved. Perhaps Andy didn't set the fire or injure Stark, but what was he hiding?

He ran a hand down his face, smoothing his beard while he questioned his motive for denying the boy his help. Was he so petty as to use Andy to get back at the judge for sentencing Wynn to prison, or Edy for marrying another man? That sounded too much like the actions of Judge Danby for his comfort. "Hold on, Andy. There's an apple pie on the kitchen counter. Get yourself a piece while I speak with your mother."

The boy glanced between Barrett and Edythe. A tiny smile of hope lit his face before he left the room.

"And stay out of trouble in there, please."

From the hall, Andy called out, "Yes, sir."

Edythe sighed and returned to the chair. "Thank you, Barrett."

"Don't thank me. I'm making no promises. You do realize your son is hiding something?"

She tilted her head. "Because he hesitated in answering some of your questions? He was recalling the scene and—"

"He was trying to decide what and how much he should say." Barrett pressed back in his chair. "Why are you convinced Andy is innocent? I wasn't here but a few days before I learned of his reputation around town."

"Because I know my son. No, he's not an angel, but when caught, he accepts responsibility. Sometimes, I think he takes pleasure in it."

She shook her head. "This time is different. This time he says he didn't do it, and I believe him."

Barrett wished he had that same confidence in the boy.

He'd believed Wynn when his brother claimed he was innocent, that the judge only wanted to punish Barrett for his relationship with his daughter. At the time, Edythe told him he had a blind spot when it came to Wynn's behavior. Not a blind spot. Trust. She had that same trust in her son.

The question was, could *Barrett* trust Andrew Westin?

Edy opened her purse and pulled out a small box, opened it, and laid it on the desk in front of him. A ring—a ruby ring with pearls. "I haven't had this appraised or the time to sell it, but I'm sure it will more than cover your fee."

Jewelry given to her by Lamar Westin? No, thanks. Just seeing it made him squirm. "I don't want your wedding ring."

"This isn't my wedding ring. It belonged to my mother."

She felt no sentiment in keeping it? One day, she might regret giving it up. "You know the fire that killed my parents left me nothing belonging to them. Your memories of your mother are tainted by her leaving. What she did wasn't right. It wasn't fair to you. But I don't want you to regret losing something that was hers. There's no such thing as a time limit on forgiveness. The day might come when you see her again and discover she's not the monster you believe her to be."

"I know why she left and can forgive her for it. What I can't forgive is the fact that she left me behind." A lifetime of hurt sharpened her voice. "My son is more important to me than a piece of jewelry."

"Be that as it may, someday, I'm certain you'll wish you had it back. Besides, money doesn't concern me."

"Then what is it? You said you liked Andrew." She closed the box and set it on the desk in front of him. "I thought you, of all people,

SANDRA ARDOIN

would understand the necessity of defending the innocent, Barrett. Didn't you always tell me that justice mattered above anything else when it came to the law?"

She would throw his words back at him, but she was a fine one to talk. Where was her plea for justice when his brother needed it? Where was her effort to influence her father's act of reprisal? "I met the judge last week."

"He told me."

"You said nothing to him about seeing Wynn at the sanitarium."

"I promised you and Wynn I wouldn't."

Barrett read nothing more in her expression than surprise at the suggestion she would go back on her word.

What harm would it do to ask a few questions at the police station? Barring the past, he supposed he owed her for keeping Wynn's secret. "I'll make some inquiries and see what I can learn. It's possible you and Andy have nothing to worry about."

She shut her eyes and blew out a breath. "Thank you."

Barrett ground his molars. He'd regret this. He already did.

Chapter Nine

B arrett justified stopping inside the doorway of City Hall with the excuse that it gave his eyes time to adjust to the dim interior. In reality, he needed a moment to vanquish the bad memories. To defeat the sudden remembrance of the night of Wynn's arrest.

As soon as he'd heard the news, Barrett rushed to this building, his heart a battering ram against his chest. He burst through the door of the police department and found his brother slumped in a hard chair, handcuffs clasped around his wrists. Barrett could smell the alcohol from five feet away. The officers explained that they'd found Wynn sleeping in the back alley adjacent to the drugstore. Dried blood spotted his hands, but despite having no money in his possession, no one believed Wynn's denial that he'd robbed the place.

Barrett shrugged off the memory and strode down the hallway. The sooner he got this over with the better. He didn't need the sign on the wall to tell him where to find the portion of the building he sought. Even with the growth of the town, the police department hadn't moved in twelve years. Expanded, perhaps, but it remained in the same place.

An officer stood behind the counter at the front of the room. He looked up when Barrett shut the door. "Help you, sir?"

"My name is Barrett Seaton. I'd like to speak with Officer Brennan."

"Wait here." The officer left his station and disappeared down a short hallway.

The name Edy had given him hadn't sounded familiar, so he supposed Brennan had been employed after Barrett left town. Good. There would be no prejudice on the man's part, no remembrance of Wynn's case to cloud their conversation.

A few minutes later, the first officer returned, accompanied by a man, fresh-faced but with the leery stare of a veteran on the force. His uniform, crisp and black with buttons of shiny brass, fit his slim frame as though tailor-made.

After introductions and a few pleasantries, Barrett got down to business. "I'd like to speak with you about the incident on the Stark property."

Officer Brennan's eyes glinted in a way that said he would not be swayed by Barrett's argument, whichever side it came down on. "Are you here on behalf of Judge Danby or his grandson?"

"His mother asked that I look into the situation."

"Then you can tell her we're still investigating the circumstances."

"You have no plans to charge him?"

"I didn't say that."

Ah, that was how this would play out—each piece of information pulled from the man's mouth like a rotted tooth. "I'd like to hear from you why he is a suspect."

"For one thing, he was hiding in the bushes not far from where Mr. Stark was sprawled unconscious on the ground."

As Wynn had been found near the scene of the robbery he'd been accused of committing.

"Then young Mr. Westin gave us a go-round when we found him. He tried to run off several times."

"It's my understanding that Andy came upon the fire and saw the man on the ground. He was frightened and unsure what to do." Barrett moderated his voice to keep from sounding as though he argued with the officer. Antagonism would get him nowhere and might hurt Andy's case. "Seeing someone unconscious, perhaps dead, would frighten a man, to say nothing of its impact on a young boy."

"I'd agree that most would take a fright at witnessing such a scene. However, Andrew has quite the reputation, Mr. Seaton, so it's no wonder he's brought suspicion upon himself."

Barrett kept his expression neutral, but inside he feared for Andy's future. "I understand your reasoning for questioning him, Officer Brennan, but a reputation for childish antics doesn't prove he injured Mr. Stark or set the man's building on fire."

"No, sir. Those childish antics you speak of include things like knocking over outhouses and trampling a flower garden. We've dealt with that kind of behavior by him in the past." Officer Brennan frowned. "Not so childish was his stealing a boat and rowing up and down the river. Eventually, he left the boat beached on one of the little islands and swam to the riverbank."

"A prank?"

"Vengeance. He was angry with the owner for making fun of his little brother. He poked a hole in the bottom of the boat. By the time the owner found it, it had almost sunk."

That was childish, too, but more serious. "What happened to him in that incident?"

The officer's mouth twisted in disgust. "Judge Danby smoothed it over with the boat's owner. I heard the boy didn't sit for a week."

Barrett couldn't imagine Edythe spanking any of her children, so the judge must have administered his own sentence and subsequent punishment. "When did this happen?"

"Last summer."

Ten years old and already infamous. "What do you think his motive was for last night? Had he had a run-in with Mr. Stark?"

"Not that we're aware of, but as I said, we're still investigating."

There was no denying Edy's son had a temper, but damaging a

boat in defense of his brother and injuring a man for seemingly no reason weren't synonymous…unless the police investigation found a reason.

"If I were you, Mr. Seaton, I wouldn't waste my time on Andrew Westin. It's my guess he'll soon be headed for the reformatory."

"We'll see. Thank you for the information."

Barrett burst into the sunshine, his mood not nearly as bright as the day. With all he'd heard and what he'd seen that day outside the barbershop, why should he believe in the boy's innocence? Andy was a thief and a troublemaker.

He was also Edythe Westin's son. To see him placed in a reform school would break her heart. How was he to tell her to prepare herself?

EDYTHE REMOVED THE top of the phonograph's case and laid it on the table alongside the machine. She slipped in a wax cylinder and turned the crank. The ballad she had chosen played for such a short time that it made no sense to sit down when she'd walk back to the machine soon to crank it again.

Standing alongside the table, she closed her eyes, letting the strains of the sentimental song act as a balm on her nerves.

It took only seconds for her mind to wander to Barrett. He'd been livid when he'd left Riverport. Why should she have been stunned to receive no letter, no visit, no evidence of any desire to see her again? All those years ago, she'd mistaken the depth of his love for her. It consisted of roots too shallow to withstand the winds of the storm they had faced. Clearly, by his attitude toward her since his return, those winds still roared.

"Demanding day, my dear?"

Even though her father sounded appropriately concerned, Edythe's mood dropped lower. "Not demanding, Father, but I won't rest easy until this situation with Andrew is resolved and the police find the person who really injured Mr. Stark."

"Even if Andrew is as innocent as he claims, he'll find something else to satisfy that troublesome spirit inside."

If only she could tell him that Andrew wasn't troubled until they moved into this house. But it would be a waste of breath. Her father only heard what he wanted to hear.

"As I said last night, Edythe, I believe the reform school will be good for the boy. He'll learn discipline and a trade."

Is that why you convinced the other attorneys in town not to help him?

"There are easier ways for a boy to learn a trade." The music stopped, but she didn't start the phonograph again.

"Only if they are willing to learn." He settled on the sofa and lit a cigar, fouling the air in the room with tobacco smoke.

"If you'll excuse me, I'll see if Mrs. Cameron needs help with supper."

On her way to the kitchen, she was tempted to keep going, straight out the back door and to Barrett's office to find out what he'd learned after speaking with the police. Would she receive another visit this evening, this time to haul her son away?

What was Andrew hiding? Barrett had recognized his hesitation. Honestly, she'd seen it too. Rather than exoneration, Andrew's silence increased the chance of conviction.

AFTER ANOTHER DISTURBED night of slumber, Edythe awoke, this time blaming Barrett for her tossing and turning. Under the circumstances, she hadn't expected him to call at the house, but he hadn't seen fit to send word of his visit to the police yesterday. He hadn't sent a message to allay her fears, which left her to imagine the worst.

She threw off the sheet and climbed out of bed. She'd left his office yesterday without reclaiming her mother's ring, and even though he'd said he hadn't wanted to take it, leaving it in his possession obligated him to work on Andrew's behalf.

Her reflection in the standing mirror revealed that wild dark strands had escaped her braid and equally wild dark eyes stared back at her.

After seeking more details from her son last night and not receiving the answers he expected, the judge had confined Andrew to his room until the situation was resolved.

Edythe shuffled through the contents of her wardrobe and chose a lovely mauve day dress. She laid it on the bed, crossed her arms, and eyed its ruffles and fancy beadwork. Releasing a huff, she carried it back to the wardrobe and grabbed a simple linen skirt with blue-gray stripes, matching jacket, and white shirtwaist. Her planned visit to see Barrett was business, not an attempt to impress him with her appearance. As he'd stated, there was nothing personal between them.

Once she had seen to her children's breakfasts and spoken to Mrs. Cameron about their care, Edythe slipped out of the house. Her father, as usual, was already gone. For someone who no longer practiced his profession, he spent many hours away from home. What he did during the day, she had no idea, nor did she care to ask.

A short time later, Edythe rapped on Barrett's door. A pretty young woman answered her knock and smiled up at Edythe while wiping her hands on her apron. "May I help you?"

"I..."

Because this woman hadn't been here on Edythe's previous two visits, she had assumed Barrett remained unmarried.

Assumptions were dangerous things...and often wrong.

In not mentioning his marriage, Barrett might as well have thrust a knife in Edythe's chest. The pain from it came swift and strong, leaving her standing speechless at his door.

Why should he have mentioned it? He left Riverport—left Edythe—of his own accord. There was no sound reason to believe he hadn't found someone else to love.

Were there children? She peeked around the woman but saw no little ones, nor did she hear a child in the background.

"Are you here to see Mr. Seaton about a legal matter?"

Edythe tried to smile, but suspected it looked more like the reaction to an abdominal cramp. "Yes, ma'am." She couldn't bring herself to refer to the woman as Mrs. Seaton. "Is he here?"

Barrett walked out of the parlor and stopped alongside the woman. Like Edythe, he towered over her. "I'll take care of this, Mrs. Quincy."

Mrs. Quincy? Not Mrs. Seaton? A closer inspection revealed a smudge of dust on the woman's cheek. A housekeeper, perhaps? Edythe had the odd urge to laugh out loud.

Mrs. Quincy glanced at Barrett, evidently sensing the tension in her employer and absurdity in Edythe. She backed down the hall. "You'll find me out back hanging the wash if you need me, Mr. Seaton."

Barrett's gaze remained on Edythe. "Thank you, Mrs. Quincy."

The woman spun around and disappeared through a doorway at the end of the hall.

When he backed away from the front door, she stepped inside and caught a whiff of a delicious aroma wafting from a nearby room. "Did I disturb your breakfast?"

"Yes."

"Mrs. Quincy must be a wonderful cook. It smells delicious."

"She does a fair job, but I made my own meal this morning."

"You cook?" That was a new side to him.

"It's Eggs à la Benedict." He glanced over his shoulder, then back at her. "Would you like to join me?"

Did he invite her out of a sense of gallantry? "Thank you. I've already eaten." She'd nibbled on a piece of toast, unable to get anything else past her nervous stomach. But it smelled so good.

"I made extra for Mrs. Quincy, but she declined for the same reason."

Edythe breathed in the aroma again and licked her lips. "Well, maybe, you might let me taste a tiny portion of yours...just to satisfy my curiosity."

"I'll bring you a plate of your own, but I don't share from mine." Humor flashed in his eyes.

Temptation overcame her. "In that case, I'll force it down."

He laughed. The pleasant sound wiped away years of her life, once more placing her on the riverbank at seventeen.

"I'm not sure whether I should take that as a compliment or an insult."

She let him ponder it as he led her through the parlor and into the dining room. The roiling stomach of earlier had vanished, and she looked forward to the breakfast.

He pulled out a chair for her. "I'll be back."

While he was gone, Edythe glanced around the room at the rich mahogany wainscoting and the wallpaper in a bold yellow print that brought to mind the egg yolks used to prepare the Hollandaise sauce.

On her first visit, she'd been surprised by the size of Barrett's house. Certainly not as large or ornate as her father's, but larger than necessary for a single man—a house that spoke of success, but one that could use a woman's touch when it came to the furnishings. In fact, she would change the wallpaper to something softer and...

Edythe closed her eyes and gathered her senses. What was she doing?

Barrett walked back into the room, carrying a tray with her breakfast, along with a cup and saucer. Once he'd set everything before her, including the coffee with its steam rising above it, he laid the tray aside. He didn't offer cream or sugar. In her already emotional state, his recollection that she drank her coffee black and strong draped her with warmth that had nothing to do with the sunshine streaming into the room from the bay window.

She blinked the sentiment away while studying the dinnerware's raised scroll work and scalloped edges. They were simple yet elegant, a perfect canvas on which to display an appetizing meal. "Thank you. It looks delicious."

"Then eat." He took his seat across the table and shook out his napkin, placing it on his lap.

Edythe cut a tiny portion of the muffin topped by bacon and egg. She swiped it in a generous dollop of the sauce before tasting it. The flavor burst in her mouth. "This is excellent. Where did you learn to cook so well?"

"It's a recent interest, one I found I enjoyed after growing tired of putting together an evening meal simply for nourishment."

"Then you're not married." Her cheeks warmed, and she focused on her food.

"No."

His short answer put a period to the subject. Just as well. She shouldn't welcome encouraging words that drove her to do something ludicrous, like pine for him a second time.

Unfortunately for her, it appeared he'd retained many of the traits she once loved about him—intelligence, confidence, self-discipline. Yet he'd lost the easy-going manner and affability he'd once shown toward her.

She eyed him. What was he thinking? That he wished he'd never seen her or her family again? More likely, that he'd never met them at all.

Regardless of how things ended between them, she couldn't say the same about him. He had always held a place in her heart and always would. Which probably qualified her as one of the most foolish women alive.

The ensuing silence between them intensified until she broke it. "How is Wynn?"

"Settling in."

"Oakcrest is a fine institution. The people there will provide him with the best care."

"It wouldn't be necessary if..." Barrett closed his mouth.

If her father hadn't sentenced him to a convict's life? Their end began with that fact. Surely, as a member of the legal profession, he understood that a jury found his brother guilty based on evidence.

Barrett glanced at her. "You never mentioned why you were at the sanitarium that day."

You never gave me an opportunity. "I sought Dr. Ellis' permission to deliver books for the patients and provide them with a library of sorts. It's a mission taken on by Widow's Might."

"Widow's Might?"

She explained the group's purpose of support, encouragement, and charitable deeds. "Two of our members are remarrying in the next couple of months. Phoebe Crain is engaged to Spence Newland."

"Of the department store Newlands?"

"Yes. Claire Kingsley will marry Mark Gregory. He's an architect, as is she."

"A woman architect?"

"A talented one from what I hear." Edythe yearned to discover her own talent, preferably if it provided a wage. "I wanted to talk about what you learned at the police station yesterday." Edythe kept any censure from her voice. Easy after a lifetime of conversing with her father.

"Not much more than what you were told. They're still looking into the incident." He paused in the midst of slicing through an egg-topped muffin and set his knife and fork on his plate.

Edythe was astute enough to realize that whatever he was about to say next wasn't good news.

Chapter Ten

B arrett's appetite fled. Despite their shattered relationship, he dreaded the idea of preparing Edy for the possibility of Andy's arrest.

But what was he to do? It would be crueler to let her think she and her son had nothing to worry about. Barrett wasn't a cruel man. He was an attorney. Their relationship was professional, not personal.

He glanced at her plate. When was the last time he'd invited a client to share his breakfast?

"You should know that the police believe in Andy's guilt. They're only waiting for more proof or for Mr. Stark to confirm it before they act."

The color disappeared from her olive-toned skin. "And if he remains unable to tell them what happened?"

"Your son has a well-known reputation in town. It hasn't helped the police to believe his story." The incident with the boat bothered Barrett to the point he struggled to believe in Andy's innocence, too.

"Then we'll find a way to prove he didn't set fire to that building or injure Mr. Stark."

"How do you propose to do that when Andy isn't being honest about what he knows?"

Light streaming through the dining room window amplified the sheen in her eyes.

Barrett contained a growl at the urge to provide her comfort.

He'd left his teen years behind long ago, which meant he could rein in this desire to be her protector, her rock. The one whose shoulder had grown damp during her times of unhappiness. He would rein it in if it killed him.

Surprisingly, she kept the tears at bay. "What's next?"

"I'll visit Stark this morning to see if he's remembered anything else."

Edy perked up. "My carriage is out front."

She thought she'd go with him? "No."

"Why not?"

"Because it isn't a good idea, Edy."

"Are you afraid I'll say something wrong? I won't. I'll remain quiet and let you do the talking."

How did he make her understand? "We don't want the Starks to suspect you're there to influence them in some way."

"Why would they think that?"

"You didn't tell me about the incident last year with the boat."

She pushed her plate away, the breakfast half-eaten. "I didn't think it was relevant."

"You were wrong." He huffed. "Edy, in a case like this, everything your son has done in the past is relevant. Fair or not, if he faces a judge, his past antics will weigh in the man's opinion. Are you prepared to offer the Starks money for their cooperation in seeing Andy cleared of wrongdoing?"

"You're talking about a bribe." She tossed her napkin on the table. "You're a representative of the law, how can you suggest it?"

"I'm not suggesting it. But it doesn't help that people know your father made last year's problem go away. If they see you, the Starks could think you're there to provide something similar."

"My father merely paid for the replacement of the boat. In my opinion, he paid more than it was worth."

"Encouraging the impression that the payment was in exchange for the owner forgetting about Andy's crime. That was what he did, Edy. Your son stole. He committed a crime."

She fidgeted in her seat. "If the Starks look forward to the same treatment, they will be disappointed. My father wants Andrew to be sent to the reform school. He claims it will make a man of him."

"Maybe it will."

Agony twisted her features.

Like the police, he leaned toward believing Andy set the fire—on purpose or not—but withheld judgment regarding Stark's injury. The boy needed someone to see he received fair treatment. His mother needed the assistance of someone who wasn't determined to send her son to a reform school. Barrett had taken on those duties whether or not he wanted them, which either made him a fool or a hero.

"To answer your question, even if I wanted to bribe the Starks I couldn't. I gave you the only thing I owned worth any money."

The ring. She hadn't taken it back yesterday. Now, he'd hang on to it for a while, not as payment for legal services, but he still believed she would regret selling it.

How had she found herself in such a financial predicament? His opinion of Lamar Westin had never been high, but knowing he left his wife and children with nothing, lowered it even further.

With his knife, Barrett pointed to her plate. "You haven't finished your breakfast."

She glanced at what remained of the Eggs à la Benedict, then propped her forehead on her palms. "I can't lose my son, Barrett." His name caught on a sob.

Instinct, not reason, sent him to kneel at her side and hold her while she cried on his shoulder. *Tears.* He could never bear seeing a woman's tears, especially not those shed by Edythe Danby. Not years ago, when her father ran roughshod over her. Not today, when her son did the same. The only time he'd ever felt truly helpless was when she cried.

"You won't lose him, so don't borrow trouble." Barrett's hand ran up and down her back, each stroke erasing a year until he returned to the day when he heard of Edy's marriage to Lamar Westin, the man of her father's choosing.

That news came too soon after Judge Danby sentenced Wynn to the Indiana State Prison in Michigan City. With an angry chip on his shoulder and a law school education waiting, Barrett abruptly left Riverport. He'd written three letters. When she never responded, he returned to town find her already married, so he went back to Valparaiso, brokenhearted, and worked his way through law school.

The sobbing ebbed. She pulled back and patted the wet spot on his suit coat. "I'm sorry."

"It needed cleaning."

A hiccupping chuckle escaped, and she used her napkin to mop at the dampness around her eyes. "You always made me laugh." She lifted her chin and her soft gaze snatched his breath.

Barrett swallowed, his mouth begging for moisture. With a gentle push, he moved her hand away from her face and dried the smooth skin over her cheekbones with his thumb. "Edy..."

Lord, help me. Not only am I calling her Edy again, but I'm on one knee and wanting nothing more in this moment than to feel those soft lips on mine.

SURELY, SHE WALKED along the edge of emotional disaster—one step away from falling off a too-familiar cliff.

How she had missed being called Edy. "Edythe" was too proper, too reminiscent of her father's demand for formality. "Edy" spoke of friendship, of familiarity.

Edythe's chest tightened, so much so, it hurt to breathe. What if she allowed Barrett to kiss her? Where would it lead? What good would come of risking her heart again?

Oh, how she wished to forget the past. She wished to start over and be swept up in renewed love for him. She wished to once again rest in the comfort and security of his arms.

Her body began a slow tilt forward, her lips almost touching his...

His expression changed, darkened, as though he'd closed the shutters on his emotions to hide any light of longing. His mouth offered, not a kiss, but the briefest trace of a reluctant smile.

Heat rushed through her. She had imagined his desire to kiss her. Now he felt sorry for her, offering her a sad smile of pity. In her distress, she had forgotten herself and let him console her. But she couldn't fool herself into thinking it meant anything more than dealing with a woman's tears.

Edythe turned and pressed her back into the hard spindles of the dining room chair until the bite of the decorative wood restored her to reality. In the future, she must be sure to use caution when around him. The comfort and security of his arms was no more reliable today than it proved to be a dozen years ago.

Barrett returned to his seat, placing the table between them. "According to my conversation with Officer Brennan, Andy purposely destroyed another person's property—the boat—over an alleged insult. Tell me about the incident."

She, too, could pretend nothing had transpired. *If you care for me at all, Father God, please don't let my voice tremble.* "Andrew took the blame and accepted the punishment my father meted out." *Thank you.*

"What do you mean he took the blame?"

She sealed off the memory of the previous few minutes and concentrated on the truth of what occurred last year. "A few days later, Timothy told me what really happened. My younger son enjoys science and experimentation. He's an intelligent child...and curious.

One day, he found a small rowboat pulled up onto the riverbank. Seeing its condition, Timothy assumed the boat had been discarded." Another wrong assumption by a Westin. "He considered it something useful in his endless quest for knowledge."

"How so?"

"The next day, he returned to the boat with a small clock, a ruler, and a drill from his grandfather's tool shed. He pushed the boat into the river and climbed in, testing it for leaks before rowing it to one of the little islands to do his"—she shivered—"experiment."

"What kind of experiment?"

She shook her head. "He sought to discover the size hole needed to sink a boat that size in ten minutes."

Barrett laughed. "Timothy drilled a hole in the bottom of the boat and timed it as it sank?"

"Yes. He'd done all the mathematics in advance." Although proud of his cleverness, she wished for her son to learn to control his urge to experiment at the drop of a hat.

"I was told Andy stole the boat and swamped it out of anger over an insult to his brother."

"The man did insult Timothy, but that took place the week before, and he denied it. If Andrew had been there, he would have defended his brother right then. He would not have waited a week."

"Are all your children...?"

He seemed to fumble for the right word, so Edythe helped him find it. "Extraordinary?"

"I can't wait to hear about the idiosyncrasies of your daughter."

"Timothy's twin. Sarah Jane." No doubt, her weighty sigh said a lot about the girl. "Yes, in her own way, she is also extraordinary."

Barrett grinned, then followed it up with a frown, as though he couldn't bear to maintain a personal conversation with her. "Let's get back to Andy. He has a temper."

"No more than anyone else. He would never purposely hurt

someone."

"You keep defending him."

"He doesn't believe I defend him enough." The snap in her voice took her aback and she apologized.

He held her gaze from across the table. "You don't need to apologize for expressing your feelings, Edy."

After the mistakes she'd made—the one she nearly made this morning—he could say that with a straight face?

I suppose I should thank you, Father, for bringing me to my senses before I gave Barrett another opportunity to walk out on me, trampling my heart in the process.

AFTER COMING TO HIS senses, setting the brake on the urge to kiss Edy, Barrett sought to offer an apology for the recklessness, not with words, but with a smile. It only managed to upset her. She'd put on an unperturbed face but he saw her wince when she pushed against the chair back.

Barrett tried to steer the conversation back to business. Somehow, it deviated once more into personal territory. This visit felt too friendly, too sociable—too much like the past. "How did Andy get involved and take the blame for the boat's destruction?"

"Evidently someone recognized the boat and told the owner. In the meantime, Andrew searched the area, looking for Timothy. Even though the river is fairly shallow in that area, he saw his brother standing on the island, too hesitant to swim back. Andrew swam out and helped Timothy to the bank. A few minutes later, the boat's owner arrived and began to confront Andrew. He didn't see Timothy, who had run away out of fear."

Why would a rebellious and angry boy take unjust blame upon himself? "Andy didn't explain the situation?"

"Timothy was only seven. He hadn't meant any harm. Andrew

wanted to protect his brother from..." Edy's explanation stalled.

"He wanted to protect Timothy from the judge's punishment?"

"Yes."

It was strange to imagine Andy Westin as a hero when he worked so hard to convince people he was a pint-sized villain.

"Though my father isn't abusive, physically, you know he is a strict authoritarian and doesn't relate well to the children, especially the boys. They try his patience, and he comes across as harsh."

More than harsh. As far as Barrett was concerned, the judge was his own brand of villain.

"I was told Andy couldn't sit for a week after the boat episode."

"That isn't true. Except for meals, my son was confined to his room. That was the extent of any physical punishment."

"And when you found out the truth?"

"Andrew opposed my interference. The incident had been handled, and he'd accepted the consequences."

"They're children, Edy. You're their mother. It should be your say."

EDYTHE HEARD THE QUESTION behind Barrett's statement. *Have you no spine?* "What good would have come from involving Timothy and seeing them both punished?"

He poured them a fresh, hot cup of coffee. "Why do you stay with the judge?"

"Your interrogation skills say much about your proficiency as a lawyer." Edythe winced at the bitterness in her voice.

The muscles in Barrett's jaw clenched. "I'm not asking these questions to meddle, Edy. I'm trying to understand what drives your son's antagonism toward you and others."

"You've already decided his guilt, so what does it matter?"

"Because it's my job. What you tell me might make a difference between Andy remaining at home or residing in a reformatory."

"Does that mean you'll continue to help us?" She counted to ten while he remained silent.

"I'll do what I can."

"Thank you." If he wanted to help Andrew, she would answer anything personal he asked, no matter how humiliating. "I stay because I have nowhere else to go."

"After your marriage, you and your husband lived with the judge?"

"No. We lived a few blocks away and didn't move in with my father until after Lamar's death."

"Were you afraid to live alone?"

"Alone? With three children?" Her laughter bordered on hysteria, and she covered her mouth until she'd brought herself under control. "As a wedding gift, my father bought us a house. When Lamar died, he sold it."

Barrett shot a perplexed glance in her direction. "Why?"

"The financial troubles of a few years ago hit my husband hard. Without telling me, Lamar borrowed money from my father to pay his debts. As guarantee for the loan, my father requested the deed to the house." She shook her head. "Afterward, we lived there through his grace. When Lamar died, the grace period ran out. My father sold the house and offered to take us in."

"What kind of father sells his daughter's house out from under her? Why didn't you find your own place?"

"With small children to feed and no skills? How could I afford it?"

"You have any number of skills."

"I can embroider. I'm not sure that would—"

"I remember you danced exceptionally well."

The compliment warmed her from the inside out. They had shared several dances on the riverbank as he hummed romantic ballads. Edythe shook off the images but allowed a smile to linger. "Perhaps I should apply for work in vaudeville."

"In that case, you'll have more than your father to contend with."

If not for Barrett's display of hostility earlier on and his rejection of her kiss, she might be tempted to believe he still cared...a little. "The idea of my working is inconsequential. When I suggested seeking employment, my father threw a tantrum. He said he wouldn't have people spreading the rumor that he refused to support his own daughter and sent her out into the working world to fend for herself."

"Yet, he stole your house. The man is a warm humanitarian."

Though the judge was her father—her flesh and blood—Edythe didn't blame Barrett for his attitude. How could she when she often agreed?

"Do you ever plan to tell the judge I'm assisting you with Andy's situation?"

Edythe hoped there would be no point, that the police would drop their suspicion of Andrew. "If it becomes necessary." She rose from her seat. "I've taken enough of your time."

He saw her to the door. "How long did it take the boat to sink?"

"Twelve minutes and twenty-three seconds."

He clucked his tongue. "So close."

"To this day, I'm not sure if Timothy was more frightened by the boat's owner or disgusted by his failure."

Barrett's laughter was a reminder of days gone by—days never to return.

EDYTHE ENTERED THE house, removed her hat and gloves, then listened for any noise from her children or her father. It was quiet. Perhaps, too quiet. In the kitchen, the housekeeper stood at the counter, kneading bread.

"Where are the children, Mrs. Cameron?"

The woman brushed a sleeve over her forehead. "Out back, Mrs. Westin."

"Were they any trouble while I was gone?" She might as well find out now, rather than be caught by surprise later.

"No, ma'am." Mrs. Cameron smiled as she wiped her hands on a dishtowel. "Miss Sarah Jane held a tea party with her animals, and Mr. Timothy kept an eye on the barometer."

"The barometer?"

"He's certain it will rain this afternoon."

"Well, maybe it will. He's generally right about those things." Edythe peeked out the kitchen window. There wasn't a cloud in the sky, but she'd learned not to doubt her son's acumen. She turned back to the housekeeper. "How is Andrew?"

Mrs. Cameron's lips drooped. It wasn't that the housekeeper disapproved of the boy. Quite the contrary. She often showed her compassion for him and—Edythe suspected—had been adding an extra serving of whatever dessert she'd prepared in the evening to the tray she carried upstairs to his room. "Not a peep out of him."

Not a peep? Instead of being comforting, that sounded ominous. "I'll go up and see him."

After a quick trip to the backyard to check on her youngest children, she walked down the hall to the foyer. She'd placed her hand on the banister and one foot on a stair tread when her father called her name.

She considered ignoring him but lowered her foot to the marble, turned, and entered the drawing room. "Yes, Father?"

He sat on the sofa, his attention on the newspaper clasped in his hands. "We'll have a guest Saturday evening."

"A guest?"

"His name is Ansel Treadway."

"The banker?" Although she'd never met Mr. Treadway, her

father talked about him on occasion. The first image that popped into her head was of the mousy, middle-aged man with a graying walrus mustache and thin face who sat near the window inside the First National Bank.

"Yes." Her father muttered, "Someone capable of managing his money."

This wasn't the first time the judge had referred to Lamar's financial failure. At first, he sang the praises of Edythe's husband, which was why he'd pushed Lamar on her. Over the years, though, he grew to lament his choice in a son-in-law, no longer seeing Lamar's promise. Edythe presumed her husband's setbacks attacked her father's pride. Yet, Lamar could hardly be blamed for the country's financial depression.

"I've already informed Mrs. Cameron to prepare a prime roast for the meal. I'd like you to wear something special." He grinned without looking at her. "Wear that new emerald gown. You're lovely in it."

Her throat constricted. The last time her father told her she looked lovely in a particular dress, she ended up with the last name of Westin. "If this is business—"

"No, it's pleasure. Ansel is a fine man—responsible and unattached. You will like him, and I'm sure we'll both be stimulated by the conversation."

The reference to liking him bore too much of a resemblance to an order, not an assumption. Was she being too suspicious in thinking Mr. Treadway was being touted as the perfect man for her father to guide into marriage?

Edythe turned the crank on the phonograph without bothering to change the cylinder and let the soothing music wash over her. For once it fell short in easing her anxiety as she saw history repeating itself. "I'm sure you'll have much to talk about together. I'll be in the way."

He peered at her over the top of the paper. "You're the hostess in this household, Edythe. Play the part well."

She tried to squeeze further argument past the lump in her throat but failed. The music ended. "If you'll excuse me, I want to speak with Andrew."

This time, her galloping feet matched her racing heart. If the judge wanted a hostess, she would "play the part well" for one night. Nothing more.

Chapter Eleven

"Mother, it's time! Come here. It's time."

Edythe rushed into the kitchen at Sarah Jane's shout. Her daughter waited in the doorway to the mudroom, bouncing as if her short legs were on springs. "Where is she?"

"Under the porch." Sarah Jane dashed out the screen door and into the evening's dusk, eager to return to the cat that probably wanted nothing more than privacy while giving birth.

Following her daughter outside, Edythe trotted down the porch steps. It was almost past her children's bedtime, but she couldn't bear for them to miss this. They had anticipated it all day.

Timothy knelt in the grass, peering under the porch, a watch in his hand.

"What are you doing, son?"

"Tracking the time between the birth of each kitten."

"It's dark under there, how can you see anything?"

"I'm listening."

Edythe bent over but refused to crawl on the ground like her children. "Sarah Jane, you'll ruin your stockings."

"Mother, I have others. This is important."

Yes, the birth of kittens was important, at least to this child. "I'll overlook it this time, but please don't make it a habit."

"No, ma'am."

From the depths of the porch cave, a tiny mewing, little more than squeaks, resonated in the darkness.

"I hear one!" Timothy eyed his watch and crawled halfway under the porch. His voice echoed back to them. "Now, I'll see how long it takes until I hear the next one. The experiment won't be scientifically accurate, because even here, I can't see too well."

Scientifically accurate? What normal eight-year-old spoke such words?

"We can't get too close, Timothy." Sarah Jane grabbed his legs and started pulling her brother from under the porch. "You'll scare Mrs. Taffy."

Ever since learning the stray cat she'd brought home weeks ago would be a mother, the little girl never failed to add "Mrs." in front of the feline's name.

"Let go, Sarah Jane." Timothy started kicking his legs in an effort to force his sister to release her hold.

"No. Come out of there."

"Children, stop." Edythe pulled her daughter away from the porch and stood her up, then did the same with her son. "Mrs. Taffy doesn't need the added strain of two squabbling children. Let her do as she must. We'll see the kittens when she's ready and not before."

"But my experiment." Timothy crawled out from under the porch and held up the watch, an old one his father had given him.

"We'll find you another experiment. Tomorrow."

Sarah Jane sat in the grass. "I wish I was a doctor."

Timothy scoffed at his sister's proclamation. "Girls aren't doctors."

"They are too! Besides, I don't want to be a people doctor. I want to make animals well."

Edythe lowered herself to the ground next to Sarah Jane, careful not to get grass stains on her skirt. "Animal doctors are called veterinarians."

She had never heard of a female veterinarian. While she preferred her child grow up to be a wife and mother, she had no doubt that if the intrepid Sarah Jane Westin sought such a vocation, she would find a way to make it happen. How had such a weak-willed woman birthed three children with such tenacity?

As they sat in the waning light, Edythe wrapped her arms around her twins and hummed to the muted sounds of a neighbor's piano. Soon, all three of them were humming the tune and rocking together from side-to-side.

This was how life was before Lamar died. It was the way it should be. Every day should bring this feeling of contentment and well-being. She sighed. There was one thing missing—one someone.

She glanced up at the second floor. Andrew watched them from his window. Trapped in his bedroom for nearly a week now, he was missing so much in life, in the lives of his siblings.

Edythe's smile only earned her a scowl from him. With the dwindling light, she assumed it was a scowl. Maybe it was what she'd expected to see, because it had become most familiar to her. Whatever his expression, it lasted mere seconds before he disappeared into the room.

This horrid situation must be resolved, because honestly, she wasn't sure which was worse for Andrew—spending his days alone and imprisoned in this house or having limited freedom to roam the grounds of a reform school.

BARRETT LAID DOWN HIS fork and pushed his plate away. He had spent over an hour in his kitchen, attempting to take his mind off this building conflict over Andy's predicament, the reunion of sorts with Edy, and more important Barrett's recent, unwelcome reactions to her.

His groan resounded off the dining room walls. He'd asked God to prevent his mouth from piercing her like a sword. He hadn't asked for their relationship to be become a feather that tickled his mind with compassion and sweet memories. Was it too much to expect something in the middle?

He left the dining room and put his half-eaten supper of steak and potatoes in the icebox. He'd save it for after church tomorrow.

Barrett entered his office, dropped into the chair, and shuffled through files of former cases scattered across his desk. Even that didn't keep the disturbing thoughts at bay.

How had Lamar Westin managed to gain Edy's respect and free her of Judge Hayden Danby's iron-fisted control? Westin succeeded where Barrett failed. In the end, though, Westin failed as well.

For the first time, Barrett acknowledged that something good had come from Wynn's arrest. Unlike Westin, Barrett had been blessed by a narrow escape. He couldn't imagine, neither would he tolerate, bowing to the judge's rule, and suspected that same rebellion against the man's dominance lay behind much of Andy's attitude.

Barrett tossed an old file aside and leaned back in his chair, hands behind his head. So why didn't his narrow escape feel like a blessing? Why did thinking of Edy bring regret?

Maybe, for her son's sake, he should stop fighting them both. That didn't mean he trusted in Andy's innocence regarding the fire and Mr. Stark's injury. It only meant that, even if he were guilty, both mother and son needed support.

Frantic pounding on his front door interrupted his thoughts. His quick steps to the foyer competed with the continued beating on the wood. "I'm coming. Don't knock the door off its hinges."

The pounding stopped, and he opened the door. Mary Quincy stood on his porch. She stared up at him with red-rimmed eyes that shouted of desperation. "Mr. Seaton, I'm sorry to bother you on a Saturday evening, but we need your help. Please, please come with me."

She'd turned toward the street when he touched her arm. "Wait.

What kind of help?"

She raised a shaky hand to her forehead. "I'm sorry. I'm not thinking clearly. The police have arrested my husband, Jeremiah, and he needs a lawyer."

Barrett stepped aside. "Please come in."

"But—"

"Your husband isn't going anywhere, Mrs. Quincy. Come in and tell me what happened." He led her to a chair in the office, urged her to sit, and took his seat behind the desk. He'd get more clarity from this woman if she followed his example and calmed down. "Now, tell me why Jeremiah was arrested."

"He's been accused of...of stabbing a man."

Barrett's muscles grew rigid. "Did he?"

"No."

Despite the vehement denial, a wife's account was certain to be biased. "Were you with him when it happened?"

"No."

"Then you can't be certain."

Her mouth pinched. "I know my husband."

Barrett picked up a pen and pulled a notebook toward him. "I'll need details."

"All I can tell you is what he told me." Mrs. Quincy ducked her head and kneaded a handkerchief in her hands. "It started when he got into a disagreement in a tavern."

The clerk at the general store had said Quincy drank too much. Was he also prone to violence? "Was it a disagreement or a fist fight?"

"He said it started as a disagreement, but the man swung at him, so he swung back."

Barrett wrote as she talked. "And?"

She shrugged. "That was it. When he knocked the man to the floor, Mr. Swain threw them both out. Jeremiah left."

"I need all the facts, Mrs. Quincy. Leaving anything out will not help me to help your husband. What was the argument about?"

She bowed her head, heralding news neither of them would find helpful to her husband. "He was fired from the brewery not long ago. The man had accused him of drinking during the day."

"Your husband knew the victim beforehand?"

She winced when he used the word victim. "His name was Claude Dulong. He worked in accounting at the brewery and claimed my husband was drunk one afternoon." Before he could ask, she rushed to say, "But he wasn't. He'd only had a beer with his lunch."

Barrett paused his scribbling, his pen suspended over the paper. "So Dulong reported him and that's when he was fired?"

"Yes."

"Is the man dead?"

She dabbed her eyes with the handkerchief and nodded.

"After Swain threw them out of the tavern did your husband go straight home?"

"The police arrested him before he..."

He cocked his head, urging her to continue.

"No, he didn't come straight home. He went to another tavern."

Barrett wrote down the name she gave him. "Was that where the police found your husband?"

"They found him at McMullin's Livery. He left the second tavern and went there to get his horse." She hesitated. "But they found Mr. Dulong by an old shack on a lot near Swain's."

"Swain's isn't far from the livery."

"No, sir."

Barrett hadn't met the husband but found it hard to picture his mild-mannered housekeeper married to—much less defending—a cold-hearted murderer. "How much had your husband had to drink before the fight?"

"He told me he'd had a couple of beers."

"And after?"

"He said he'd only gotten to the second place when he turned around to come home."

Barrett smoothed his close-cropped beard. Two beers, maybe three. Personally, he'd never cared for the taste of alcohol in any form, but if Quincy told his wife the truth, Barrett figured that amount probably wasn't enough to stab someone in a drunken rage—especially if that someone was accustomed to drink. "Do you believe your husband is innocent?"

"With all my heart."

The strength of her answer gave him hope, but he'd heard such proclamations from spouses in the past. He'd heard similar from Edy in her defense of her son.

"My husband is not a drunk or a violent man, Mr. Seaton. It's true that he likes to visit a tavern now and then."

"Why go to a second tavern?"

"The quarrel shook him up."

"And he was angry?"

"I suppose." The admission was a whisper. "But he said by the time he got there he'd calmed down and wanted to go home."

Good old Jeremiah had an answer for everything, but how truthful were those answers? Was he as innocent as his wife believed?

"Will you help my Jeremiah, Mr. Seaton?"

He dropped the pen and stood. "You go home, Mrs. Quincy, and I'll meet with your husband."

A relieved smile graced her face. "Thank you, Mr. Seaton."

At least the prospect of a new case would take Barrett's mind off Edy for a while.

THE EMERALD-COLORED earrings dangled from Edythe's ears, a present from Lamar on their last anniversary. Flicking the right one, she watched its reflection swing in the dressing table mirror. She'd learned years ago the jewels were nothing but paste.

At breakfast, Edythe's father had reiterated his command that she wear the emerald gown this evening. His cheerful charge only served to heighten her nerves. The clock in her bedroom read six thirty, but how she wished to crawl into her bed and pull the covers over her head.

Weakness. I must no longer appear weak.

The last time she found herself in the position of fending off her father's idea of a suitor, she'd expected to fight it knowing Barrett would be at her side. The expectation turned out to be as false as his promise to write to her weekly.

In her mind, she heard Verbenia urge her to pray for wisdom, but prayer had done nothing the last time the judge chose her groom. How was she to trust in prayer when God had decreed that children obey their parents? When, through His inaction, He took her father's side against her?

She straightened the gown's neckline and plumped up the puffed sleeves. She'd adored this gown, one of the last sewn by Madame Marie before the doors of her shop closed. Now, she wished she hadn't bought it.

Her father burst into her room without knocking, his face a masterpiece of mottled anger. "What is the meaning of your behavior, Edythe?"

Skittish over his tone, she turned to face the mirror, away from his glower. "What have I done?"

He seized her wrist and wrenched her around. "Don't turn away from me."

She tried to pull away. "You're hurting me, Father."

He eyed his hold on her and let her go with a hint of regret in his expression and a slight shove away from him. She bumped the dressing table, caught her balance, and rubbed her throbbing wrist.

Already, a bruise rose, along with the fear she tried to hold back. "You've never hurt me, not even when I was a child."

"I'm sor..." His voice faded on what sounded like the start of an apology. "Had I been more prone to physical discipline, it might have taught you not to sneak around with a man behind my back."

Edythe wanted to deny her father's claim, but his words were true. Long ago, she'd met Barrett without his knowledge, certain he wouldn't have approved of his daughter courting a man whose ambition was to become a lawyer. How ironic that the judge never found himself to be as loathsome as others in the profession.

"No matter the work I put into raising you as a proper young lady, Edythe, you grew into a woman as deceitful as your mother."

"I've done nothing wrong."

"Then I suppose you thought I would approve of you hiring Barrett Seaton."

Edythe's throat grew dry. "It's to help Andrew." Could she sound any more like a scared five-year-old?

"You cannot help someone bent on self-destruction."

"Andrew is my son. I'll never give up on him."

"If you insist upon letting Seaton worm his way back into your life and the boy's, so be it. But mark my words. If I see that man anywhere near this house, I will have him arrested for trespassing."

He marched out of the room. The door slammed and Edythe flinched.

Her fingers quivered as she reached up to restore a curl displaced when her father shoved her. She was nothing like her mother. For one thing, she would never abandon her children, no matter what they had done.

She walked out of the room more certain than ever that she and her children didn't belong in this house. That certainty was all she and her mother had in common.

Edythe's steps faltered. Maybe she was more like Mary Ellen

Danby than she wished to believe. Her mother had shown no more courage in confronting the judge than Edythe, so she escaped this house with someone else and never returned.

If only she had taken her child with her.

Chapter Twelve

In a small room inside the police department, Barrett questioned the officer who had arrested Jeremiah Quincy. "What about witnesses?"

"No witnesses to the stabbing." Officer Souter picked a piece of lint off his uniform as though bored by the conversation. "Plenty of witnesses to the fight inside the tavern."

Barrett scribbled in his notebook. "And the stabbing took place near Swain's?"

"Behind an outbuilding on a lot about fifty yards away."

"What happened after the fight?"

"Mr. Swain tossed them out. He said they went their separate ways. Dulong turned down an alley close by. Quincy went the other direction."

"He watched them leave?"

"Not for long. He went back inside."

Had Jeremiah turned around and followed Dulong? "I was told Mr. Quincy went straight to another tavern after the fight."

Office Souter shrugged. "If so, he didn't go inside."

"Did anyone see Mr. Dulong cut through the alley to the lot on the other side? Was that the direction he'd take to his house?"

"No one's come forward to say they saw him, sir, and he'd have gone in the opposite direction to go home."

"So, there are no witnesses to say the men exchanged words in that lot or after they went their separate ways?"

"No witnesses to another conflict, though Quincy claims he bumped into a man near the head of the alley on his way to the livery."

Barrett frowned. "Who?"

"No idea, sir. We've found no one to support his statement. As far as we can surmise, the men carried on their disagreement in the shack where Quincy stabbed Dulong. Simple as that." The officer's voice had taken on an edge.

"What about the weapon involved? A knife?"

"Yes. We found it near the body."

"May I see it?"

Barrett waited until the officer fetched the knife. He examined the six-inch blade and the burled-wood handle. "A nice piece." If it weren't coated in dried blood.

"The man was stabbed six times."

His pencil slid across the paper. Six? Mary Quincy hadn't mentioned that fact. "You arrested Mr. Quincy at the livery?"

"Yes, sir. He was wearing bloody clothing. He said it was from a livery horse."

Barrett made a note to talk to the livery owner about an injured horse. "What was Mr. Quincy doing when you found him in the livery?"

"Saddling his horse."

"Did he seem in a hurry?"

"No, sir."

"Was he combative when you arrested him?"

Souter leaned back in his seat. "No. He came along peaceable."

"So he was calm?"

"I wouldn't call it calm, but he didn't fight us."

Barrett tapped the end of his pencil on the notebook. "Did you find it peculiar that a man would stab someone so many times—indicating rage—then a few minutes later calmly saddle his horse, and when arrested, accompany the officers without a struggle?"

The policeman shrugged. "I've been doing this job for over fifteen years, sir. It doesn't take long to learn there's no such thing as peculiar. People do odd things for odd reasons."

"Have you spoken with the livery owner?"

"Yes, sir. The livery was closed all day. Quincy told us he left his horse in the corral and a few coins in a box McMullin keeps in his tack room. We didn't find any money." Souter crossed his arms, signaling an unwillingness to consider Quincy's innocence. "Anything else?"

"One more question. Has Mr. Quincy ever been in legal trouble before?"

"Not that we have record of. Not in Riverport, anyway."

"Thank you, Officer Souter. I'd like to speak with Mr. Quincy now."

While he waited for Quincy, Barrett wrote down the timeline as he'd heard it thus far. Jeremiah left his horse at the livery, then went to Swain's, which was only a few buildings away. He and Dulong saw one another, had words and an altercation, then each went his own way.

He stopped writing. Why had Dulong cut through the alley and entered a vacant lot when he lived in the opposite direction? Where was he going?

WHEN READY, EDYTHE descended the stairs and entered the drawing room to find her father in conversation with a man standing in front of the fireplace.

She'd erred in her identification of the banker. Rather than the mousy little man she often spotted through the window at the bank, the gentleman who stood before her was neither little nor mousy. In fact, he was at least Barrett's height and had the same solid build. His charming grin could captivate even the most churlish matron.

She would fight to keep from becoming one of them.

"There you are, Edythe. Come in and meet Mr. Treadway."

Despite her intention to remain aloof, her gaze never left the face of their guest. She stopped, keeping the length of the sofa between her and the men—close enough to be polite, yet far enough to be safe from the confidence oozing from the banker. "Good evening, Mr. Treadway."

He closed the distance in two strides, took her hand, and pressed a kiss to the back of it. Along with talcum powder to hide the redness on her wrist, she'd slipped on a bangle bracelet. He showed no curiosity, no sign of having spotted the discoloration on her skin. "I'm honored to meet you, Mrs. Westin."

She forced a smile and managed to take part in frivolous conversation until she glimpsed the cook's signal. "If you gentlemen are ready, I believe Mrs. Cameron has our supper prepared."

Mr. Treadway crooked his elbow. After a subtle glance at her father, she took the man's arm and directed him to the dining room.

She had to admit, Ansel Treadway was a far cry from the man she had expected to meet tonight.

OFFICER SOUTER USHERED a man into the small room where Barrett waited, then left, shutting the door behind him. Barrett was six feet, one inch, but Jeremiah Quincy had another four inches on him, which left a strange picture in Barrett's mind when it came to this giant having such a petite wife.

He shook the man's hand. "I'm Barrett Seaton."

"The attorney Mary keeps house for. She said she'd talk to you. Did she tell you I ain't got much money for a lawyer?"

"Let's take one thing at a time. I haven't agreed to represent you yet." Barrett studied him from the top of his head to the toes of his dirty boots. His beard was scruffy and his hair stood on end, as though he'd pulled on both.

Barrett pointed to the dried stain on the bib of the man's coveralls. "Where did you get that?"

Quincy dipped his head and pulled on the bib. "When I went to the livery, I noticed one of the draft horses in the corral had cut herself on the neck. It looked like a deep gash. I was trying to get a better look, and she got cantankerous. She pushed me against the barn wall, got blood on me, and near broke a rib. The police think it's that man's blood, but it ain't."

Barrett gestured to the chair the policeman had vacated. "Have a seat, Mr. Quincy. I have more questions for you."

The man cocked his head. Wariness filled his expression.

Barrett spent the next half hour conferring with Jeremiah. He compared the man's answers to the notes he'd taken in his office and during his questioning of the police officer. So far, Jeremiah hadn't deviated from the story he'd told his wife.

Still, there was that blood smear on his clothing. Not as much as Barrett would expect to see after such a gruesome stabbing, but enough to raise doubts about Jeremiah's version of the truth.

"How tall was Mr. Dulong?"

"He was a whippersnapper." The chair scraped the floor as Quincy stood and placed his hand to an area below his throat. "Didn't come up no taller than this on me."

"According to you, you hit him at Swain's after he tried to strike you."

"Yes, sir, but I ain't one to go hitting a man unless it's to protect me or mine."

"What about stabbing him?"

Quincy's eyes widened. "No, sir! I ain't never stabbed nobody and never would." He held up a fist. "I already admitted that I hit

Dulong, but it only took one blow to bloody his nose. Why hit him again? I proved my point. Why would I kill him?"

"Because he had you fired?"

"I only worked at the brewery a couple days a week to add a little money to the coffers. I'll admit I didn't look on him favorably for what he done, but we'll get by. I never saw him after I left Swain's, and that's the truth of it."

The victim had been stabbed several times in the abdomen and chest. "Dulong was found face down. If you stabbed him—"

"I didn't."

"If you stabbed him and he fell against you, bleeding on you, the stain would be at your waist or below, not up here." Barrett poked at the blood near the top of the bib.

The light of understanding lit Quincy's eyes. "That makes sense. Ain't that enough to get me outta here?"

"I'm afraid not." But the case intrigued Barrett. "What did you argue about?"

"I seen him as soon as he come in to the tavern. He was looking for a fight."

"Why do you say that?"

"His face. Hard and mean-like. He wasn't a happy man. He saw me,"—Quincy snorted—"I ain't exactly hard to miss. Next thing I know, he starts talking about men like me being no good and a bad influence on others, then he takes a swing at me."

"What about the man you bumped into? Was he coming out of the alley?"

"Can't say for sure. I was walking down the sidewalk, thinking about a fence that needed mending and didn't see him. I guess no one else did either, 'cause the police say they can't find him."

"Describe him."

The farmer raised both shackled arms and scratched the days-old beard covering his face. "He looked to be in his fifties, and kinda wiry. Honestly, I don't remember much."

Did Jeremiah Quincy really bump into someone near the alley? If so, such a vague description would make it nearly impossible to find him.

Barrett studied the man and said a silent prayer for guidance. Even during times when he questioned God's concern over earthly justice, he'd developed a habit to pray before taking on a client. Throughout the entire case, really. He had broken that habit when he involved himself in Andy Westin's legal problem. Maybe he hadn't wanted to know if his impetuous agreement had been a mistake.

Sensing no objection, Barrett stuffed the small notebook and pencil in his coat pocket and stood. "All right, Mr. Quincy. I'll do my best for you."

Relief smoothed the lines on the man's face. "Can you get me outta here? I got a farm to run and cows to milk. My wife can't do it all."

"I'm afraid not. The court frowns on bail for murder."

"Does that mean I won't get out until the trial is over?"

At least his new client had confidence in his acquittal. "Perhaps things won't go that far."

Barrett walked out of the police department into a moonlit night. He had another client whose guilt seemed assured. Before he changed his mind, Barrett strode toward the Danby house, hopeful Edy's father wouldn't deny him the chance to speak with his daughter or grandson.

WITH THE MEAL FINISHED and dinner plates cleared, Edythe sipped her coffee while the two men discussed financial matters.

"I'm afraid we've bored you, Mrs. Westin." Mr. Treadway's face flushed with apology.

Not only was he handsome, he was kind. She placed her cup on the saucer. "Not at all." In fact, she had enjoyed his deep and soothing voice—a little like listening to her music.

The muted chimes of the grandfather clock in the foyer announced the top of the hour.

Mr. Treadway set his napkin on the table and pushed away the empty dessert plate. "It's nine o'clock. I had no idea we'd been sitting here for two hours. It was a splendid meal and good company, but I should take my leave before I wear out my welcome."

"Don't be in such a hurry, Ansel." Her father stood. "It's the perfect night for a walk. Why don't you take my daughter for a stroll around the neighborhood?"

"Father, I—"

"I'd be honored to accompany you on a stroll, Mrs. Westin." The banker rose from his seat to stand alongside her. He held out his hand.

Edythe stared at it, wanting to take it, yet wanting to defy her father's obvious attempt to play matchmaker—to control her future.

Beaming, Mr. Treadway waited patiently. His delight waned when she hesitated to take his hand.

What harm would come from it? She let him help her to her feet.

He closed the front door behind him, drew in a deep breath, and released it. "Are those roses I smell?"

"From the bushes at each corner of the house."

"Roses suit you." As if he sensed her discomfort, he turned toward the street. "Your father was right. It is a lovely night."

"Yes, it is." He was correct in using the term night to describe the time. The sun had set and she had no desire to walk the streets with a man in the dark. What had her father been thinking? "If you don't mind, why don't we sit on the porch?"

At least, the lamps shining from the drawing room provided a little light, and she wouldn't feel as susceptible to both the possible wiles of a handsome stranger and neighborhood gossip.

Edythe eased into one wicker chair and motioned for him to occupy the other. A potted ivy plant draped the top of the small table separating them. Now what? It had been years since she'd been alone with a man. Alone in this way. She didn't count the time she spent with Barrett two days ago. In fact, she tried to forget it.

Mr. Treadway twisted in the chair to face her, the light from the drawing room painting a golden glow on his face. "I've looked forward to this evening, Mrs. Westin. Whenever your father visits the bank, he never fails to sing your praises. Now that we've met, I understand why."

"Thank you, Mr. Treadway." If her father held her in such high regard, why had she been forced to cover up the consequences of their earlier confrontation?

"I would be honored if you would call me Ansel."

She responded with a noncommittal smile.

Insects played a background serenade in the silence between the two of them. A bat wheeled through the air.

Edythe struggled for something to say to ease the awkwardness. "How do you like your work?"

"It's an honorable profession and what I was meant to do. One day, I hope to run the bank."

"You sound confident in your ambition."

He laughed. "As I told your father last week, my plans have been set in stone for a decade, and I'm well on my way to achieving them."

"Then I'm sure you will succeed."

Undoubtedly, her father chose this man because he saw success in him.

Movement along the street caught her eye. A figure stood in the dark, staring at her father's house, his face partially illuminated by a gas lamp in the neighbor's yard.

Barrett.

She silently willed him to leave before her father saw him. If he stepped one foot on Danby property, the judge wouldn't hesitate to see he was jailed.

"You know that fellow?" Mr. Treadway had followed her gaze.

The question was filled with complex implications. At one time, Edythe would have said she knew Barrett well—his likes, dislikes, moods.

Did she know the Barrett of today? Based on her mistaken impression at breakfast, she had to say no. "That man you see is a stranger."

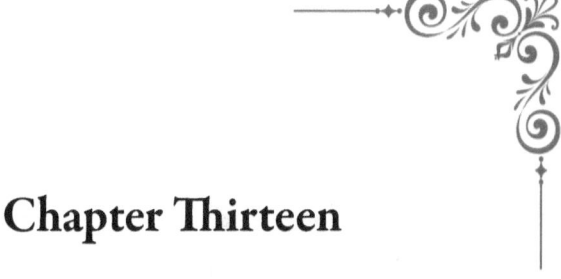

Chapter Thirteen

Edythe sat propped against the bed's headboard. She pressed a cool, damp cloth to her forehead, hoping to convince the carpenters in her head to stop hammering on her skull.

The strain of the past week's events sent her to her bedroom after church. In the past hours, neither rest nor willow bark tea had lessened her headache.

Last night, when pressed by her father, she'd admitted that Ansel Treadway seemed like a nice man, which increased his smug grin. But she'd agreed to act only as hostess to her father's guest, not as a potential bride, something she'd failed to verbalize at the time.

She had found Ansel pleasant and attractive, hadn't she? And he had shown an interest in her. Yet...

Oh, why had Barrett returned to Riverport and complicated her emotions? Her heart had no business fluttering when near him. Her mind had no right to keep bringing up thoughts of him.

"Mrs. Westin?" Mrs. Cameron knocked on the bedroom door.

Edythe lowered the cloth. "Yes?"

"You have visitors, ma'am."

Edythe groaned and left the bed. She dropped the damp cloth on the marble top of her washstand and opened the door. "Who is it, Mrs. Cameron?"

"Two ladies—Mrs. Jensen and Mrs. Kingsley."

Verbenia and Claire? Of course. It was Sunday, and Edythe had missed the Widow's Might meeting. "Please show them to the sitting room and tell them I'll be down shortly. I'm sure they would like some of that cake you served last night."

"Yes, ma'am."

Edythe peered into the dressing table mirror to fix her hair. The edge of her sleeve slid upward, revealing a bluish splotch on her skin. She tugged it back down. The small bruise, though not painful, was not something she cared to display.

A few minutes later, Edythe stood in the doorway to the sitting room, listening to her guests' vibrant and carefree conversation. Both women noticed her presence and rose, their brows twisted with concern.

Verbenia studied Edythe. "Are you ill?"

Edythe would shake her head if it weren't for the concern it might fall off. "A mere headache."

"Perhaps we should have put off our visit, dear, but we were concerned when you didn't join us today."

"I'm sorry I didn't send word."

Claire guided her to the small sofa. "Sit before you fall down. What can we do for you?"

"You can tell me what I missed and how everyone has fared this week."

While they partook of the refreshments, the women discussed Ruby Kelly's new job at the post office, Louisa Gruhn's absence due to her daughter's summer cold, and Claire's plan to make next Sunday her last meeting with the Widow's Might circle.

Edythe had formed friendships with all the women in the group but felt closest to Claire and Phoebe. Maybe because both women possessed traits Edythe admired. They were talented, intelligent, outgoing. They stood up for themselves and what they wanted. In many ways, they were her heroines. "You and Mark aren't marrying until the end of October."

"True, but Phoebe already left, making room for Louisa. Since our group is limited to seven"—Claire gestured toward their mentor—"eight with Verbenia, I feel it's time I make room for someone else."

"I'm sorry to see you go."

Claire laughed. "Oh, you won't get rid of me that easily. If it's all right, I'd like to visit you on occasion, and you're always welcome to visit me."

"I would like that." Edythe turned her attention to Verbenia. "At the moment, I'm not aware of anyone who would fit into our circle, are you?" Widowhood wasn't a qualification most young women aspired to achieve.

"Actually, we do have a candidate and voted this afternoon. However, with member approval required to be unanimous, we won't ask her until we receive your vote."

"Who is she?"

Verbenia exchanged a glance with Claire. "Roslyn Malone."

"Mrs. Malone?" Edythe's only knowledge of the woman consisted of the rumors surrounding her missing husband's embezzlement months ago and Claire's decision to move out of her parents' house and in with the woman. "I hadn't heard that her husband had died."

"He's still missing." Claire shook her head. "Roslyn is not a widow as far as she or anyone else is aware."

"Then, I don't understand why we would consider her." Both Claire and Verbenia had worked with the woman at Newland's. They knew her well, so despite her concern, Edythe would take their suggestion seriously.

"Since Gil Malone's theft and betrayal last Christmas, people have mistrusted her. Some believe she assisted him in his embezzlement at Newland's." Claire scowled at the cake on the plate in her lap. "A ridiculous and unfair notion."

"If that were the case, I would have expected her to flee Riverport with him." Why did people insist on jumping to the worst conclusions about others?

"Exactly. His crime caught her as much by surprise as it did the Newlands. Fortunately, they don't believe the rumors any more than I do." Claire set her plate on a nearby table. "She's lonely, Edythe. She could use what Widow's Might offers. Camaraderie and helping other women are the cornerstones of our group. Everything we do is built on that."

Edythe hid a tiny smile. Leave it to Claire, an architect, to explain things in construction terms. "How did the others vote?"

Verbenia also set her plate aside. "We'd rather not influence your decision."

It was possible Widow's Might was a fit for Roslyn Malone, but was Roslyn Malone a fit for Widow's Might?

Edythe addressed Claire. "No one has heard from Gil Malone since he left?"

"No."

"So as a matter of practicality, she lives as a widow, correct?"

"Yes."

"Then I won't object to her membership in the group until we're sure of her marital status."

Claire grinned at Verbenia. "I told you she wouldn't say no."

Was she that easily read? "What about Louisa?"

"We've already spoken with her. She agreed." Claire sighed. "I'm going to miss you ladies more than you'll ever realize, but I'm happy that you'll welcome Roslyn and treat her with respect. She's not as tough as she pretends."

"We'll do our best, Claire."

Whether real or imagined, it seemed Verbenia's shrewd gaze narrowed in on Edythe's wrist. Her instinct was to tug on the edge of her sleeve. Her friend started to say something but Edythe's father entered the sitting room and drew everyone's attention.

"I wasn't aware we were entertaining." His beard filled out his lean face. Her father was a handsome man when he chose to charm others. "I don't believe we've met. I'm Hayden Danby, Edythe's father."

Edythe introduced Verbenia and Claire. "They missed me at the meeting this afternoon and came to see that I was well."

Verbenia stood. "We were about to leave and let your daughter get some rest. It was nice to meet you, Judge Danby."

"Must you go so soon? It's a pleasure to finally meet my daughter's friends. She speaks of you often."

A pleasure to meet her friends?

"It's clear that Edythe isn't feeling well."

"Is that true, Edythe?" The judge's performance could earn him a role on the stage.

"Merely a headache, Father." One that had almost vanished with the visit by her friends. Now, it raged once more.

His eyes narrowed. "Then I agree. It is better if she rests. I'll see you ladies to the door." Her father led them from the room.

Verbenia glanced over her shoulder. "If you need *anything*, my dear, I'm always available."

Edythe's eyes stung. Had God given her friend special insight into the needs of all the women she mentored?

As soon as her father shut the door, she crossed the foyer to the staircase, intent on spending some time with Andrew.

"I'd like to speak with you before you return to your room."

She sighed and followed the judge into the drawing room. He prompted her to sit in the armchair by the fireplace. For a moment, she considered rebelling by sitting on the sofa. But what good did it do to fight the petty skirmishes of a war when there were larger battles to wage?

He stood beside her. "Let me see your arm."

He needn't indicate which one. Before she could push back her sleeve, he lifted her wrist and did it for her. Grimacing at the bruise, he ran a finger over it, his touch light and tender. "I'm sorry for having been rough with you. It won't happen again."

Edythe stared at her father, not sure what to say. How long had it been since he'd shown her the type of regret and thoughtfulness she heard in his quiet words? How long would the contrite attitude last?

More to the point, what did he want in return for it?

GOOD SENSE AND BARRETT'S emotions had parted ways Saturday evening. He'd suffered for it ever since, unable to free his mind of the image of Edy on the porch, calm and comfortable as she entertained a visitor—a male visitor whose laughter had scraped Barrett's eardrums. He imagined the clod salivating over the opportunity to keep company with such a beautiful woman as Edythe Westin.

Maybe he had erred in turning around without saying a word but the memories, the past anguish, took control of his actions...and his feet.

He entered the police department and approached the front desk. "I'd like to speak with my client, Jeremiah Quincy."

"Wait here, sir."

Once the sergeant left, Barrett tripped on a chair along the wall and nearly fell onto the seat. *Clumsy oaf.* He almost kicked the chair, then wanted to kick himself for being preoccupied with Edy's love life when she meant nothing to him.

She should mean nothing to him.

Barrett rested his elbow on the chair's arm and propped his chin on his hand. He needed to pull himself together before something dire happened—to him or someone in his path.

His thoughts had been scattered this morning. He burned his breakfast, lost his temper with Mrs. Quincy for no good reason, and misplaced the book with his notes on her husband's case. The latter could have proved disastrous for Jeremiah. Fortunately, Barrett had found it in—of all places—the icebox.

Being out of sorts because another man courted Edy made no sense. He'd survived this situation before. He'd survive this time.

And why shouldn't she enjoy someone else's interest? What business was it of Barrett's? He'd lost her favor years ago. At least, at the time, he'd thought she favored him. He'd learned the truth the hard way. No wonder she'd never answered his letters back then.

Barrett looked up to find the sergeant waiting for him. "Your client is ready for you, Mr. Seaton."

After being escorted to a private room, Barrett found Jeremiah inside, wearing clean coveralls, iron cuffs on his wrists, and a befuddled look on his face.

"Did they decide I ain't guilty?"

"No, Jeremiah." Barrett shut the door. "I want to talk about your time at McMullin's livery. You left your horse there."

"In the corral."

"Since McMullin closed the livery for the day on Saturday, you placed the fee in a box in the tack room." Barrett eyed the man as he fidgeted in the chair.

Jeremiah jerked his hands apart, pulling taut the chain holding the handcuffs together. "I reckon that's something I wasn't truthful about. I guess I didn't want to admit to not having paid and give them something else to charge me with."

Barrett drew in a breath and released it, which helped him control his tone. "Don't ever lie to the police, Jeremiah, and don't ever lie to me."

"No, sir." He shook his head. "I've been thinking about that man I bumped into and remembered something about him."

"What?"

"I knocked the fella down and his hat flew off. He had a crooked gray streak running through his hair." Jeremiah pointed to his head, indicating the area with the discoloration. "Reminded me of a lightning bolt."

A gray lightning bolt? Considering Jeremiah had lied about the livery fee and suddenly recalled the mystery man's prominent feature, Barrett wasn't sure he could trust what his client told him. "Is there anything else you remember about the man you knocked down or your actions that day?"

"No, sir. I reckon not."

"This is important, Jeremiah. Anything might help."

The man sat straight. "I'll think on it some more, but I told you everything I remember."

Barrett left, less convinced of his client's innocence, but he'd pay a visit to the scene where the crime took place and to the livery.

Despite the discovery of Jeremiah's lie, working had eased some of the tension in Barrett's gut.

EDYTHE STRUGGLED TO lift the crate of books from the carriage seat. It had taken two of them to put it in the vehicle, and even with her height, she needed leverage to raise the heavy box. She should have brought two smaller crates instead of packing this one so full at Verbenia's.

What if she pulled it across the seat until it reached the edge and fell into her hands? No. She might mar the leather, which would only antagonize her father. He still hadn't let her forget the incident with the banister.

She turned to ask for assistance inside and ran into a human wall. Each of them stepped back. "Wynn. I mean Ned." She glanced behind him to be sure no one heard her call him by his real name.

He stepped back. "It's all right. My guess is I'll be found out sooner or later. I hoped to protect Barrett until he got a good start with his law office." A half-grin brightened his wan face. "I was sitting in one of those chairs on the porch when you drove up. It looked like you were having some trouble. Thought I'd help you out."

She feared overtaxing him. "Are you sure? It's heavy."

He picked up the crate and grimaced. "You're right about that, but I'll manage." Back slumped, he appeared fragile, looking as though he should do nothing more strenuous than rest in bed, but he didn't buckle under the weight of the books.

She remained at Wynn's side in case she was needed. He carried the crate into the sanitarium. The muscles in his thin arms shook from bearing the weight. There was a time when his muscular build outshone his younger brother's slim frame. Now, the opposite was true.

"Where to, Edy?"

"In the parlor, please. Dr. Ellis agreed to let us set up a library of sorts in there." Fortunately, it was the first doorway on the right, so he hadn't far to go.

With a grunt, he set the crate on a table in the center of the room. His breathing strained harder and faster than it should for a man in his early thirties. "I heard about your husband. I'm sorry."

"Thank you." She pulled several books from the crate. Wynn stepped back once more, as though protecting her from his illness. His concern clutched at her heart.

The years and consumption had changed the Wynn Seaton she remembered. He was subdued, the opposite of the young man who'd always had something to do, somewhere to go, or something to say. He'd been a bit too wild for her taste, but Barrett never seemed to see that side of his brother. He had admired Wynn in much the same way Timothy revered Andrew.

"Were you happy with him?"

She hugged the books to her body, searching for a proper response to a question she'd rather not answer. "Our marriage blessed each of us."

Unnerved by what he might see through his steadfast gaze, Edythe carried the books a few at a time to one of the built-in shelves the staff had cleaned off and arranged them in alphabetical order. Once the Widow's Might ladies had accumulated a better-sized collection, she would organize everything by type of reading material.

Wynn's footsteps shuffled across the bare floor, but he kept his distance. "I apologize, Edy."

She turned. Whatever was on his mind dragged down the corners of his mouth and crinkled his brow. "For what?"

He glanced around the room, then behind him. Making sure they were alone? "What happened back then...I came between you and Barrett and ruined your happiness."

Her relationship with Barrett changed when the police arrested Wynn. Yes, she'd been bitter toward Wynn for a while, but Barrett left her of his own volition. Even if he hadn't, her father's hostility and her inability to stand up to him might have torn them apart eventually anyway. "The problem between Barrett and me wasn't your fault, Wynn."

"If it weren't for me, the two of you would have married...had children...been happy together. You both deserved that."

Barrett had condemned her father—continued to condemn him—for the influence he believed the judge exerted in Wynn's arrest and conviction. That condemnation had trickled down to include her. "It's in the past. Let's not dredge it up again."

"That's just it." He hung his head. "I need to tell you something before it's too late. When I do, you'll probably hate me."

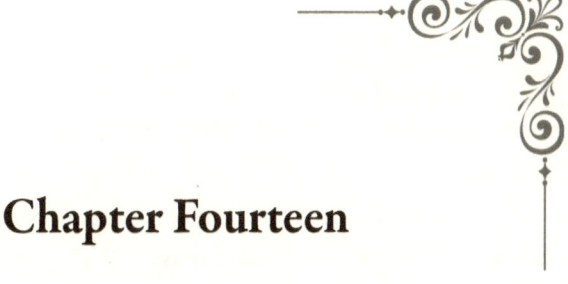

Chapter Fourteen

Edythe looked up from the stack of books awaiting placement on the shelf, her spine stiff with dread. Wynn continued to avoid looking at her, and the seconds ticked by without him saying what was on his mind, why he thought she would hate him. "What's bothering you?"

His toe scuffed the floor, reminding her of a child expecting chastisement. "I've been looking for a way to tell Barrett. So far, I've been too big a coward." He shrugged. "He's had such faith in me, you know."

"He always looked up to you."

"Which makes the truth even harder to say." He turned away from her, dragged a handkerchief from his trousers pocket, and covered his mouth as he coughed. His shoulders shook emphasizing the thinness of his body.

Poor man.

When he'd finished, looking pale and even more frail, he dropped into the nearest chair.

"What's this about, Wynn?"

He peered up at her. "How do I tell my little brother that he's been wrong about me all these years, Edy? He still believes I was innocent of the robbery."

She placed a hand against the commotion in her stomach. His confession wasn't a surprise. She'd always thought him guilty, but he'd refused to admit it.

"My brother thinks your father railroaded me into prison because of him."

"He believed what you told him."

"It wasn't all a lie. I didn't hurt that man, but I was there. I took the money."

"If you didn't hurt him are you saying there was someone else with you?" The police only accused Wynn, who had denied the involvement of anyone else.

He nodded. "Don't ask me for a name."

"Why not speak up at the time?"

"What good would it have done?"

"You might have received a lesser sentence."

He turned away and coughed again, the wracking sound distressing. "Maybe I didn't hit that druggist, but I was guilty of theft. The jury would have said so, and your father would have sentenced me to those years anyway."

"And your partner? You're content to let him get away with no punishment?"

"What happened is long past done, and she's dead. There's no point in upsetting her family."

"A woman?"

His rueful grin reminded Edythe of the old Wynn. "Another of my sins."

And one she'd be happy for him to refrain from confessing. "They found no money on you."

The grin faded. "She took it from me."

"Why, Wynn? You had plans for your life. Good plans. You had the possibility of a successful future. Why throw it all away?"

"I was drunk, Edy. As you know, I liked my liquor in those days." He spat the words out.

From the way his hands slid up and down his thighs, she understood he aimed the explosive words at himself, not her. His

132

reckless actions of yesterday drew his self-condemnation today.

He hung his head. "But I trusted her. I loved her."

And love often led to foolhardy behavior.

"After my arrest, I couldn't bear to disappoint my brother, so when he accused your father of influencing the police and prosecuting attorney, I went along with it."

"Oh, Wynn. Why tell me this? Barrett is the one who needs to hear it."

"I've tried a hundred times to tell him. Each time I lose my nerve. Your pa isn't the only one to convict me of my sins. God got His hold on me in prison. The only difference is I know God has forgiven me." He blew out a breath. "I'm telling you all this, because I'm humbly asking for your forgiveness."

"Mine?"

"If I'd told the truth back then, Barrett would have accepted my guilt. He'd have stayed here and fought the judge for you."

Edythe stared out the window at the view of the rear yard and its colorful flower garden, its cheery blooms a contradiction to the purpose of this building...to her state of mind. The only man she had ever wished to speak vows with was Barrett Seaton. If only he had loved her as she had loved him. "Your brother had other plans—plans to become a lawyer. He was going to leave one way or another."

"But not without you...not for so long."

Could she grant Wynn her forgiveness? Years ago, she would have said no. It no longer mattered, and she would help him find peace. "I do forgive you, but your brother deserves to hear the truth."

"I know." He rose from the chair. "I'd appreciate it if you'd keep what I said to yourself and let me tell him in my own time."

She nodded. "This is a family matter. It isn't up to me to say anything." Not that Barrett would listen to her, in any case.

"There was a time when I thought you'd be family. You two have a second chance. Don't let what I did in the past keep you apart now." Again, he flashed that rueful smile. "I found the courage easier to come by when it came to confessing to God. I'll have to work myself up to being truthful with Barrett."

She couldn't help the slight smile on her own face. "Telling me was a rehearsal?"

"Not intentional. Well, maybe." Wynn lumbered across the room. Pausing in the doorway, he turned, shoulders hunched so that he appeared twice his age. "You've always had a sweet spirit, Edy. I'm truly sorry to have caused you trouble."

Once he'd left the room, she finished placing all the books on the shelf without worrying about alphabetizing them. Detailed focus eluded her. Wynn's apology was unnecessary, but his news would break Barrett's heart.

Before leaving the sanitarium, Edythe told the matron to expect another book delivery in the next couple of weeks. She stepped onto the porch and peered at the groups of chairs set up on each end. Several patients lounged in them, taking advantage of the fresh air that doctors said was key to recovering their strength or maintaining their health. None of the patients was Wynn Seaton.

She settled on the seat of her father's carriage and gave the reins a gentle slap against Jester's gray hindquarters. As the horse headed toward town, she prayed for guidance in dealing with Andrew. She prayed that her belief in her son's innocence was not as misplaced as Barrett's faith in Wynn's.

And she prayed for the faith to believe those prayers mattered to God.

BARRETT SCOURED THE alley near Swain's, looking for anything that might pertain to his case, anything to help him identify the man Jeremiah said he bumped into. He peered in and behind crates, kicked empty liquor bottles, examined smudged shoeprints in the dirt. Nothing useful.

Moving into the grassy lot, he headed toward the small shack where Dulong met his death—a tumble-down structure he recalled from his days growing up. One of the earliest buildings in town, it hadn't seen a resident since the '70s and attracted all manner of visitors, mostly those who stumbled into it after a few hours at Swain's.

He pushed open the door. The police had already searched the building, but it didn't hurt for another set of eyes to go over it.

The stench inside the one-room shack nearly knocked him over. Pulling a handkerchief from his coat pocket, he pressed it to his face. Clearly, people had abused the place over the years—using it for sleeping, as a shelter against the cold or rain, to empty their stomachs after too much alcohol, even as a latrine. What the shack lacked in comfort and cleanliness, it made up for in broken furniture, boxes, and more liquor bottles.

Barrett caught a whiff of the iron scent of blood. Or maybe he imagined that last smell based on the dark stains splattered across the floor.

Eager to accomplish his task and leave, he combed through the room in the same methodical way he had the alley. His investigation ended with equally disappointing results.

Standing near the door with his hands on his hips, his gaze skimmed the room one more time—around the walls, up to the ceiling, down to the floor and the...

Barrett took two steps, reached down, and pulled out a ragged scrap of paper caught in a crack between the bottom of the wall and the floorboards. Somewhat triangular-shaped, it looked like a small portion of a telegram containing the handwritten words "hard," "Major," "U. S.," and the partial words "Subj—," "Dru—," and "Arm—." With the slight flourish under the "m" and its location to the right of "U. S.," Barrett read the last word as Army, though he couldn't be sure.

Not dry or yellowed, the paper didn't appear to have been there too long. Someone could have dropped it yesterday or months ago.

He balled it up in the same hand that held his handkerchief and took one more look around the shack. Intuition told him Jeremiah was not a murderer. But how to prove it, especially with his client's admission of a lie to the police?

After leaving the location where Dulong was murdered, Barrett walked a few doors down to a sizable two-story building. Recently painted letters, still a jaunty white, flaunted the name "McMullin's Livery" above the double barn doors.

He entered the shady structure and inhaled the earthiness and strong aromas of old wood, hay, and grain. The smells brought back fond memories of growing up on his grandfather's farm after his parents died.

It had taken a few months for his six-year-old self to feel comfortable around the old man. After all, he'd never met his grandfather before the day after the funerals when he and Wynn arrived in Riverport. Once he accepted the strict boundaries Grandpa Kirby set, he learned to appreciate them as being for his own good.

Wynn never settled in as well as Barrett. While his brother respected their grandfather, there was always something in him that refused to accept his new home on the farm.

At the same time, Barrett couldn't help but draw a connection between the Seaton brothers' experience and that of the Westin boys. Far from the dictatorial methods of Judge Danby, his grandfather led by faith and example. Until the day he died, he instilled discipline, respect, and wisdom in the boys. They worked hard around the farm, and when their chores were done, they played hard with his blessing.

Barrett attended law school with the money he'd inherited after

Grandpa passed on. Wynn's portion had been enough to open the store he'd always wanted and solidified Barrett's belief in his brother's innocence. Why steal with no need to do so?

"You looking for something, mister?" A shaggy-haired, bowlegged man stood at the other end of the barn's aisle. His silver handlebar mustache quivered with humor, presumably over Barrett's daydreaming.

"Yes, sir. I'm looking for Mr. McMullin."

"Well, don't look too far, or you'll miss him."

"You're Mr. McMullin?"

The man met him halfway down the aisle. "For the past six plus decades. You wanting a horse or buggy? Got me a couple of them bicycles if you're looking to travel in that fashion."

Bicycles? Off and on, Barrett had considered purchasing one and learning how to ride it. Surely, it wasn't hard. One day, perhaps. "I'm afraid I'm not here to rent transportation."

"Shame. I got some of the best horses in the county."

Barrett declined to say he used the other livery in town for his needs, since it was closer to his house. "My name is Barrett Seaton. I'm Jeremiah Quincy's attorney."

"He the one who stabbed the man a few places over?" He jerked his head in the direction of the lot.

"He's suspected of it. I understand you were closed Saturday."

"My granddaughter got married." Mr. McMullin reached over a stall partition and rubbed the face of a large bay tethered to a ring in the wall. The animal turned his head, begging for continued attention. The man seemed willing to give the animal all he sought.

"My client left his horse in your corral that afternoon." Barrett leaned against the other side of the narrow stall and rubbed the horse's back, hoping for the approval of the livery owner. He'd get more cooperation from someone who saw him as kindhearted and friendly rather than some shyster ready to twist the words of a witness. "Was anyone here that day? An employee?"

"I only got two boys that work for me on Saturdays. I sent 'em home Saturday morning after they finished cleaning stalls. Leave 'em on their own, and they'll get themselves in trouble."

"I understand. You live on the premises?"

"Upstairs, which I keep locked. Most folks know I don't lock a side door in case there's a fire and, of course, I can't lock the corral. Anyone who wanted to could get inside."

To leave their livery fee. "By the way, how is your horse? The one with the cut on his neck?"

The man drew back. "How'd you know about that?"

"My client saw the injury and tried to help her, but she pushed him against the barn wall."

McMullin cackled. "Just like her. She's more mule than mare and thinks it's fun to trap a body against something. She's a big'un. He get hurt?"

"Nothing serious." So Jeremiah probably told the truth about the blood stain. "Have you ever seen a man around the place—fifties, small in stature, and with a silver streak in his hair? Crooked like lightning."

McMullin shook his head. "Don't think so. Of course, I get a lot of people in here, and if the fella was wearing a hat when I saw him..." He shrugged.

"If he should come in, I'd appreciate knowing about it."

"I'll keep my eyes open."

Barrett stepped away from the stall. "Thank you for your time, Mr. McMullin. You've been helpful."

"You come on back for another visit." He pointed to the bay. "It appears this fella found a new friend."

Laughing, Barrett shook the man's hand. "I might do that, sir."

He left the barn, squinting in the sunlight. He'd make one more stop before returning home, not expecting this one to go as well.

Chapter Fifteen

Edythe rejected the idea of Andrew being to blame for the fire and injury to Mr. Stark. Barrett claimed her son hadn't told them the full truth, but when she'd asked Andrew about it, he denied knowing more.

Too often, she had all but abandoned the discipline of her children to the dictates of their grandfather, yet she had a keen sense of when they told a lie. Right now, that sense told her he lied about knowing more but told the truth about his guilt. What was he hiding?

She stepped away from his room—his prison cell where her father had incarcerated Andrew before he'd been found responsible for a crime. Whatever happened to the tenet in the law that insisted upon innocence until proof of guilt?

Five days was long enough for her father to get his point across. Andrew would not spend another twenty-four hours in a well-furnished cell.

This newfound strength of conviction left Edythe curious as to its source...almost as though Barrett's return had restored some of the past daring required to meet him in secret.

She wasn't naive. Confronting her father required more than daring.

Of course, she could simply walk back to her son's room, open the door, and order him out. That was a temporary solution at best.

"Daydreaming about a certain banker, my dear?"

SANDRA ARDOIN

She looked up to see the judge standing at the bottom of the stairs, making a show of reading the newspaper. *Five days of imprisonment.* Now was her opportunity. Her time.

If it were physically possible, she'd swear her heart raced her feet down those stairs. "Not daydreaming. However, I would like to speak with you."

The lines between his eyes deepened with a guarded look. "About?"

"Andrew."

Her father closed and folded the newspaper. "I suppose he's whined to you about being confined to his room."

"In fact, he hasn't complained once. That worries me."

"Worrying is a waste of energy."

She'd read that advice in the Bible. It never seemed to stop her, not with a seemingly endless list of things to worry about.

Edythe followed her father down the hall toward the kitchen. "Don't you think his confinement has gone on long enough?"

"You want me to release him on bail?" A corner of his mouth slid up with his sarcasm.

"He hasn't been accused of anything and should be allowed his freedom."

"So he can cause more trouble than he already has? I'm doing him a favor by keeping him away from temptation." He entered the kitchen and slapped the newspaper on the counter. "Andrew receives three meals a day and a fine roof over his head. He's more fortunate than many boys his age. I'm simply giving him a tiny taste of his future in the event he does not turn his life around."

Andrew is your child, your responsibility.

She owed her son loyalty and strength. She owed all of her children a mother who refused to shrink away from others like a timid wallflower.

"That is not *your* duty." When was the last time she had spoken

140

to him in such an emphatic manner? It felt good. She stepped forward, ignoring the scowl on his face that narrowed his dark eyes. "As of now, Father, Andrew's punishment is over."

Her father gripped the edge of the counter until his knuckles turned white. His voice rose to match hers. "This is *my* house. While you and your children live here, you are under *my* authority. I say whether the child will go free to ravage society, and I say no."

"Then you've left me no choice but to take my children and go." The threat tumbled from her mouth without forethought. Unlike her husband, she was not a gambler. What would she do if her father called her bluff?

For an instant, his jaw dropped in disbelief. She thought he might relent, but his shock lasted only a moment before it gave way to a smirk. "Just where do you think you will go, Edythe? Are you forgetting who provides for your needs? If it weren't for me, the four of you would be huddled in some alley, begging for scraps from strangers. Instead, I provide you shelter, sustenance, and a generous allowance you can spend on the charity projects those Widow's Might women rope you into paying for."

She ignored the insinuation that her friends used her. "If it weren't for your selfishness, Father, we still would have a house—our own house." Her chest heaved with years of pent-up resentment. It bubbled up from some hidden place inside her like water from a hot spring. It pushed its way through a crack in her reserve, breaching the dam that normally held back her emotions. "You're the one who chose to sell my home out from under me. Why? Why treat me as you do? It wasn't my fault that Mother..." Her lips clinched tight, plugging the fissure about to gush with the ugliness of the past.

He stared at her, but she hardened her expression. Silence stretched between them.

Finally, her father opened the icebox and pulled out a pitcher. He poured a glass of milk and carried it toward the hall, then paused, turning at the kitchen door. "Free your child, but do not come crying to me the next time he gets into trouble."

Once he had gone, Edythe sank against the counter, drained of energy. She had done it. It had been a gamble on her part, but she'd argued with her father and won. How many times in the past might she have prevailed against him if she'd only stood her ground?

It energized her. It motivated her. One day she would gain the courage to confront the two people who had abandoned her in the past—Barrett and her mother, if she ever saw the woman again.

Edythe tipped her head back and stared at the ceiling. *Someday, I'll feel strong enough to take you to task, too, God.* She would ask Him why He never felt a need to fight for her as she had just done for her son. But she could only cope with one battle at a time.

Someday, though. Someday.

BARRETT HADN'T COME to the Danby house to eavesdrop, but the open window at the kitchen and the raised voices flowing from it had provided ample opportunity.

A few minutes ago, he'd approached the front walk, prepared to talk to Andy again. Timmy jumped off the porch with all the enthusiasm of an eight-year-old boy and insisted Barrett follow him to see his latest experiment.

In the rear yard, he let the boy take his hand, press his index finger on an ink pad, and press it again on a sheet of paper lying on a small table in the yard. Timmy did the same with Barrett's thumb. Above his marks were smaller such images marked "Timothy" and "Sarah Jane."

"What are you doing?"

"Getting your fingerprints." Under Barrett's inky swirls, Timmy wrote "Mr. B. J." and closed the lid on the ink pad.

Barrett tried to rub away the ink coating his skin but only

managed to splotch the other fingers. "Why do you want my fingerprints?"

"My teacher says everyone's are different, so I'm collecting them from people I know."

Barrett was aware of the science of fingerprinting people but also aware they were inadmissible in court. What Timothy planned to do with the fingerprints was a mystery.

He started to pat the boy's head, then remembered the ink. Staining Timmy's blond hair would not please his mother. "That's clever of you."

Now, the raised voices of Edy and her father flowed through the screen of the open kitchen window. Barrett, the Westin twins, and a dog that drooled on his shoes stood silent in the yard, listening to the argument inside the house.

The children's eyes bulged and their lips parted. Barrett worked hard not to follow suit. Silently, he cheered Edy on and prayed for her strength of conviction. What a fine thing to hear her stand up for herself and her son.

Sarah Jane leaned toward her brother and whispered, "She's giving it to him."

Timmy whispered back, "I wonder what will happen next."

"I don't know. Do you think she meant it when she said we'd leave Grandfather's house?"

Her brother shrugged. "I hope so."

"Me, too."

Why couldn't the judge see that his dictatorial conduct had cost him the love and respect of his daughter and grandchildren?

Barrett worked to associate the incensed woman of the moment with the girl who was more apt to cry over her father's injustice than rage against it. Feelings he'd thought long buried awakened—feelings he couldn't afford to resurrect.

The voices quieted, and Barrett's conscience pricked him.

Concerned Edy would catch them listening, he gestured for the children to step away from the window.

He followed them into the middle of the yard. While Timmy carried on about the uniqueness of a person's finger marks, Barrett only half listened. His thoughts returned to the argument and Sarah Jane's question. Would this prompt Edy to move out? Without employment and three children, where would she go?

Something poked his leg, then grabbed hold of his trousers and pulled. He looked down and jerked his leg away from a white, well-fed goose—one that would make quite an impression on a platter at Christmastime.

"He does that to everybody but Grandfather. I guess he knows his goose would be cooked if he did." Timmy guffawed over his joke. He shooed the bird away and returned to his experiment while Sarah Jane chastised her brother for scaring her precious Snowman.

Edy was right. Her children were extraordinary, each in their own way.

Barrett eyed the goose, waiting for it to attack a second time. "I'll be going now."

Sarah Jane stopped chasing the goose and cocked her head. "I thought you wanted to talk to Mother."

After what he'd overheard, it wasn't a good time to confront Edy or Andrew. "It can wait. Let's keep this visit and what we overheard to ourselves for now, all right?"

"All right."

As he turned to go, he spotted two boys watching from a rear corner of the Danby property—the same boys he'd seen at the river the day he'd first met Andy and Timmy. He followed their line of sight to a window on the second floor of the house. Andy stood there, looking back at the boys as if he wished to jump through the glass and pummel them. Interesting.

Barrett tipped his head toward the visitors. "Timmy, do you

know those boys?"

Timmy made a face and turned his back on them. "Yes, sir, I know them."

"Who are they?"

"I call them the Trouble Brothers, because that's what they are."

If any boys looked like trouble, it was those two. "What are their real names?"

"The big one's Tad Larson. His little brother is Hollis."

As if sensing they were being talked about, the Larson brothers turned and bolted away. "Andy knows them, too?"

Timmy shrugged, but it was a hesitant shrug, the kind that said yes without having to verbally link his brother to more turmoil. "I told Andy to stay away from them."

Years ago, Barrett had warned Wynn away from certain bad influences. "Has he?"

"Sometimes."

It hadn't always worked with Wynn, either.

"What kind of trouble has he gotten into with the Larson brothers?"

"After Mother got mad because he'd been smoking, Andy laughed about it and told me he could smoke cigarettes anytime he wanted to. He'd just ask the Trouble Brothers for them."

Barrett drew in a sharp breath. Smoking? Edy had known of her son's activity and hadn't mentioned it.

Had Andy been smoking at the Stark farm? It was possible Stark caught the boy with a cigarette on his property and they'd had words.

Timmy hung his head. A moment later, he sniffled and wiped his nose on his sleeve. "Will my brother go away to that school, Mr. B. J.?"

He laid a hand on the boy's shoulder. "Your mother and I will do whatever we can to prevent it, Timmy." For the sake of the younger brother—a boy who reminded him of himself—Barrett vowed to do all in his power for Andy Westin.

A chill skittered up Barrett's back and his gaze slid to the second floor of the Danby house. Andy no longer stood at the window. In his place Judge Hayden Danby stared down at Barrett. If the judge's hostile expression were a sword, it would have sliced him in two.

Barrett stared back, determined to show the man that any effort at intimidation would fail. He'd stand in this spot for hours to prove he was no longer a young man crushed by an older man's power. The judge might rule his house with an iron fist, but he didn't rule Barrett's life.

The man disappeared from behind the glass, which meant the judge had lost a battle twice in a matter of minutes. Like a wounded bear, the indignity made him more dangerous and unpredictable. That begged the question...most dangerous to whom? Barrett or Edy?

Possibly both of them.

Chapter Sixteen

"Mother, I'm going outside."

Edythe looked up from her embroidery to see Andrew standing in the foyer. He was a different child now that he had the run of the house again. "Fine, but don't leave the yard."

"I won't." He scuffed the toe of his shoe over the marble.

"Is there something else?"

"I...uh...I'm sorry."

Edythe dropped the tablecloth on the sofa. Joy, curiosity, relief—all the motherly emotions combined in a swirl of eagerness that sent her to her son. She barely contained her steps to a walk when she really wanted to run to him. "What are you sorry for?" She held her breath, awaiting his answer.

"Doing stupid things and causing you problems."

If only an apology would save him from the possibility of reform school.

"Honest, I only smoked one time—that day you caught me—and it made me sick to my stomach. I didn't burn that shed, either, or hit Mr. Stark."

The passion in his confession brought the assurance she'd longed for since the whole debacle began. "But you were there. Why?"

He stared at his shoes and shrugged. "I told you. I was mad."

Edythe dropped to her knees in front of him and clasped his hands. "Andrew, the past few years have been difficult for all of us. I know I haven't handled everything as I should. I haven't stood up for you and the twins enough. I'm so sorry. Things will change. I will change."

After a slight hesitation, he wrapped his arms around her neck, nearly choking her. She leaned back and pulled him onto her lap. The weight strained her knees and the hard marble dug into them, but she didn't care. "I love you, Andy."

"I love you, too, Ma...ma. I do."

Edythe laughed. "Ma. Mama. Mother. I'll answer to it all."

The twins rushed down the stairs and dropped on each side of her, their arms encircling their brother and her. Together, the four of them sat bunched in a circle on the floor. Smiling. Happy. Momentarily free of fear and dread.

She had argued with her father and won. Amazing. More amazing was how it had earned her the renewed regard of her children.

A knock on the front door separated them. Decked in their cheeriest mood in days, the children bolted down the hall toward the kitchen. The door off the mudroom slammed.

Edythe opened the front door to find a boy on the porch.

He held out an envelope. "Are you Mrs. Westin?"

"Yes."

"I was asked to deliver this, ma'am."

She took the message and thanked him.

"I'm to wait for a reply."

Edythe turned the envelope over, slid her finger under the flap, and pulled out a piece of note paper. Unfolding it, she sought the signature and wasn't surprised to learn it was from Mr. Treadway.

My dear Mrs. Westin,

Please accept my sincere appreciation for the delicious meal you served Saturday evening. I must also thank Judge Danby for allowing me the pleasure of sharing the company of his lovely daughter.

As such, I would consider it a delight to escort you to supper in the restaurant of the Patton Place Hotel on Saturday evening. Should you honor me with your acceptance, I will arrive at your home at seven o'clock.

I am ever hopeful,

Ansel

Supper with the banker? Edythe's stomach muscles tightened.

"Ma'am?"

The question broke through her pondering. Before she could respond, her father climbed the porch steps and stood behind the boy. "I see you received Ansel's invitation."

Edythe held up the note. "You know about this?"

"We spoke at the bank a short time ago. This boy had already left, but I took the liberty of accepting for you." He paid the messenger and gestured for him to run along.

She followed her father into the drawing room. "You accepted this invitation for me?"

"Yes. You deserve an evening away from the children...a quiet evening with an adult."

An adult man. Her spirits deflated. This sounded too much like her father arranging her future yet again. This time, she hadn't the possibility of Barrett saving her from his choice of husbands—not that it had done her any good last time. "Did you even consider asking me if I wanted to go to supper with Mr. Treadway?"

"Don't get on your high horse, Edythe. Of course, you'll go. I saw the two of you on Saturday. A perfect couple."

"We are not a couple."

"Give him a chance." He glared at her and spoke as though she had no choice in the matter.

Only minutes earlier she'd promised Andrew she would be a different person. But could she win another argument against her father so soon, or was it best to choose her skirmishes more wisely? After all, it was only supper. Ansel was a gentleman, and it wasn't as though other men had called on her.

It wasn't as though Barrett cared who she saw.

The image of Ansel sitting on the porch Saturday evening faded, replaced by Barrett sitting across the table from her as they ate Eggs à la Benedict and discussed Andrew's situation. Notwithstanding the topic of conversation, it was much as she'd imagined many times when she was younger.

Edythe shut her eyes, willing the image to go away. She couldn't do this again. She couldn't allow Barrett to tiptoe into her emotions and her life. She couldn't allow him the opportunity to abandon her again. "Yes, I'll go to supper with Ansel."

She opened her eyes to see a satisfied grin on her father's face.

BARRETT REINED IN THE carriage horse at the curb in front of the Danby residence. He sat inside the conveyance finalizing what he would say should the judge answer his knock. In that event, he expected to be told Edy wasn't home—not to him.

Before he left the carriage, the front door opened. Edy descended the porch steps and followed the walkway toward the street. Head down, she focused on the bricks under her feet rather than her surroundings.

In all their years apart, he'd never found her equal in elegance, in kindness—in appeal. Truth be told, he'd rarely taken the time to look.

When she finally glanced up, she halted, her eyes wide. "I see you made it all the way to the house this time."

Barrett controlled his grin. Evidently, her recent victory over her father had sharpened her tongue.

Before their lives turned upside down, he had enjoyed playing the part of Edy's protector, her strength. Having her lean on him for comfort made his younger self feel more like a man, the only one she could count on. But, honestly, this side of her was something to behold and drove him to test how far he could push her.

He left the carriage and closed the distance between them, stopping within breathing distance of the flowery perfume she wore. "Who was I to disturb your Saturday evening visit with your beau?"

"He is not my beau." Just as the resentment in her voice brought a surprising warmth to his insides, a tiny smile formed on her face. "Not yet."

Maybe he preferred her to be less sure of herself.

She glanced over her shoulder at the house. "You shouldn't be here."

Barrett clasped her elbow. "If it's too uncomfortable to ask me in, let's take a ride."

She raised her arm to pull away, then relaxed and allowed him to lead her to the carriage.

They said little while he drove to a quiet spot by the river. He'd had no idea what she'd been thinking as she stared ahead. As for him, his thoughts swirled, bouncing off one side of his brain, then the other.

They strolled down a narrow and winding path to their old meeting place on the bank. Unsure where to start their conversation, he picked up a small stone and skimmed it across the surface of the water. It bounced half a dozen times before it sank, leaving ripples to fan out over the surface. "Remember when I taught you how to do that?"

Edy wrapped her arms around her waist. "I was never very good at it."

"I hear your father's belittling voice."

She bent down and picked up a stone. Positioning her fingers around it as he'd taught her, she gave it a quick side-arm toss. It skipped once, twice, three times before it plopped and sank to the bottom. She glanced at him and shrugged her shoulders.

"Not bad." He stared at a squirrel digging in the dirt on the other side of the river, probably burying an acorn. He should have taken Edy straight to his office. They could talk in a business setting rather than this spot where they had spent so much time in years past.

"Tell me about Andy's smoking habit."

Her eyes flashed. "How did you find out?"

"It doesn't matter. What matters is that you're honest with me."

Her lips drew taut. "I caught him with cigarettes a few weeks ago and took them away."

"And since then?"

"That was the only time."

What about times she hadn't caught him? According to Timmy, Andy could get more of the tobacco whenever he wanted it. "If what happened was an accident and Andy admits to it, things might go better for him."

She crossed her arms. "You're convinced my son set that fire?"

"You have proof otherwise?"

"If I did, I would have gone to the police. When the Stark incident occurred, I asked my son if he had been smoking again. He denied having smoked at all around the Stark property." She bit her bottom lip when it began to tremble. "I think you're right to say he's not telling me everything. Do you understand how awful it is to think you can't trust in your own son's word?"

He had an inkling of the pain and guilt. He'd suffered through moments when he dealt with his own doubts about Wynn's truthfulness concerning the robbery.

"But I do *not* think my son was responsible for the fire, Barrett, or the injury to Mr. Stark."

"How do you know?"

"We talked on Monday...really talked. He was adamant that he hadn't smoked since the day I caught him with cigarettes. That was before the incident at the Stark property. He said he didn't even like smoking and had only done it the one time." Her chin rose with confidence. "He's a different boy, so yes, I believe him."

"I'd like to think he told the truth about what happened, but you should be prepared in case the police provide evidence that your son set the fire."

Edy rubbed the area above her eye as though her head hurt. "What about the injury to Mr. Stark?"

Yes, there was that. "I don't know."

"He might have set his own shed on fire by accident." Her voice rose with hope.

"It's possible." Anything was possible at this stage.

"Oh, Barrett, if it were that simple."

If. The world was filled with "ifs."

If Wynn hadn't paid the price for Barrett's deceit.

If the judge weren't so bitter and domineering.

If his brother had not been drunk that night and been in the wrong place at the wrong time.

Most of all, if Barrett had never fallen in love with Edy.

Even as he wanted nothing more in this moment than to take her in his arms, repeating the past was a mistake. Things would never work between them if he couldn't trust in her devotion.

Chapter Seventeen

Barrett tapped a pencil on the paper in front of him. For the past hour, he'd studied the book on the desk, taking notes on cases that might help him with Jeremiah's. At least, he'd tried to take notes.

Bouncing up from the chair, he was eager to get away from the thoughts that spun round and round like a whirlpool inside his head—thoughts having no business being there. For two days, he'd fought to concentrate on something other than those few minutes with Edy beside the river and how he'd longed for more than a business relationship.

He needed someone to converse with, someone who understood what agitated him. Wynn. His big brother always knew how to take his mind off whatever bothered him.

An hour later, Barrett parked his carriage in front of the sanitarium. He hopped to the ground, snatching a package from the seat.

Nurse Hammond met him in the front hall, her bearing inflexible and disapproving. "Good evening, Mr. Seaton. It's a little late for a visit."

"I apologize, ma'am. I won't stay long, but may I see Ned?" Would he ever get used to calling his brother by that name? He held up the bag. "I brought him something to cheer him up."

"What is it?"

"Gumdrops. They're his favorite candy."

Her head waggled side to side. "That isn't part of his approved diet."

He thought to argue that it wouldn't hurt to let Wynn have something enjoyable once in a while, but he'd brought his brother here to improve his health not contribute to its decline.

She held out her hand and stared at him until he handed over the bag. What good would it do his brother for Barrett to ignore the rules?

"Mr. Flannigan is in his room. Please don't stay long. It hasn't been a good day for him."

"He's worse?"

"The tuberculosis is weakening him."

"I brought my...Mr. Flannigan here based on the good reports I heard about Oakcrest. Dr. Ellis is well-known for successful treatments. Is Ned not responding to them?"

For the first time since his arrival, her authoritative expression slipped into something softer, more sympathetic. "The doctor keeps a careful eye on the progress of all his patients, but as he informed you, tuberculosis is an incurable disease and your friend was in poor health when he arrived."

She needn't remind him it was a killer.

"Don't be discouraged, Mr. Seaton. With faith comes hope."

Now faith is the substance of things hoped for, the evidence of things not seen.

Yet faith and hope weren't the same as assurance, and Barrett wanted the assurance that Wynn would survive for many years, even with this breath-stealing disease. While he asked for a miracle for Wynn, Barrett also asked God to make the judge understand what he had done to the Seatons.

"Thank you, Nurse Hammond. I won't stay long." He strode down the hallway to his brother's room before she could barrage him with more well-meaning platitudes.

Barrett studied Wynn, who lay in a semi-upright position in the bed, his frail body not much more than a series of lumps under the covers. His chest rose and fell as though he'd finished a sprint around the sanitarium's building mere moments ago. The darkened skin of sickness and fatigue ringed his closed eyes, and his cheekbones stood out like spikes under his skin.

God, he's getting worse, not better. Is my faith too small to save him?

Maybe his desire for Wynn's survival—even with the illness—was a selfish one.

Barrett's throat tightened, threatening to cut off his own supply of air. As much as he despised Edy's father, he despised himself even more for having failed his brother.

"Stop it...Barrett."

He started at the weak voice. Immersed in self-pity, he hadn't noticed that Wynn had opened his eyes. He whipped off his hat and pasted a smile on his face. "I was about to leave and let you sleep."

Wynn snorted. "Plenty of time...for that...later."

"I brought you a bag of gumdrops." Barrett glanced over his shoulder. The hall was empty. "The dragon at the door snatched it from me."

His brother's chest bounced a couple of times and one side of his mouth drifted up. "Don't worry...I'll get them. She can't...resist my sweet talk."

Barrett laughed. "I've no doubt. You've always had a silver tongue." This was the reason he drove out to visit his brother this evening. Based on Wynn's condition, though, he shouldn't stay. "You're tired, and I promised Nurse Hammond I wouldn't be long."

"I'm glad you came." Wynn drew in a deep breath and coughed. "I saw Edy...a few days ago."

"She came to visit you?" Her coming to see Wynn would only draw attention to him. It wouldn't be long before his brother's identity was revealed.

"No. She brought books...for a library." He coughed again. "I told her I was sorry."

"Sorry? For what?" Wynn was the last person to owe anyone an apology.

"I need to tell you..." Deep, wracking coughs interrupted him, snatching his breath and leaving Barrett struggling to know how to help.

As he ventured farther into the room, Nurse Hammond rushed past him as if she'd been loitering outside, her face covered with a cloth mask. She helped Wynn to sit straighter and propped another pillow behind his back. During the continued coughs, she eyed Barrett. "Please leave, Mr. Seaton."

"But—"

"He'll be fine and ready to see you in a few days. For now, he needs less talk and more rest."

Barrett slapped the hat on his head. "I'll be back when you've built your strength, Wy...Ned."

He escaped out the front door and onto the wide porch, his chest heaving as much as Wynn's. He leaned his forehead against a column, wanting to forget the pitiful sight of the man he once believed to be stronger than anyone he'd ever met.

"I'm trying to have patience, God, but when does Your justice take hold?"

EDYTHE PLACED HER HAND in Ansel's as she stepped from the carriage in front of the Patton Place Hotel. He tucked her arm around his and led her inside the building, keeping hold of her as if he worried she'd run back home. It had crossed her mind.

The headwaiter ushered them into the dining room, a long and somewhat narrow room with tables arranged against the side walls and separated by Roman-style columns. A straight line of large chandeliers spaced several feet apart hung from the ceiling, and colorful carpeting muffled their footsteps. Starched white tablecloths, polished silver, and crystal glassware awaited diners.

The hotel's restaurant was not an eating establishment the majority of Riverport frequented. Hopefully, Ansel could afford the meal and wasn't simply trying to impress her.

On the way to their table, Edythe dipped her head in greeting to a number of people she knew or recognized. Most were friends of her father. Surely, their tongues would wag for the next few days as they speculated on seeing her accompanied by Ansel.

They had barely been seated when two shadows passed over the table. Phoebe Crain and Spence Newland approached. Ansel pushed back from the table and sprang to his feet.

"I told Spence I thought I saw you enter the room." Phoebe clung to the arm of her fiancé and slid a curious glance toward Edythe's companion.

"I'd like to introduce you to Mr. Ansel Treadway. Mr. Treadway, these are my friends, Mrs. Phoebe Crain and Mr. Spence Newland."

Ansel nodded a greeting. "It's an honor to meet you, Mrs. Crain. I had the pleasure of attending your July Fourth concert and was quite taken with your talent. Superb."

Phoebe's gift as a concert pianist had gained her acclaim throughout the Midwest until a man's deceit ended her career. Why did love too often end in betrayal?

"Thank you, Mr. Treadway."

He reached out and shook Spence's hand. "Mr. Newland, it's a pleasure to see you again, sir. I understand you and Mrs. Crain became engaged on Independence Day. I offer you my congratulations."

Spence grinned. "When a man finds the right woman, he takes the necessary steps to keep her from getting away."

Ansel gazed at Edythe. Her cheeks flared like a flambéed Cherries Jubilee. She liked the gentleman, but he wasn't—

Her jaw tightened. No, Ansel Treadway was not Barrett Seaton. Shouldn't she consider that a good thing?

Phoebe exchanged an amused glance with Spence. "We should go."

Ansel's attention whipped back to Edythe's friends. "Won't you join us?"

"No, thank you," said Spence. "We've finished our meal. Maura's bedtime is coming soon and Phoebe wants to tuck her in." Clearly, Phoebe's fiancé would enjoy his role as papa to her child.

Barrett had his doubts about Andrew's innocence with regard to the Stark incident, but her son's respect for him said much about their newly formed relationship. Even Timmy and Sarah Jane spoke about him as though he were a hero.

Oh, for heaven's sake. If she didn't stop snatching at every opportunity to think of Barrett, she might scream.

Left to themselves again, Ansel settled back in his chair. "Nice couple."

"Yes." Edythe turned her attention to the evening's menu.

"Of course, I knew Mr. Newland from his visits to the bank."

"Really?" *Really?* Even with her natural timidity, Edythe had been taught to provide more scintillating and intelligent conversation in a discussion. She focused on Ansel. "He is a nice man." *No better.* "I'm sure he finds your assistance..."—her brow furrowed—"helpful."

"I hope so. The bank's president is leaving soon. As a substantial investor and one of its board members, I'm sure your father must have mentioned it."

"No, he didn't." Her father rarely spoke to her of anything regarding his business dealings.

"It's rumored that I am certain to take his place." His chest puffed out like a Thanksgiving turkey's.

"Congratulations."

"We'll see. It all depends..." The sentence faded as though the words had fallen over a cliff. He raised his menu, his gaze moving up and down it with enthusiasm. "What would you like, Edythe?"

She would like to know who told him the bank presidency might be his and why this sudden chill had overtaken her.

WYNN WAS ASLEEP WHEN Barrett returned to Oakcrest on Sunday afternoon, so he hadn't stayed. On Tuesday, he received a message from Dr. Ellis telling him that Ned Flannigan was feeling much better, dissolving the solid clump of anxiety he'd struggled to breathe around for days.

Mrs. Quincy appeared in the doorway to his office. "Mr. Seaton, a gentleman is here to see you."

Barrett checked his schedule to be sure he hadn't forgotten an appointment. Still new in town, there hadn't been many yet. As expected, nothing was written in the small agenda he kept open on a corner of his desk. "Thank you, Mrs. Quincy. Show him in, please."

"Yes, sir." She disappeared momentarily and reappeared, followed by a well-dressed man near his own age.

Barrett met him in the middle of the room.

His guest removed his hat. "Mr. Seaton?"

"I'm Barrett Seaton. What can I do for you?" Barrett gestured for the man to take the chair near the desk and returned to his own seat.

"My name is Mark Gregory. I'm an architect here in town."

Someone drumming up business? "I'm afraid I'm not in the market for an architect's services, Mr. Gregory."

The man grinned. Confidence oozed from him. "Well, if you ever find yourself in that market, come see me. My office is on Commerce Street." He lost the grin. "Actually, I'm not here regarding my business. I'm here about yours, or I should say, that of Jeremiah Quincy."

Barrett leaned forward and rested his forearms on the desk. "What about Mr. Quincy?"

"I spoke with Mr. McMullin earlier. He's like a gossipy old woman when it comes to the disturbing event that happened near his livery."

"I can't blame him for considering it disturbing."

Mr. Gregory grimaced. "As is learning you're looking for a man who once lived under my roof."

Barrett bolted upright. "He's a relative of yours?"

"By the grace of God, no."

"But you know who he is."

"I believe he's a man by the name of Alec Olesky. He rented a room from my mother in July. He's in his fifties, thin, and has a jagged gray streak in his hair. About here." Mark Gregory ran a finger down the front portion of his brown hair.

"That's the description Jeremiah gave me."

"And the one Mr. McMullin gave me."

Stopping to talk to the friendly livery owner might have been Barrett's best move in this case so far.

He wrote down the name he'd been given, then studied his guest. Though seemingly self-assured, he didn't appear to be the type of person to make up a story in order to assert himself into a criminal case. However, one never knew. Barrett had met such men—and women—in his line of work. They sought the notoriety.

No, Mr. Gregory didn't look the type, but he couldn't dismiss the possibility. "To be clear, if the man I'm looking for is this Mr. Olesky, no one has accused him of taking part in Dulong's murder. At this point, I'd categorize him as a potential witness."

"I don't like to think the worst of people, yet I always felt there was something not quite right about Olesky."

"In what way?"

He shrugged. "Call it a feeling."

"I see." Feelings weren't fact and definitely not evidence of wrongdoing. "Your mother owns a boardinghouse?"

"Not a boardinghouse. It's a long story, but she rented the room to him thinking to help ease my financial burden while I established my business here."

"So, you're new in Riverport."

"We've been here a few months."

"Mr. Olesky still resides with you?"

Gregory shook his head. "When I informed him I would marry in October and he should find another place to live, he moved out that night without a word. I haven't seen him since."

"Strange." And disappointing.

"No stranger than the man himself. I didn't pay much attention to McMullin's gossip until he mentioned the gray streak in the man's hair."

"Have you given this information to the police?"

"I stopped there before coming here. They listened and wrote down his name, but I'm not sure they considered my information as being important."

"Which prompted you to come see me."

Mr. Gregory bobbed his head. "When speaking with the officer in charge, I sensed he'd made up his mind about the murder and wasn't looking elsewhere. Perhaps I'm imagining it, but I'm afraid his lack of desire in investigating the facts might stem from your client being a frequent visitor of the local taverns."

"Why? What did he say to you?"

"It wasn't what he said. It was more the way he grimaced each time he mentioned that Quincy was a 'drinking man.'" Gregory leaned forward. "My partner in my company is a woman and my fiancée. I've seen the prejudice she's encountered as a female architect. It almost ruined my business and our relationship."

This man was the fiancé of Edy's friend? What was her name?

The name Claire came to mind.

"I don't know if Mr. Quincy is innocent or guilty, but I do know he deserves a fair trial and not one based on someone's bias."

"We agree." Barrett admired the passion and sincerity in Mark Gregory's voice. It was obvious he'd taken his fiancée's troubles to heart. "Do you know where Mr. Olesky lived before he rented a room from you? Was he new to town?"

"All I know is he told my mother he was a widower whose children had moved away. He said he didn't like living by himself, yet the whole time he stayed in my house, he rarely interacted with us." He rubbed his chin. "He did talk about Peru in one of our conversations. I got the impression he'd lived there not long ago."

Peru was a good-sized town a short train ride from Riverport. Barrett would make his inquiries around here first and, if necessary, travel to Peru. "Would your mother have any other information?"

"I'm afraid I've told you all she knows." He settled the bowler on his head. "If you have no more questions for me, I've been gone from the office long enough."

"I'm grateful for your help, Mr. Gregory."

"Mark. Please." He rose from his seat, and Barrett accompanied him to the front door. "If you need anything further from me, as I said, my office is on Commerce."

"I'll keep that in mind. Thank you for coming to see me, Mark."

The man nodded again and walked away.

Barrett returned to his office and reviewed the notes he'd taken, grateful for the help from the architect. Nothing pinpointed Alec Olesky's present whereabouts, but there was enough to get Barrett started on inquiries.

He marched to the foyer and grabbed his hat from the hall tree. "Mrs. Quincy, I'm going out. I'll return later this afternoon."

A faint "Yes, sir" came from the kitchen, barely heard as he walked out the door.

If the man he sought was Olesky, Barrett would find him. He prayed that, when he did, it would be to Jeremiah's benefit.

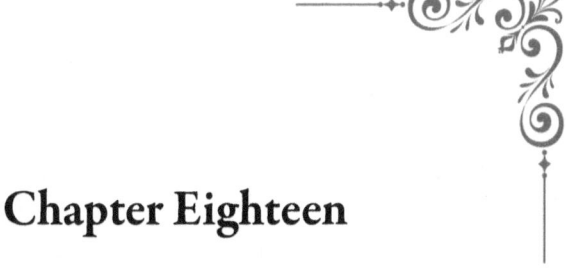

Chapter Eighteen

Barrett eyed the sign for the Homestead Hotel on Webster Street, a narrow brick building squeezed between two broader structures. He'd visited the boardinghouses and the other hotels in town, including the Patton Place, which was a long shot. This was his last chance to find Olesky.

The name painted on the window lacked the "H" in hotel, and the door stuck when he pushed on it. In contrast, the inside appeared clean and orderly, if devoid of much in the way of furniture and natural light.

Barrett walked up to the clerk behind the counter. "Do you have an Alec Olesky staying here?"

"Olesky?" The young clerk, not much past twenty, tilted his red head, then shook it. "No, sir. That name isn't familiar."

"Maybe he isn't here now but stayed in the past, say May or June? It's important that I talk to him."

The clerk's mouth twisted with indecision, and he glanced right to left as if expecting his employer to be listening. "Giving out information about our guests is not regular."

"My name is Barrett Seaton. I'm an attorney. The man I'm looking for might be a witness to a crime." Barrett described Olesky.

When he mentioned the streak in the man's hair, the hotel clerk's eyes widened. He grabbed the register and flipped the pages, skimming each one. He tapped a line. "Here." He turned the book around for Barrett to see. "This man fits that description. He checked out on August fourteenth."

The day of the murder.

Barrett studied the signature. "Osbourne?" Asa Osborne. Alec Olesky. The same man? If Mark had seen Olesky's handwriting, he might identify it as matching Osbourne's signature in the register. After Barrett left here, he'd stop at the architect's office and ask him to take a look when he had a chance.

"If you want confirmation that they're one and the same, the first time he stayed here—I'm thinking it was last fall or winter—he wanted to know where he could get a haircut. I sent him to Mr. Ferris' place. The barber might remember Mr. Osbourne."

It was worth checking. He pushed the register back toward the clerk. "Did you see him with anyone? Maybe he checked in with a companion?"

"No, sir. If he met anyone here, I didn't see."

"Nothing was found in his room after he checked out? He didn't mention where he might go from here?"

"Nothing, and he didn't tell me his plans."

"Sounds like he made quite an impression on you." And not a good one.

"Yes, sir."

"What is your name?"

"Curtis, sir."

Barrett tapped the counter, satisfied he'd gotten all the answers available from the young man. He pulled out his card and laid it on the counter. "Thank you, Curtis. You've been a big help. If you think of anything else, please send word to that address."

"I hope you find him, Mr. Seaton. The truth is, he did make an impression on me. There was something about him, you know? Something shady."

That said a lot considering the type of clientele a place like the Homestead must attract.

Curtis curled his lip. "He was unemotional, like he had no feelings, or if he expressed any, they weren't real. Know what I mean?"

"I do." In his dealings, Barrett had met one or two people so coldhearted they sent a shiver down his spine.

If Olesky and Osbourne were one and the same, he was glad the man no longer lived under the Gregory roof.

EDYTHE KNOCKED ON VERBENIA'S door. She'd looked forward to this Widow's Might meeting all morning, needing the time away from her father. He'd interrogated her over her supper with Ansel last night. His self-satisfied smile had given her another headache, this time not so serious as to keep her from enjoying the company of her friends.

"Good afternoon."

Edythe glanced over her shoulder to see a woman approaching the porch—a blonde several years younger than her. Composed and direct with her eye contact, the woman stood at the edge of the porch steps. "Good afternoon...Mrs. Malone?"

"Roslyn, yes. Claire encouraged me to come today. I really don't know what to expect." She looked Edythe up and down. "I apologize. Though I've seen you before, probably at Newland's, I can't recall your name." As fast as Roslyn Malone talked, her fingers tapped the front of her purse even faster.

"I'm Edythe Westin. We're happy you're able to join us."

The door opened and Verbenia grinned, her cheeks as broad as her stout figure. "Good afternoon, Edythe." She glanced at Roslyn. "Good afternoon, Roslyn. Welcome and please come in."

The other ladies already occupied the parlor. Introductions were made, and Roslyn sat in a dining room chair next to Edythe.

Verbenia stood nearby. "Of course, we're acquainted from our work at the store, but these ladies want to know you, Roslyn. Tell them a little about yourself."

Roslyn glanced from one woman to another until she'd taken in all the faces staring at her. "As you know, Claire suggested I visit one of your meetings. To be clear, I'm not a widow. At least, I don't think I am." She crossed her arms, and her facial features grew taut. "My husband is Gil Malone. He disappeared last December—ran out, I'd say—after stealing from Newland's Department Store. Contrary to the opinions of some people, I had nothing to do with it. Even the Newlands don't believe the rumors, which I'm sure is the only reason I still work at the perfume counter in the store."

Edythe generally avoided chatterboxes. Her head spun with the effort to keep up.

Verbenia laid a hand on Roslyn's shoulder. "We aren't here to judge you, dear, or dwell on rumor. We each have our troubles and choose to support one another rather than tear each other apart."

Roslyn unfolded her arms and her expression relaxed. "Thank you. I do appreciate the invitation to join you. Even if I can't claim the title of widow, I feel like one."

None of them in the room would prefer to claim the title of widow. Neither would they want to walk in Roslyn's shoes. What was it like to have a missing husband, one who was accused of a crime? Anything similar to having a child accused of criminal mischief?

"Edythe?"

She blinked at Verbenia's raised voice. "Yes?"

The older woman's sharp eyes seemed to penetrate Edythe's thoughts. "I asked how the book delivery went? Do you know if our little library has been accepted by the residents at Oakcrest?"

"I haven't returned to the sanitarium since delivering the first collection." Since Wynn confessed to her his guilt in the robbery. Had he told Barrett yet? It seemed, lately, stories of illegal behavior surrounded her. "I'll make another delivery this week and speak with the matron."

Verbenia nodded, though she still regarded Edythe with undue interest. "Would you like one of us to go with you? Perhaps Roslyn would care to see firsthand the type of work we do."

Not one for idle conversation with a stranger, Edythe shrank from the idea of traveling to the sanitarium and back with someone she hardly knew. Neither could she allow her timidity to deny Roslyn an opportunity to take part in their endeavor. She shifted on her chair to address their new member. "I'd planned to drive out there Tuesday morning."

Roslyn shook her head. "Thank you for the offer, but I can't that day. I have my work at the store, and I'm sure it will be busy. Newland's begins a sale this week and people come from miles around for the bargains."

Edythe breathed easier. "Perhaps another time."

"Now that our business is over, let's carry on with our study." Verbenia turned to Jenny. "I believe it's your turn, dear."

Jenny stood and opened her Bible. This was the portion of their time together Edythe preferred to miss. Not that she minded the reading of scripture. However, the ladies rotated sharing a short passage that had meaning to them—one they would then discuss. Every eighth Sunday was Edythe's turn.

She dreaded her Sundays. Speaking before others was hard enough for her, but choosing scripture of special meaning when she lacked the insight expected by the others... That made her responsibility doubly difficult.

Jenny read with gusto from Romans 8. "'For as many as are led by the Spirit of God, they are the sons of God. For ye have not received the spirit of bondage again to fear; but ye have received the Spirit of adoption, whereby we cry, Abba, Father. The Spirit itself beareth witness with our spirit, that we are the children of God...'"

Children of God. Abba, Father. *Am I your child, God? Why don't I feel like it?*

After their discussion, they filed into the dining room for cookies, apple pie, and coffee. Edythe nibbled on a sugar cookie while listening to the conversations around her and responding when necessary. How she'd come to love these women—Louisa, Mavis, Ruby, Jenny, Lucy, and, of course, Verbenia. At the same time, she missed Phoebe's quiet self-assurance and Claire's sense of humor.

She slid a glance at Roslyn, who chatted with Mavis and Lucy as though she'd known them a lifetime. Evidently not one to meet a stranger, Roslyn would fit well into their circle. But what if her husband returned? Perhaps, in some ways, knowing the fate of a husband made life easier, even if he no longer resided on this earth.

Lamar would never return, but Barrett had. He had returned and set her world spinning topsy-turvy.

She carried her empty plate, cup, and saucer to the kitchen sink. Verbenia followed and set her plate on the counter. "Are you all right?"

Edythe turned to look into her mentor's face. "Yes. Why do ask?"

"You went a little pale when Jenny read her choice in passages. I offered to be a sounding board should you need one. That offer remains open."

Verbenia took her responsibility for her younger charges seriously, providing guidance and help where needed. It was her mission, her purpose.

"You know, if you'd prefer not to discuss it with me, Edythe, keep in mind you have a heavenly Father who encourages you to tell Him of your concerns. He'll always listen."

"Really? It's my experience that fathers rarely listen to or care for their children's concerns and wishes." Edythe looked away. How dare she speak that way. Verbenia must think her a heathen. Sometimes, she wished she were, then guilt over her attitude wouldn't cling to her like a shadow. She wouldn't expect a lightning bolt to strike her dead at any time. "I'm sorry for my outburst."

A small smile tilted Verbenia's lips. "We are all permitted one on occasion."

"But God—"

"But God...two of the most encouraging words in the Bible." Verbenia rested a hand on Edythe's arm. "He knows your heart. He knows you speak from whatever hurt you've experienced, and He's big and strong enough to let you beat on His chest now and then. I can tell you He's taken plenty of my blows over the years."

"And afterwards?" What consequences had rained down upon Verbenia?

"Afterwards, I ask forgiveness for my doubts and fears and rest in the knowledge that 'all things work together for good to them that love God, to them who are the called according to His purpose.'" Verbenia quoted one of the verses read by Jenny.

Edythe quoted another. "'If God be for us, who can be against us?'"

"So true."

If only she had the faith that God considered her one of His children. "That's my problem, Verbenia. I don't always believe God is for me, that He works for my good rather than working against me." Once she started her confession, Edythe couldn't seem to stop. "How can I believe He cares for me when I think He only wants to exert power over me, to show me I'm nothing without Him?"

"We are nothing without Him, my dear. With Him we become more than we ever imagined ourselves being." Verbenia frowned. "Forgive my boldness, but are you sure you're not confusing God's judgment with man's?"

A bitter chuckle escaped. "You mean they're not one and the same?"

"God's judgment is righteous. His discipline is meant to bring

SANDRA ARDOIN

His people back to Him, not drive them away or punish them for pleasure." Verbenia laid a hand on Edythe's arm. "Sometimes, we can't understand someone until we've taken the time to get to know him. There's a difference between knowing about God and being one of His children. Perhaps, before you accuse the Father of being what He is not, you need to develop a closer relationship with Him. The way to do that is through the Son."

"But I..." Had she ever truly sought to know Jesus, or had she only assumed she knew Him because she'd attended church her whole life? When was the last time she read—intently studied—the Bible that sat on her bedroom dresser? What did she know of God in the deepest part of her, other than the character she had assigned Him?

Edythe swallowed the lump that clogged her throat, leaned over, and wrapped Verbenia in a hug. "Thank you."

Verbenia clung to her and whispered in her ear, "I love every one of you dear ladies like you were my own children, and I'll always be here for you."

She would always be there for Edythe and the others...like a loving mother. The type of mother Edythe had never known.

If she truly sought to understand Him, would she find that God was the type of father she'd never known?

THE TIP OF BARRETT'S pencil broke. When he reached into the desk drawer for another one, his fingers brushed the small jeweler's box Edy had given him. He hadn't wanted her mother's ring and should have kept it in a safer place for her.

He pulled out the box and set it on top of the papers that littered his desk. Though Barrett didn't approve of the apparent circumstances, he understood why the judge's wife left her husband. If only Edy could find a way to leave her father.

172

Lifting the lid revealed the exquisite and valuable ring that had belonged to Mary Ellen Danby. Merely looking at it brought back the overheard argument between Edy and her father. The judge had lorded over her the fact that she had nowhere else to go.

Nothing prevented Barrett from returning the ring to her, from encouraging her to use it to provide for her children. Nothing but the fact that each time he saw Edy, he slipped further into those feelings he'd had for her years ago.

He'd thought the passing of time and his bitterness over their parting had destroyed this longing to be with her. Before returning to Riverport, he'd deemed his previous love for her unsalvageable. But in being here, seeing her, time rewound and the bitterness dissolved like sugar in warm water.

Barrett closed the box and tossed it in the air. It landed on his palm, and he sealed it in his fist. Was sentimentality more important than freedom? His wounded pride more vital than the emotional welfare of three children?

Chapter Nineteen

After knocking on the front door of the Danby house, Barrett waited until Edy opened the door, ready to take on her father if necessary. When she didn't glance over her shoulder or whisper for him to go away, he deduced the judge wasn't home.

"What are you doing here, Barrett?"

"Is that any way to greet your attorney?"

"You're Andrew's attorney."

She'd grown more guarded toward him since the day she shared his breakfast and he'd made the mistake of nearly kissing her. Or had his mistake come in backing away?

He'd fought daily to safeguard his heart since returning to Riverport, but with the way it pummeled his chest right now, it was a lost cause.

"I came to return this." He took her hand with its long, graceful fingers, turned it over, and laid the box on the flat of her palm.

She eyed the jeweler's box as if expecting it to bite. "You're returning the ring? You said you'd help my son."

"And I will."

"Then why?"

"You said it yourself, I'm *Andy's* attorney. Since he has no money of his own, my services must be provided *pro bono publico*."

She stared at the box again. "My father thinks a lawyer who provides his services without charge has more money than sense."

Barrett laughed. "And with that nonsensical thinking, I know

I'm in the right. I told you before, there's not much I can do for Andy as an attorney. But I can help him as a friend."

Her tiny smile provided a bit of relief to his churning gut.

"Maybe you can use that for a new start, somewhere to live other than this house."

"Weren't you the one who said I should keep the ring out of sentimentality?"

"Sentiment only takes a person so far. Sometimes, events call for practicality."

She appeared to deliberate a moment, then wrapped those long, slender fingers around the box, one at a time. "Thank you."

A boy of about sixteen sailed past them on a bicycle, the bell on the handlebars trilling. Barrett laughed when the boy let go of the handlebars but continued to glide down the street. "Look at him. He's having fun."

"Lamar owned a bicycle."

The reminder of Westin pained him like a sore that never healed.

"He taught me to ride it."

"Edythe Westin riding a bicycle. That must have been something to see." Barrett tried to picture her rolling along, the wind in her smiling face. Carefree and...simply free.

She laughed. "I'll have you know I was a natural."

"Bloomers and all?"

"I wasn't that devoted." She stuffed the jewelers' box in the small pocket in her skirt. "I have a little money saved to pay you. It won't be much, but..."

Back to business. "I'll agree to take payment in a different way." Barrett paused to second guess what he was about to say when he had no right even thinking it.

Suspicion narrowed her eyes. "A different way?"

He clasped her elbow in an attempt to lead her down the walkway to the street. "I'll show you. Let's go."

"Go? Where?" Her heels dug into the brick, and she lifted her regal chin. "Where are you taking me this time, Barrett?"

"Mr. McMullin's livery."

"A livery? That still doesn't tell me where we're going."

"Wherever we want, Edy." When she continued to look at him with those cow eyes, he grinned. "The man rents bicycles."

"You want to ride a bicycle?"

"I do. There's only one problem."

She studied him and her lips stretched into a smile. "You don't know how to ride a bicycle."

He shrugged. "I need an expert to teach me, and I've recently learned of one."

BARRETT ROLLED THE bicycle away from the livery, walking on one side of it while Edy kept pace on the other side. It was true that he'd never ridden one of the contraptions, but he didn't need her to teach him. Surely, it wasn't that hard...mainly a matter of balance.

His imagination jumped ahead, showing him a picture of them together, both pedaling down the road on a long, leisurely ride in the country.

Not today.

Today, she had refused his offer to rent a second bicycle for her, saying this was his lesson, and she wasn't dressed for riding, anyway. Before hauling her away from her home, he should have suggested she change into something less formal than the day dress she wore with its frills and layers of material.

They strolled down a macadam road leading out of town and toward flat farmland where no one would see him wobbling about on two wheels. No one but Edy Westin.

She gazed up at the cloudless sky. "Timothy insisted it will rain this afternoon. He's rarely wrong."

Barrett didn't doubt it. "Then we should hurry."

A wagon trail meandered off the road toward the east, a surprisingly smooth path that ran between a field of corn on one side and a shallow tree line on the other. A private path. He pointed to the trail. "How about there?"

"Hmm. Nice, soft dirt for your landings."

Barrett had forgotten how playful she could be when she was comfortable and relaxed. It was almost like the old days. But they were no longer young and as foolish as they were then. No longer young, anyhow. But how foolish was it for him to expose his heart for a second time to a love that once nearly broke him?

He answered her teasing with a mock scowl. "There will be no landing other than one made of my own free will."

"We'll see."

After swinging his leg over the bicycle, Barrett squirmed on the seat. Gripping each side of the handlebar, he followed Edy's instruction and placed one foot on the pedal closest to the ground. Good...so far.

Edy stood at his side, her arms up as though ready to catch him. Didn't she realize he could crush her if he fell? "All right, now balance, then put your other foot on the pedal and push down."

"Before I go too far, how do I stop it?"

"Drag your feet."

So much for the fresh shine on his shoes. "Here I go." He lifted his foot and placed it on the pedal. The handlebars wriggled back and forth and, with them, the front wheel. He dropped his foot. "A natural, huh? Maybe you should show me."

She raised an eyebrow. "Try again."

After several minutes of practice and Edy's encouraging words—along with a couple of those embarrassing soft landings—he wheeled down the path, the tires maintaining a fairly steady line, even as the pedals spun faster than his confidence allowed. "This isn't so hard."

"You're doing well."

He still hadn't mastered the ability to stop the bicycle with ease and dignity, nor were his turns smooth, but he would conquer those problems in time. "One day I'll ride without gripping the handlebar, like the boy we saw earlier."

She covered her eyes with her hand, mimicking terror. "I don't want to be around for that."

Barrett rolled toward her. A gust of wind blew down the path, sending biting dust into the air and tearing loose tendrils of raven hair from under her hat. She brushed them aside, revealing rosy cheeks and a broad smile. She'd always been the loveliest girl he had ever seen—sophisticated, stately, gentle in both movement and spirit.

Her mouth formed a pretty O and those brown velvet eyes grew round. "Look out, Barrett!"

His focus jerked to the path ahead of him...and the tree he careened toward.

Barrett steered left. The bicycle wobbled and shook, this time heading straight for Edy. He managed to avoid her by a hair but lost his balance. The bicycle slid and he tumbled into Edy. They both fell to the ground with Barrett sprawled across her. Too shocked to move, all he could do was stare into her face.

Beneath him, her ribcage expanded and contracted rapidly. Those dark eyes blinked several times as though she grappled with the reality of their situation.

Heat seared his insides. Days of keeping his distance, physically and emotionally, disintegrated with a single accidental, off-balance moment.

"This is your idea of a free will landing?" Huskiness altered her normally smooth voice.

He eased his weight off her lungs but planted his arms on either side of her. He leaned closer, eager to make good on what he'd denied himself at breakfast over two weeks ago.

Edy turned her head, freezing his movement. "I can't do this."

"You can't do what?" She couldn't kiss him or couldn't bear to be close to him?

He scooted sideways and propped his elbow in the dirt, his head on his palm, hoping to display a nonchalance rather than the current of frustration running through him.

She scrambled backward to widen the distance between them and sat in the dirt, her arms wrapped around her knees like a caterpillar seeking the safety of its cocoon. "I can't let you break my heart a second time."

Barrett shot up into a sitting position, doubtful he'd heard her right. After rerunning the words through his mind, his back teeth clenched. "*Me* break *your* heart?"

Chapter Twenty

From the moment he fell from the bicycle to land on top of her, Edythe realized how little had changed for her when it came to Barrett.

As a mother, she was accustomed to cleaning up messes and bringing order to chaos. Spilled milk. Dirty clothing. A child's sickness. She had no idea how to clean up this mess. No idea how to ignore the fact that she'd lain beneath Barrett on the ground, yearning to turn back the clock, to once again feel his arms around her, his kisses on her lips.

Then the past intervened, ruining her dreams, her future, her trust.

"Of course, you broke my heart. What other man cared so little that he teased me with false intentions, then abandoned me?"

"If anyone was guilty of false intentions and abandonment, it was you, Edy." His face darkened like the thunderclouds above them. "On second thought, I'd say you were guilty of infidelity."

If he hadn't tantalized her with the same smoldering gaze she'd almost given in to days ago, they could have passed the afternoon in a civilized manner.

That was her way, wasn't it? Civilized. Silent. Run over.

No more. It was time she stopped playing the part of a helpless little girl to men who cared little for her feelings. It was time she took matters into her own hands and told Barrett how badly he had hurt her.

"You accuse me of infidelity?" Resentment ruled her tongue. "I am not the one who moved away for a dozen years."

"No, you're the one who married another man before my prints in the dust had blown away."

"What did you expect when you left me no choice?"

"I didn't force you to marry Lamar, Edy."

"You didn't stop me."

"Because I didn't know." He leaned closer. She leaned back. "You should have waited for me."

"You promised to write."

He ran a hand over his hair. "I did write to you, Edy—three times that first month."

He wrote to her? The need to lash out withered. "I received no letters. Not one."

His brow furrowed. "I'm telling you the truth."

With his denial, a horrible suspicion took hold. "My father."

Barrett glared at the building clouds as if her father hid in the midst of them to eavesdrop on their quarrel. "I should have expected it. I waited for a response that never came."

"I had no address to write you." If only she had taken the initiative to collect the mail first. "Why didn't you take me with you? We could have married."

His voice softened. "I wanted nothing more than to marry you. One day. That wasn't the right time for us. With my schooling, I couldn't support us in the way you deserved. I thought you understood that. Then when your father sentenced Wynn to prison—"

Edythe pushed to her feet, her attempt at composure drowned by a wild surge of exasperation. "You blamed me."

Barrett's scowl turned fierce. "I blamed the judge, never you. But forgive me if I didn't understand that you were so eager to escape your father that you'd marry someone else within two months."

She'd never wanted to marry Barrett simply to escape life with her father. She'd wanted him. Only him. "I had no choice."

"Of course, you did. I told you I'd come back for you. When I received no response to my letters, I returned to Riverport to learn why. That's when I discovered you'd married Westin. *That's* when I blamed you. Why didn't you wait for me, Edy?"

"You always spoke of justice...swore to bring justice to those who were innocent. Didn't you think to grant me that same justice? Did you even ask yourself why I had a sudden change of heart?"

"I asked." Pain lined his face. "I asked myself over and over. I assumed you—"

"You assumed I was too weak to fight my father. I can't deny it." Too tired to argue any longer, she turned her back on him. "It's in the past, Barrett. All that concerns me right now is Andrew's future."

With a hand on each shoulder, he turned her around. "Well, it's not all that concerns me. We've started this conversation. Let's finish it. What happened, Edy? What did I miss?"

A line of ants paraded through the dirt at her feet as though she and Barrett were nothing more than tunnel walls for them to pass through. "Twelve years and three children?"

"Sarcasm isn't helpful." With a curled finger under her jaw, he tried to lift her chin, but like a mule sitting on its hindquarters, she rejected the attempt. He dropped his hand and picked up the bicycle from where it had fallen on the ground. "Forget it. I think I've had my fill of lessons today."

As he walked away from her, possibly for good, Edythe's stubbornness melted. Maybe Barrett was right. Maybe it was time they cleared the air. "After you left, my father tried to convince me you weren't coming back. When I didn't receive any word from you, I believed him. Then, he said if I didn't marry Lamar, he'd send me to my grandfather in California."

Barrett stilled. "Your grandfather? You were terrified of him after the day he locked you in the cellar."

She nodded, unable to express how the dark and musty-smelling hole in the ground had petrified her as a five-year-old. Even now, her stomach often twisted at the smell of fresh dirt turned with a gardening spade. When her father found her trapped by her grandfather's cruel joke, his curses against the old man had blistered the air. She hadn't seen her grandfather since that day.

Her father may have bluffed with his threat, but she hadn't had the courage to test him. "I'd rather have married a stranger than live with that man, Barrett."

He walked the bicycle back to her and laid it down. "I remember him pushing a courtship between you and Westin. I never dreamed he'd go so far."

What she said next either would drive a deeper wedge between them or help them move past the hurt. "I discovered something about Lamar that my father wasn't aware of. He had a weak heart. For years, he believed he wouldn't live long enough to marry and raise a family."

"You married him and had his children out of pity?" Disgust flooded his voice. "Or was it because you figured it wouldn't last long?"

She deserved that last part, because the thought had crossed her mind at the time. She swept blowing hair from her face. "Lamar was a kind man. He wanted me as his wife."

"*I* wanted you." He shook his head. "I thought long and hard about coming back here, knowing I'd see you again—see you with Westin. I didn't realize he'd died."

"But you returned for Wynn's sake." Not hers.

"I owed him."

"You still believe the judge sentenced Wynn to prison because of us?"

"That's part of it." He stuffed his hands in his trouser pockets, his gaze aimed at something over her shoulder. "I'd promised to meet him the night of the robbery."

Edythe gasped. "You and Wynn planned to...?"

His features contorted as though he considered her question ridiculous. "No. I had no plans to rob anyone and neither did Wynn. We were to spend time together...checkers or something."

"Instead, you met with me."

Barrett sighed. "If I'd kept my promise, there would have been no charges against Wynn, and your father would have had no excuse to send him to prison where he contracted consumption."

So he'd returned to Riverport out of guilt.

The tip of Edythe's tongue ached with the desire to tell him of Wynn's confession, to erase a portion of that guilt. She would if she hadn't agreed to let Wynn tell him in his own way and time. Clearly, the man hadn't followed through yet. If he didn't tell Barrett soon, she would tell him herself rather than see him continue to beat himself up.

"It was never my intention to desert you, Edy. You're right. I was angry over what happened to Wynn, but I should have given you the benefit of the doubt and guessed your father was behind your decision." His fingers combed through his hair. "After the way he treated my brother, I shouldn't have put it past him to do something evil where you were concerned."

She'd never considered her father truly evil, just callous and domineering—a man wanting his way in everything. Maybe that was a definition of evil.

But keeping Barrett's letters from her? She'd been foolhardy not to consider it before now.

"I loved you and appreciated that you worried about your brother. If I'd been sure of *your* love, Barrett, I would have given you all the time you needed, despite my father's threat and Lamar's poor health." Even if meant remaining in her father's house until Barrett came for her.

"The truth is, I waded so deep in my own guilt and misery, I couldn't focus on much else. I've always loved you, Edy, ever since that first day I saw you sitting forlorn on the riverbank. I wanted to carry you away and protect you." He eased her into an embrace so firm, yet tender, that she could barely breathe for the emotion it wrought. "Will you forgive me for not trusting that you returned that love and for acting like a cretin since my homecoming?"

She and Barrett wasted years of happiness because of her father's interference—years better spent growing together, loving one another, raising children. There was no reason to waste more time when the prospect of a future together lay ahead.

"Will you forgive me for not seeing how deeply Wynn's situation affected you, for letting my father convince me you didn't love me enough to remain with me, and for marrying Lamar out of fear?" Edythe snuggled closer. "You were my bold knight, Barrett. I never felt so safe, so loved as when we were together."

Another sigh blew past her ear. "And I failed you, just as I failed Wynn."

She couldn't let him continue to flog himself unnecessarily over his brother's guilt. "Barrett, there's something you should—"

"No knight worth his salt fails to protect his lady from the dragon. It's the way I see that father of yours, Edy, and I'll never forgive myself for leaving you to suffer through his dominance."

He cupped both sides of her face with hands that were big and stalwart. Hands that warmed and soothed. Those hands whisked away her every thought, except the reminder that he held each corner of her heart and always had.

When he leaned in, brushing her lips with his own, Edythe welcomed the kiss that resurrected all the love she'd stuffed deep inside, the type of love she'd thought to experience no more except in her dreams of him.

Freedom. Joy. Passion. And a beautiful hope that had lingered in the background for too long.

SOMEWHERE IN THE BACK of Barrett's mind a voice shouted that if he didn't gain control over this raging thirst for Edy—one he'd never imagined feeling a second time—there would be no turning back for either of them. He wanted more for her and for them. Much more. He always had.

He eased away and inhaled a lungful of the country air that had grown more humid as the afternoon wore on. His words spilled out in a breathless manner. "Never again say you have no talent, Mrs. Westin, because I've found something you excel in."

She stroked the hairs of his beard, her trembling fingers revealing nerves that were every bit as raw as his. "The last time you kissed me, you didn't have a mustache and beard."

"If they're a bother, I'll shave." He'd do anything to please her. How was it that she shrank from most everyone, but her comfort and confidence with him could twist him around her little finger like he was a limp strand of yarn?

"Don't. I like the new look. It's a reminder that so much has changed over the years, that we've grown and..."

"We're different."

She pulled away. "In some ways. In other ways, our circumstances have not changed. What about my father? He won't welcome a relationship between us now any more than he did before. I don't want him making things difficult for any of us." Her furrowed brow foreshadowed her tumble into the old fear.

"You're an adult, Edy. He should have no control over your life, and I know he has no control over mine."

He overrode the impulse to ask her to marry him. Right here, right now. It was too soon. She had a point. They had changed.

What if he had changed too much for her? What if they found their individual growth had produced differences too insurmountable for a lifetime together?

"I want to court you. This time it will be out in the open. I won't sneak around behind the judge's back. When I take you home, I'll talk to him."

She pushed against his chest. "No. Give me time to talk to him first. I don't care about me, but I can't afford to make life worse for my children."

It pained him to see her give her father power over her for any reason. Contrary to his claim otherwise, would they fall back into their previous pattern of hiding their relationship from the judge and everyone else in Riverport? "I heard you plead Andy's case for freedom."

"You were at the house?"

"Out back with the twins after Timmy waylaid me. The kitchen window was open." Barrett straightened her hat. It had tipped sideways with her fall to the ground. What he longed to do was remove it, along with the pins that held that silky hair on top of her head—a number of which had worked loose, promising to relieve themselves of their burden.

"What if my father had seen you? He threatened to have you arrested for trespassing."

"He saw me." Why hadn't he followed through with his threat? Had Edy's argument shaken his confidence?

"He never said anything." She chewed on her lip. "That worries me."

"Maybe he never mentioned it because you'd stood up for yourself and Andy. Your courage didn't get past your other children. We were all proud of you."

"I had to do it for the good of my son."

Years ago, she'd often fixated too much on herself and her

circumstances. He liked seeing this motherly side of her—the concern for her children. "And you won. In fact, you put up quite an argument. Have you ever considered becoming a lawyer?"

She scoffed. "Not for a moment."

"You have something against lawyers?"

A spark of humor lit her face. "Not at all. In fact, I have great respect and...admiration...for one particular lawyer."

"Only admiration?" That wasn't exactly the term he'd hoped to hear.

"It's never been just admiration, Barrett. It never will be."

A drop of rain landed on his hand, another in the dirt at their feet. She looked up. "Maybe we should return to town before we become drenched."

Barrett enclosed her in his arms, unable to stop himself. "Rain brings cleansing, Edy. It brings a freshness to everything it touches."

"Sometimes, it brings a storm."

"I choose to see this shower as a sign from God. He's telling us we've been given a fresh start, a cleansing from the past and a new beginning."

Her sigh expressed doubt, but she burrowed closer to him. "I hope you're right, because I couldn't bear the beginning of another tempest."

"I'll give you time to talk to your father, but don't take long."

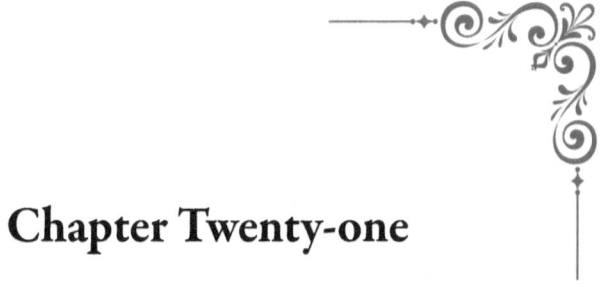

Chapter Twenty-one

E dythe entered her father's house with her clothing and the ends of her hair dripping from the rain. A glance at the face of the grandfather clock in the foyer revealed it was later than she'd realized—almost time for supper.

She touched her lips, astounded by the fact they still tingled from Barrett's goodbye kiss. Astounded and ever so thankful for new beginnings. She hoped—no, she prayed—he was right in saying God had given them a new start.

In some ways, Barrett was a different person from the one she remembered—stronger, more serious and self-assured. No doubt the years, the circumstances of their separation, had changed both of them, but their attraction remained, one that transcended time.

She frowned when it occurred to her she hadn't told him about the robbery involving his brother. Perhaps it was for the best. That story belonged to Wynn.

"For Pete's sake, Edythe." Her father's voice yanked her from her thoughts. His mouth gaped as he observed her sodden appearance from the doorway of the drawing room. "Where have you been?"

"I helped a friend learn to ride a bicycle."

"In the rain?"

She stood mute while the deluge drummed against the roof.

I want to court you. This time it will be out in the open. I won't sneak around behind the judge's back.

Edythe had told Barrett she would do nothing that might cause more hurt for her babies. That included blurting out her activities that afternoon without concocting a reasonable argument against her father's objections.

Her smile wobbled like Barrett's bicycle. Normally a capable man in control, seeing him struggle to master something new exposed his humanity and endeared her to him even more. Now, it was her turn to show that determination and control. "I'd like to speak with you, Father."

He waved a hand. "Another time. Go upstairs and change into dry clothes before you flood the foyer."

She looked down. Water puddled on the marble floor around her. She hurried to the stairs, remorseful over having made more work for Mrs. Cameron.

"And Edythe."

She paused on the stairs without turning. "Yes, Father?"

"Wear something worthy of a guest. Ansel is here. I've invited him for supper."

She restrained a groan. Ansel was the last person she wanted to see today of all days.

Edythe would worry about her father's obsession over her relationship with the banker later...when she sat him down and told him about Barrett.

EDYTHE PUSHED THE CAULIFLOWER around her plate. Mrs. Cameron knew she despised the vegetable, but the judge had ordered it, the housekeeper told her, because it was Mr. Treadway's favorite, providing an additional—if not irrational—reason *not* to court the man.

After her time with Barrett, she didn't care what Ansel Treadway liked or didn't like and would have preferred eating with her children. At another order by her father, Andrew and the twins were fed in the kitchen earlier and sent to their rooms, forcing her to dine in the company of the two men.

Since joining her children wasn't possible and the men talked business, she occupied herself by reliving the time spent with Barrett on that secluded wagon path, paying little attention to the conversation taking place in the room.

"You find it amusing, Edythe?"

At the mention of her name, the warmth that flowed through her a moment before turned to a chill. "Find what amusing, Father?"

"I hardly think Ansel's story of losing his parents as a child called for a smile."

Oh, how awful if Ansel had mistaken her happiness as being directed toward his misfortune. "No, of course not. My apologies, Ansel. I..." What excuse could she give for her blunder? Perhaps it was better to not offer one than open her mouth and spout something imprudent.

"It's quite all right, Edythe." Looking not in the least bit wounded, Ansel said, "Forgive us for monopolizing the conversation with our talk of business. I understand how a woman's mind might wander when faced with certain complex subjects."

Yes, blame it on the simplicity of a woman's mind rather than a man's penchant for boring supper topics.

Regardless, guilt gnawed at her. "I'm sorry to learn of the deaths of your parents."

The two men shared a laugh. "Oh, I assure you, they are alive and well."

She dropped her fork, knocking one of the dreadful cauliflowers off the plate.

"I told your father of the day we became separated during a trip to Chicago." Ansel's laugh said he forgave her. "Realizing you weren't listening, your father couldn't help teasing you."

Edythe glanced at the judge and puckered a brow at his smirk.

Perhaps Barrett was right in saying Hayden Danby was evil. Her gaze slid to Ansel's grinning face across the table from her. It left her equally unsure of his saintliness.

"The rain has let up. Why don't you show her your new house, Ansel? I'm sure she'll find it charming."

She turned to their guest. "You bought a house?"

His chest inflated like a balloon. "Yes. In fact, it's near here. I'd be honored to show you."

At his eagerness, warning bells drowned out his final words. "It's getting late, Ansel. Perhaps we could do it another time. I should say goodnight to the children."

"Nonsense. You'll be back before they go to bed." Her father rose from his place at the table.

"Father, we wouldn't want to find ourselves the subject of unwarranted gossip should Ansel and I enter his house without a chaperone."

Ansel's enthusiasm fell. "Oh, yes. I hadn't considered someone might misconstrue our visit."

"I see no impropriety in Ansel showing you the front exterior."

Edythe glanced at her father. Though she had no interest in furthering the banker's hopes, what harm was there in letting him show her his new residence? The sooner she agreed, the sooner she would be rid of him for the evening.

She dropped her napkin on the table and stood. "I suppose that would be fine."

They walked a mere two streets over, dodging puddles along the way. "When you said your new home was nearby, I didn't imagine how close."

She stood at the edge of the walk and studied the two-story structure in the twilight. With embellished gables and a broad wraparound porch, it was nothing as elaborate or large as her father's house, but spacious and welcoming nonetheless.

"Naturally, it isn't the same neighborhood. I'm not yet able to afford something on your street."

But he'd found something close enough to smell the wealth? Edythe chastised herself for her unkind thought. There was nothing wrong with ambition if applied in a moral and wise manner.

"I happened to mention to Judge Danby that I was looking for a house, and he directed me here."

Of course, he did. Better to continue his reign over her family.

Ansel turned toward her. "Do you like it, Edythe?"

"You have good taste."

"To be honest, I'm not sure what to do with it. I mean, numerical figures and loans are my strong point, not paint or wallpaper or knick-knacks."

"I'm sure whatever you do, it will be lovely."

"It needs a woman's touch."

A pulsing ache began at the back of her head. A few weeks ago, she might have eventually seen him as a way to find freedom for herself and her children. After her time with Barrett this afternoon, that disgraceful notion was an impossibility. "You'll find the right person to give it an interior beauty befitting the outside. Now, I really should go. It's been a busy day."

With a last disenchanted glance at the house, Ansel took her arm. "I'll walk you home."

She didn't argue. Letting him escort her would prevent her father from questioning why she returned alone.

EDYTHE KNOCKED ON BARRETT'S door. When she received no answer, she turned the knob and poked her head inside the house, hoping to see Mrs. Quincy. "Hello?"

Hearing muffled voices coming from behind the closed door of his office, she stepped into the foyer and paused. Even if she must wait in the drawing room for an hour, she had to see Barrett and convince herself their time in the country had been no dream.

The door to Barrett's office opened and Mrs. Quincy's voice drifted into the hallway. "You'll find the man who really murdered Mr. Dulong, Mr. Seaton. I know you will. My husband doesn't deserve to be punished for something he didn't do."

"I'll do my best, Mrs. Quincy."

It was too late to duck into the drawing room and let them have their privacy, so Edythe opened her mouth to make her presence known, but the housekeeper wasn't through. "I can't tell you how much Jeremiah and me appreciate your help. You, too, Mr. Gregory."

Gregory? The only Gregory she knew was Claire's fiancé, but he was an architect. What had he to do with finding a murderer, and how dangerous was that for both men?

"Jeremiah is no killer." Mrs. Quincy's voice trembled. "He's a good man."

Jeremiah Quincy. Edythe had heard the name of the housekeeper's husband once before, but where?

Ah, yes. Somewhere in the lengthy conversation she'd tried to ignore last Monday, her father and Ansel spoke of a man charged with murdering someone. Without naming the lawyer, her father mentioned that Jeremiah Quincy had hired a fool for an attorney. Every muscle along Edythe's spine stiffened. Naturally he would say that, since that lawyer must be Barrett.

Edythe tapped on the front door, announcing her presence.

The housekeeper jumped and peered at Edythe with glossy eyes. She turned back to the office. "Mrs. Westin is here, sir."

After a pause and a rumbling, unintelligible mumble, Barrett called out, "Come in, Edy."

Edythe stopped at the door of his office, hesitant to enter the room and disturb Barrett's meeting. Both men rose. "I'm sorry. I didn't mean to interrupt. Mark, I didn't expect to see you here."

"Good afternoon, Edythe." He glanced at Barrett and back to her, grinning. "You're a surprise too."

"He's helping with a legal matter." Edythe's cheeks warmed at the defensiveness in her outburst. She focused her attention on Barrett. "I believe I told you about my friend, Claire Kingsley, and her fiancé."

Mark picked up his hat from a corner of Barrett's desk. "That reminds me. Claire is waiting for me to go over some plans. I don't want to be late and give her an excuse to back out of our partnership—business or personal." He grinned.

"Please tell her I said hello and I miss her at our meetings."

"I'll do it." He turned to Barrett. "I'll meet you at the station Thursday afternoon."

Once Mark left, Edythe walked across the room for an explanation. "You're leaving?" She despised the weakness in her voice.

"Just a short trip to Peru to look into a possible witness in the Dulong murder. We'll be back on Friday." Barrett's brow crimped. "How long have you been out there?"

Was he asking if she'd overheard the previous conversation? "I came in a few seconds before Mrs. Quincy opened your office door. I didn't intentionally listen but heard enough to know that you're representing her husband."

"I'm convinced of Jeremiah's innocence."

"If she needs another woman to talk to, she's welcome to visit me."

He moved closer and rested a hand against her cheek. She leaned into his touch. "It's thoughtful of you to offer a listening ear. Your kind spirit is one of the things I've always loved about you."

The sincerity in his voice eased some of her concern. "Mark is going to Peru with you?"

"He's helping me with Jeremiah's case. I really can't say more than that it's possible he can identify the man I'm looking for."

"Oh." At Mrs. Quincy's voice coming from the doorway, Barrett dropped his hand and Edythe stepped back. The housekeeper clutched a broom in one hand and a rag in the other. "Pardon me for interrupting, Mr. Seaton."

"It's all right, Mrs. Quincy."

"Under the circumstances, I don't mind Mrs. Westin knowing about my husband's case. The details will come out eventually."

Under what circumstances?

Thinking back on Barrett's words and touch to her cheek, Edythe understood. On one hand, it thrilled her to let others know of their renewed relationship. On the other, she hadn't told her father yet. Having him hear rumors about them brought back her anxiety.

Mrs. Quincy smiled at her. "I don't spread gossip, ma'am."

Edythe nodded, taking the woman at her word. "I wish the best for your husband. He has a fine lawyer."

"We're grateful to Mr. Seaton, but I believe God will walk beside Jeremiah and the truth will come out."

"I admire your faith, Mrs. Quincy. The only details I need pertain to Mr. Seaton's absence, though as I told him, if you'd like another woman to confide in, I'll be happy to listen."

"I'll keep that in mind, ma'am. For now, I'll let you two talk in private. I have a porch to sweep." She slipped by them and the front door closed.

Barrett took Edythe in his arms. "I've missed you."

"I've missed you too." She ran a hand down the side of his bearded face. A month ago, she'd never thought to see that face again. "Please be careful. The idea of you looking for and finding a murder suspect is too frightful to imagine."

"I didn't say he was a suspect."

"Not with your words, but I heard it in your voice. You think he has something to do with that man's death."

"Possibly. For now, I only want to have a conversation with him. Mark and I will be fine. This isn't my first criminal case, Edy."

She sighed. "Yes, well, I didn't know about those."

He chuckled. "I'm afraid you'll need to get used to the way I work, because when I return, we're going to discuss our future."

When he returned. Words she longed to hear.

Warmth spread through her. "Then hurry."

Barrett's gaze drifted over her face as though he was memorizing it. His look of longing ignited in her a yearning to return to that out-of-the-way cornfield and resume those kisses that spoke of restored love and trust. "Would you like another bicycle-riding lesson?"

He laughed, but a glance toward the hallway said he doubted the wisdom of taking her up on the offer today. "One day soon, but for now, remaining here is probably safer." He gestured to the chair Mark had occupied. Once she sat, he settled behind his desk. "How is Andy?"

She lamented the change in topic, yet appreciated his concern for her son. "It's been almost three weeks with no charges. Surely, the police aren't still considering his guilt."

"I spoke to the officer Saturday. Mrs. Stark has made herself a nuisance at the police station, insisting they charge someone, and Andy is their only suspect."

Edythe scooted forward on the seat. "No one saw anything and Mr. Stark doesn't remember what happened. How can she expect the police to arrest my son with no witnesses?"

"The officer assured me they were no closer to doing so than they were the night of the fire. Trust in the legal system. Trust in God's providence. He knows the truth."

He leaned back in his chair, his gaze drilling into her. "Have you told him yet?"

SANDRA ARDOIN

He had no need to remind her of the identity of *him*. "Not yet."

He closed his eyes as though counting to ten, then opened them. "Tell him soon or I will."

"Barrett—"

"Unless you have no intention of proceeding with our relationship. If that's the case, let me know now."

"I want nothing more than for us to be together, but Ansel was at the house when I got back the other day and—"

"Who's Ansel?" He dropped back against the office chair. "The man on the porch. Is this another effort to see you married?"

"I'm afraid it might be. He's a nice man, but—"

"That's what you said about Lamar Westin."

Rather than be perturbed at his irritation, she found it enlightening. It was flattering to see a man's jealousy, but she couldn't let him think there was a basis for it. "I have no interest in him, Barrett. Father will hear that as soon as I can find him."

"Find him?"

"After Ansel left the other evening, he disappeared. I haven't seen him since."

Barrett stepped around the desk and helped her to her feet. His voice softened. "Then tell him when he returns."

She couldn't lose this man again. She couldn't allow her father to continue to dictate everything about her life. "I will."

Edythe walked out the front door a few minutes later, his kisses still delighting her. She raised a silent prayer for her son's name to be cleared and added one more, asking for the right time and right words to tell her father of her love for Barrett.

Throughout her life, she'd often presented God with her intercessions for others, but asking God for anything of a personal nature amounted to little more than a passive hope. With Verbenia's encouragement, Edythe was seeking that relationship her friend spoke of. She'd begun to strengthen her faith by realizing she'd never drawn close enough to God to comprehend the depth of His love. Rather, she'd measured His compassion for His children based on her father's lack of such.

Mrs. Quincy paused in her task of sweeping the porch and glanced at the front door. "He's a good man."

Edythe glanced over her shoulder as though she could see Barrett through the wood. "Yes, he is."

She added one more prayer to her list, a request that God watch over both Barrett and Mark in their travels, and that they find the object of their search.

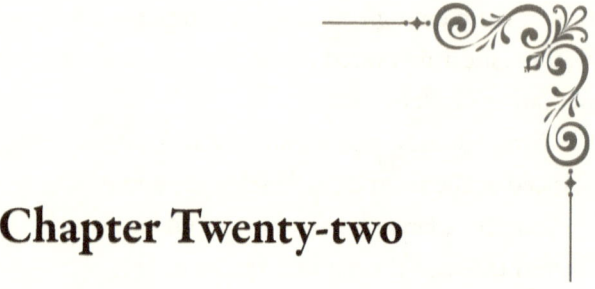

Chapter Twenty-two

B arrett paused outside his Peru hotel room. "How about if we meet for supper in half an hour?"

"Sounds good. I'm famished. In the meantime, I'll wash some of this soot and dust off." Mark Gregory entered his room and shut the door.

Eager to follow suit, Barrett finished cleaning up a few minutes later.

He looked out the window at the people coming and going along the sidewalks. Peru was the winter headquarters for the Wallace circus. It'd be nice to take Edy's children to the circus one day. Sarah Jane, especially, would enjoy the exotic animals. Timothy's mind would whirl with mathematical equations linking weight and height and whatever else was involved in walking a tightrope. No doubt, if given a chance, Andy would balance on that tightrope.

But this trip's priority was not to explore the circus grounds. It was to find information regarding the man whose name might or might not be Asa Osbourne and ascertain whether he had a role in the death of Claude Dulong—as witness or suspect.

Not only did he want to bring Jeremiah and Mary good news, those few minutes he and Edy spent together in his office yesterday weren't enough to satisfy him. It was strange how after years of separation and resentment, he now felt incomplete without her.

Help me find the truth, Lord, for the sake of the Quincys. He stopped before asking God to hurry up.

Inside his leather case sat the mail he'd retrieved from the post office before leaving Riverport. He shuffled through it, stopping at a square envelope Mrs. Quincy had added to the stack, one she'd said had been hand delivered.

Barrett tore it open, pulled out a card, and read the invitation. Disbelieving what he read, he blinked and mumbled through the words a second time. "The Company of Mr. Barrett Seaton is requested at a reception to be held at the home of Judge Hayden Danby of Riverport on Tuesday, the seventh of September at seven o'clock in the evening."

With the card clasped behind his back, Barrett paced from the head of the bed to the foot. Why would the judge invite him to his home for any reason, particularly for an event that required a printed invitation? Odd that Edy hadn't mentioned a reception yesterday, or that he was invited. That alone made the hairs on the back of his neck stand up...unless she sent it. If so, she'd told her father about them. He let out a loud *whoop*.

Barrett tossed the invitation on the bed. It landed printed side down, revealing a handwritten note on the back. *Discretion is requested with regard to your attendance. This event is a surprise for my daughter. Judge H. Danby*

A surprise for Edy? He frowned. That answered his question as to why she never mentioned it. Left unexplained was the judge's purpose in inviting a man with whom he shared a mutual dislike. Unless she *had* talked to him and this was his way of saying he approved of their relationship.

Barrett stuffed the invitation back into the envelope. Was he so far gone he'd grasp at any dubious excuse to imagine a future together with Edy?

He joined Mark for supper in the small but pleasant dining room. Around them, quiet conversation and occasional laughter gave the room a cozy atmosphere.

SANDRA ARDOIN

After finishing his apple pie, Mark leaned back in his chair. "It was nice to see Edythe again. She's a fine woman. Claire counts her as a good friend."

"I wasn't aware you two knew one another before yesterday."

"Until recently, Claire was part of the Widow's Might group. Earlier in the summer, the ladies took on a repair project for a woman who is now also a member." Mark laughed. "I can tell you that Mrs. Westin wields an authoritative crowbar on porch planks."

Barrett wiped the corner of his mouth. "A crowbar? Edy?" He had difficulty picturing her holding the tool, much less prying up boards in an authoritarian manner.

"I got the idea the two of you were longtime friends." When Barrett didn't respond to the subtle inquiry, Mark pushed the dessert plate away and crossed his arms on the table. "Look, it isn't my business, so forgive me for meddling, but Claire is concerned about the family."

"Why?"

"She believes Mrs. Westin uses her time with the Widow's Might group as an escape from the pressures she faces at home. Evidently, Judge Danby can be rather...intense."

Barrett laughed. "That's one word for him. Have you met the man?"

"I haven't had the pleasure."

"Believe me, it's no pleasure."

Mark frowned and told a tale of his mother's immigration from Poland and the misery she'd suffered and caused. "Bitterness makes everyone miserable."

Did Mark aim that sage wisdom at the judge or him? True, he was bitter toward Edy's father for what he'd done to her, as well as to Wynn. Right or wrong, he'd never deny it to himself or even to God.

Finding Mark easy to talk to, a potential good friend, Barrett gave an abbreviated version of his past relationship with Edy and experience with the judge. "Because of him, we spent a dozen years apart. Now, he's sent me an invitation to a reception on the seventh, and I'm not sure what to make of it."

"What did Edythe say?"

"It's supposed to be a surprise for her, something else I can't comprehend. Edy despises large social gatherings."

"Do you think this invitation might be Danby's way of issuing a truce?"

"I considered it." Barrett wanted to believe that was the case. He wanted to believe in peace between the Seatons and Judge Danby but that bitterness Mark spoke of—on both sides— generated too much doubt. "Why a sudden about-face?"

"From what you've told me, I'd wonder the same thing." Mark frowned. "I recall mentioning the businessman who refused to work with Claire in designing his building, simply because she was a woman. I'm not generally prone to pessimism, but people like that enjoy their power and control. If he sent your brother to prison to make a point, he's already proven himself to be devious. Tread carefully."

The only way to learn the judge's true motive for the invitation was to accept, but would that reveal a trap as damaging as the one set years ago for Wynn?

ON HER WAY TO THE KITCHEN, Edythe spotted her father in the dining room. He'd awakened later than usual and was eating his breakfast a full hour after she and the children had finished. She hadn't seen him in days, and a blessed peace had fallen over the house while he was gone.

Now that he presented her with an opportunity to talk to him, she owed it to Barrett to keep her promise. She owed it to herself and her children to not display any weakness.

After Sarah Jane and Timothy passed her on their way to the backyard, Edythe fought to gain control of her breathing and entered the room. "Good morning, Father."

"Good morning."

"I didn't realize you'd returned."

"I arrived late last night."

That explained his haggard look—the deepened creases around his eyes and mouth.

She poured herself a cup of coffee from the urn on the sideboard and sat at the opposite end of the table, the memory of her bruised arm still fresh. The cup rattled on the saucer, testifying to her nerves. With his silence, he didn't appear to notice. "There's something I'd like to discuss with you."

"What is it?" The judge sliced into a piece of ham and stabbed it with his fork.

The best attack was one from the front. Wasn't it?

She took a sip of coffee, and its warmth bolstered her courage to get to the point. "Before you hear it from someone else, you should know that I've been—"

A high-pitched scream ruptured Edythe's confession. She and her father stared at one another, then he bolted out of the dining room with Edythe close behind. They rushed through the kitchen and out the back door, their footsteps accompanied by two more screams.

Sarah Jane stood in the middle of the yard, the heels of her hands pressed against her eyes and her goose honking as though he were dying.

"What is all this noise?" The judge stopped short.

Edythe peered over his shoulder. Timothy knelt in the grass beside Sarah Jane, holding to Snowman. Someone had painted the red circles of a bullseye on the feathers of the bird's back.

She reached for her wailing daughter, pressing Sarah Jane against

204

her middle to hide from her the sight of the sullied white goose. Smoothing a hand over her distraught child's hair, Edythe fought tears of her own. Not that the mean-spirited Snowman deserved her sympathy, but she hurt for the way in which the large and crude drawing affected her children. Who would do such a horrid thing to her daughter's pet? Why?

"He's hurt." Sarah Jane pointed to the crimson line running down the side of the goose. "Snowman's bleeding."

"No, sweetheart. It's only paint." The goose might be fine, but her father's pale features worried her. "Someone played a joke on us. That's all. He's fine."

"If it was blood, it wouldn't be in circles." Despite his bold statement, Timothy pushed to his feet and latched on to Edythe's side.

Snowman waddled a few feet away, honking his usual disdain for all of them.

"Don't fret, Sarah Jane." Edythe's father ran a hand over the girl's hair. The gesture was both touching and awkward.

"What's the matter?" The back door slammed, and Andrew ran toward them from the house. He jerked to a halt at seeing the goose, his eyes wide and troubled.

Her father regained his composure. "Was this *your* doing, young man?"

Andrew stepped back. "No, sir. I wouldn't do something like that to my sister." At the same time, Edythe saw panic in her son's wide eyes. She believed his claim that he had nothing to do with painting the goose but couldn't shake the impression that he feared more than his grandfather's reaction.

The judge didn't press the accusation. Instead, he turned to her. "If Andrew didn't do it, my guess is Seaton did."

"Why would you think something like that?"

"Because he has an ax to grind against me. It's probably his response to what happened years ago."

"You're wrong."

"You were always blinded to his character." Before she could think of a suitable reply, he grabbed hold of the noisy goose. "Take the children inside. I'll see if I can clean off the paint without plucking all his feathers."

Edythe urged the children toward the house. She glanced back as her father picked up the goose. Surprisingly, it didn't fight him. Cradling it in his arms—almost as though he carried an infant—he disappeared behind the small barn at the rear of the property. He had treated Snowman with a care and respect she would not have anticipated him showing a bad-tempered bird. More care and respect than he often showed people.

The sight returned to her off and on throughout the day as she attempted to console Sarah Jane and the boys. With it came the memory of the day her grandfather trapped her in the cellar and the image of her father cradling her in his arms in much the same way as he had the goose.

AFTER A QUICK BREAKFAST in the hotel restaurant on Friday, Barrett and Mark walked into the sheriff's office. They introduced themselves to the deputy at the front counter.

Barrett said, "We'd like to speak with someone about a man we believe lived here not long ago."

"Who?"

"It's possible he went by the name of Alec Olesky."

"Never heard of him."

Mark moved closer to the counter. "What about Asa Osbourne?"

The young deputy shook his head, but his frown deepened the creases between his eyes. "What do you want with him?"

"I think he might know something about a crime committed in Riverport last month."

They were approached by an older lawman, probably in his early fifties, about the same age as the man they sought. "Did you say Osbourne?"

"Yes, sir. Do you know him?"

"When I was a boy, a family named Osbourne lived about five miles outside of town. We never saw them much. Strange lot." He rubbed his bearded chin as he thought. "Seems to me they moved away about twenty-five or thirty years ago."

The family might have moved but that didn't mean Asa hadn't been back. "Have you seen any of them lately?"

"No. Sorry."

"Will you check to be certain there's no record of Asa Osbourne or Alec Olesky being arrested here in the last few years?"

"You said Asa? I think I remember him. He's not just a witness, is he?"

"I can't say for certain and am not accusing him of anything. At this point, I simply have questions for him."

"Give me a few minutes." The man returned five minutes later. "Nothing."

Barrett schooled his features, trying not to show his disappointment. An arrest record might have made his job easier, especially if Osbourne—or Olesky—had been arrested for a violent crime.

"You might talk to one of the former neighbors."

"That's a long ride for a slim possibility," said Mark. "We're only here for the day."

"Then I'd start with Harold Tanner. He grew up on the farm next to the Osbourne place and returned to town about a year ago. I've been thinking about it, and if I remember right, he was friends with Asa. He might know where the family moved."

Barrett's nails drummed the counter. It wasn't likely Mr. Tanner and Asa Osbourne had kept in touch after so many years, but it couldn't hurt to talk to him. "Where will we find him?"

The deputy checked the clock on the wall. "Can't say where he'll be this morning, but about noon, try the saloon on Broadway and 2nd Streets. I gotta warn you. The man isn't always in a pleasant mood these days."

Mark cocked his head. "What do you mean?"

"He left town a few years back a respectable citizen. My understanding is he worked as an accountant for some factory in Indianapolis. About a year ago, he quit his job and come back here. He took to drinking at night and causing trouble. Now, he survives on odd jobs around town."

"What changed?"

"No telling. He's not telling, anyway. He's spent more than one night in the hoosegow for fighting."

Barrett had second thoughts about leading Mark into the unpredictable situation. "You can't think of anyone else we might talk to for information?"

"You can always ask around at some of the businesses. Otherwise, no, sir."

Barrett glanced at each deputy and bobbed his head. "Thank you, gentlemen."

When they left the building, Barrett stopped Mark. "It sounds like this man could be erratic. Why don't you wait for me at the hotel?"

A cloud darkened Mark's face. "I grew up knowing how to use my fists. You might need my help."

"Just remember you volunteered."

Mark grinned. "So speaks the lawyer."

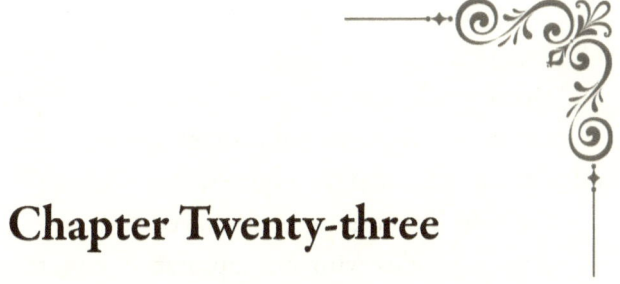

Chapter Twenty-three

Barrett and Mark visited several of the store owners in town, along with the editor at the newspaper, and the clerks in the hotels. No one in Peru had heard of Alec Olesky, though some of the older residents said the name Osbourne sounded familiar. However, their recollection was from years past, nothing current.

Barrett pulled out his watch. His legs ached from all the walking they had done around town. "It's almost noon. We're not doing much good this way. Let's head over to the saloon and try to find Tanner."

They entered the building and paused by the door to look around. Electric ceiling fixtures lit the faces of the customers. All morning, Mark had scrutinized people they met or passed on the street, looking for his former boarder. Barrett turned to him now, his question unspoken.

Mark shook his head. "No. I don't see Olesky."

"I knew it couldn't be that easy."

They moved farther into the room and approached the man behind the bar. "Good afternoon, sir. I was told I'd find a man named Harold Tanner here. Have you seen him?"

The bartender poured an amber liquid into a small glass and passed it to a man standing next to Mark. "Why do you ask?"

"It's private business. Is he here?"

The man paused, then tipped his head toward the back. Barrett eased around and spotted a man in worn coveralls, sitting alone at a table along the wall. He appeared clean but despondent as he stared at his empty glass.

"Thank you."

Barrett and Mark weaved through the tables filled with patrons and stopped in front of their quarry. "Mr. Tanner?"

"Yes." His bloodshot eyes narrowed. "What can I do for you?" His speech, at odds with his appearance, confirmed the deputy's description of Tanner being an educated man.

"We're looking for someone named Asa Osbourne," said Barrett.

The man paled.

"I understand you were neigh—"

Tanner bolted from his seat and sprinted toward the door, shoving people out of his way. Caught off guard, he and Mark were slow to respond.

"Interesting." Mark moved first, excusing himself to every customer he shoved as he darted across the room.

Barrett caught up to his friend, and they burst onto the sidewalk, looking both ways. He pointed to the corner. "There."

Dodging traffic, they pursued Tanner across the street and down an alley, catching up to him in an empty lot a block away. Barrett grabbed the sleeve of the man's shirt and yanked, ripping the material at the shoulder, but he maintained his grip and jerked Tanner to a stop.

Tanner breathed hard while he struggled to free himself from Barrett's hold. "Let go. Never heard of anyone named Osbourne."

"The fact that you ran tells me a different story."

Mark stood in front of the man, blocking his escape.

"I've nothing to say to you."

Barrett let Tanner go, prepared to pursue the man should he flee again. Tanner simply wilted.

After introducing himself and Mark, Barrett got down to business, not sure when the man might choose to run again. "We were told you grew up with Osbourne."

"That was a long time ago." The answer came out on a whine. "Now, leave me alone."

"But you've seen him lately." A guess, but one that fit Tanner's reaction. Barrett thought over what they had been told by the deputy. "Maybe a year ago?"

The tendons in Tanner's neck tightened when he clamped his mouth shut.

"A man's future—his life—is at stake. It's possible Asa Osbourne has information that can help me defend my client."

The answer came first as a shrill laugh. "Help you? You have no idea who you're dealing with, mister."

What was Osbourne like that he instilled such alarm in others? "Tell me."

A far-off look filled the man's eyes, as though he were seeing something from the past. "Osbourne ruined my life. I once thought he was a friend, and he ruined me."

Barrett exchanged a confused glance with Mark. "How?"

After several mild and disregarded threats by Barrett, Mark finally spoke up. "I believe Osbourne rented a room from my mother under a different name. Olesky. Does that sound familiar?"

Tanner shook his head.

"Look, I had to live with the man for a while." Mark's voice took on an urgency. "If he's anywhere around Riverport, I want to know who I'm dealing with if he shows up at my home again. My mother's safety is paramount to me."

With a slow glance in Mark's direction, Harold Tanner whispered, "Keep away from him. Keep your mother away from him."

Everything the man had said thus far had proven to Barrett the value of this trip. "Why? What did he do to you?"

A moan broke free. "Every day I go to that saloon and consider the worthlessness of my life. Nearly every day, I go in there to forget how I got to this point. At night, I think I'll be safe if I get drunk enough to be taken to jail. The trouble is, I'm out in the morning and it starts over again. I'm too cowardly to do anything serious to land me in prison." A strident laugh pierced the air. "If I wasn't, I'd have ended this torture years ago."

"What did Osbourne do that has you so shaken you wish to spend time in jail?" Barrett softened his voice. "If we know what he's capable of, it might help us to find him."

The man had covered his face, muffling his words. "I doubt it. He's a ghost."

"Take it from me, man, you'll never have peace unless you help us find him." Mark laid a hand on Tanner's shoulder. "Let Mr. Seaton see to it Osbourne doesn't bother you again."

Barrett opened his mouth to tell Mark he couldn't guarantee anything of the kind, but he decided to wait for Tanner's answer.

The man stared at Mark a moment, then shifted his watery gaze to Barrett. "Blackmail. He threatened to reveal something that happened when we were young and blame me if I didn't steal for him from my employer." A mirthless chuckle escaped. "The thing is, I didn't do what he would have accused me of. He did." His eyes glossed over with tears. "But I was there. I saw it. He has proof."

"What happened back then? A man's life might depend on what you tell us."

Tanner lowered his hands. "Asa killed someone, a drifter—a down-on-his-luck old man no one would miss."

Mark sucked in a breath.

"Asa showed no anger, no regret, no emotion whatsoever. The boy was cold, the man colder. That day, he ended a life with no more regard than someone putting his shoes on in the morning. One minute he's tormenting the man." Tanner jabbed his eyes with the heels of his hands as if he jabbed at a barbaric vision. "The next he shoves a knife in his belly."

A knife to the belly. Had Osbourne done the same to Dulong?

Barrett pressed his lips together to keep from asking more questions while he waited for Harold Tanner to continue. It was a short wait.

"We were fourteen. I wish I'd understood how evil Asa was back then. Instead, I followed him around like a faithful mutt. Part of me sensed the danger. Part of me enjoyed walking on the edge of it." He looked up. "Do you understand?"

Walking on the edge of danger. Barrett swallowed. In his relationship with Edy all those years ago, he'd been aware he walked that line between being a respectable suitor and being someone who enjoyed the challenge of frustrating her father. Yes, he'd loved her and wanted to protect her, but there was something about the secrecy—the idea that the judge had no control over Barrett and Edy's relationship—that had given it added excitement.

"You said he has proof that you were there when the man was stabbed. What kind of proof?"

"I was in shock and leaned over the man—I don't even know his name—in order to see if he was alive. In the process, I got blood on my shirt. Asa stole it from where I buried it. He still has it."

"You could have denied it was yours." Not that Barrett would encourage anyone to lie to the authorities, but with such old and scant evidence, he wondered why Tanner let that threat affect him.

"My ma had sewn my name in it. She used to do things like that."

"Osbourne wanted you to steal from your employer and used the shirt as a way to coerce you. Is that why you left your employment in Indianapolis and returned here?"

"Like I said, I'm too cowardly to commit a crime."

Barrett decided now was not the time to inform him he'd done so by not reporting the drifter's murder. "What happened then?"

"He was furious and told me the only reason he didn't kill me was because I'd befriended him all those years ago. Other than me, he had no friends growing up."

What a surprise.

"It's why I ran from you. If he finds out I talked to anyone about him, he will kill me."

Mark moved a little closer. "Why stay here? Why not leave town and go somewhere he can't find you?"

A sad smile lined the man's face. "Why bother? He'll track me down if he wants me bad enough. After I'd gone to Indianapolis, he charmed my mother into telling him where to find me. Besides, she needs me...for whatever good I am to her."

Barrett took a moment to review the conversation. If Osbourne tried to blackmail Tanner into theft had he done the same with Dulong? Or was Barrett grasping for answers with no merit? "Are you aware of Osbourne blackmailing anyone else?"

"He didn't mention names but said I was the first to turn him down, that most men were greedy enough to take their share. I think in some twisted way, he admired what I did."

Barrett admired it too. "You work odd jobs these days so he can't blackmail you again?"

"If I have no access to anything Asa wants, he'll leave me alone."

"You're a braver man than you believe, Mr. Tanner."

"I'm hoping talking to you—confessing—will take some of the load off my conscience."

"We aren't the only ones who need to hear your story."

"But my ma's safety..."

"If you tell all you know, Osbourne will have no reason to threaten either of you." Barrett prayed he spoke the truth, and Asa Osbourne wasn't so far gone he'd take some type of revenge before he was found.

Tanner turned his attention north toward the sheriff's office but said nothing for a while. Barrett let him think.

"I suppose it is time for me to do what I can to stop him. Do you think they'll arrest me for the death of that man?"

"I can't say, but let's find you a lawyer first."

Tanner groaned as he stood. "You know, it's already a relief."

After finding a lawyer willing to go with Harold Tanner to the sheriff's office, Barrett and Mark walked back to the hotel.

Mark opened the door to the lobby. "What do you think?"

"I think Osbourne has given us a gift."

"In what way?"

"Tanner mentioned there being more blackmail victims than himself. He was an accountant. Dulong was an accountant. If the Riverport police dig deeper into Dulong's life, I'm hoping they'll find out something that proves he was being blackmailed into stealing from his employer. At the least, they should investigate other such crimes in the state."

Realizing he was talking to himself, Barrett turned to find Mark standing in the middle of the lobby, his brow furrowed with whatever thoughts ran through his head. "What's wrong?"

"It might be nothing, but Claire lives with Roslyn Malone. She's the wife of Gil Malone."

"And?"

"From what Claire has told me, last Christmas Gil Malone embezzled money from his employer, Newland's Department Store. He disappeared before he could be arrested."

"Let me guess. He was an accountant."

"The head man."

BARRETT SAT ON A LOG on the bank of the Wabash River, one foot propped on the fallen tree trunk. The other rested on the ground. He dropped his line in the water and relaxed, enjoying the smell of the approaching autumn—the hint of dying leaves mixed with river water and damp soil. The sun shone bright, a vestige of the fading summer warmth. The bobber on his fishing line floated with the current.

Whether or not he caught anything this afternoon didn't matter. Being here gave him time to think.

After spending much of Friday afternoon helping Harold Tanner locate a lawyer, he and Mark stayed a second night in Peru before returning to Riverport yesterday.

Barrett was disappointed over not finding a solid lead in locating Osbourne, but Tanner's story gave him added reason to believe Jeremiah.

It didn't seem a stretch. If Asa Osbourne killed a man with a knife at fourteen, threatened his boyhood friend, and coerced others into committing crimes, it wasn't illogical to believe he had stabbed Dulong. Barrett's job now was to find a connection between Osbourne and Dulong. Even if they never found Osbourne, it might help to persuade a jury of reasonable doubt in Jeremiah's case...if the presiding judge allowed it to be presented.

Lots of "ifs."

Something rustled the brush behind Barrett. He swiveled on the log as a large, familiar dog loped through the grass ahead of Andy and his siblings. Mr. Peters jumped up and placed his big paws on Barrett's leg, leaving both brown hairs and large, dirty prints on his pants. The dog's tongue dripped like a leaking hand pump.

He pushed the animal off him and patted his monstrous head. "It's good to see you, too."

Andy carried a fishing pole and a tin can holding what Barrett assumed were worms for bait. "Hello, Mr. B. J. Catch anything?"

The Westin boys plopped onto the ground nearby. Sarah Jane settled on the log beside him. A cloud seemed to hang over all three of them.

"Not yet. Does your mother know you're here, Andy?" Barrett

glanced behind him, hoping she'd accompanied her children.

Andy grimaced. "Timothy and Sarah Jane are supposed to make sure I don't get into trouble. But I told Mama I thought you'd be here, so how could I?"

In less than ten seconds, Barrett had gone from lawyer to nursemaid. He didn't mind this time. If he and Edy were to have a future, it would include her children, so he might as well get used to having them around. Besides, they were more entertaining than watching a drifting bobber while pondering murders.

Another "if" to add to the list that kept growing.

After the boys baited their hooks, they cast their lines into the water. Barrett turned his attention to Sarah Jane. Her shoulders dragged and her mouth drooped. Mr. Peters laid his head in the child's lap and released a long, canine groan.

"What's wrong, Sarah Jane?"

A tear ran down the cheek facing him. "Someone bad hurt Snowman."

Snowman? Barrett searched his memory, trying to recall which of Sarah Jane's animals had that name.

"Her goose." Timothy shot his sister a sympathetic look.

Someone hurt that nasty bird? Out of self-defense, most likely. "How did they hurt him?"

Timmy dropped his pole and shuffled over to the log. "They painted a sign on his back."

"A sign?"

"A red bullseye."

Barrett leaned back, his fishing line and Jeremiah's case forgotten.

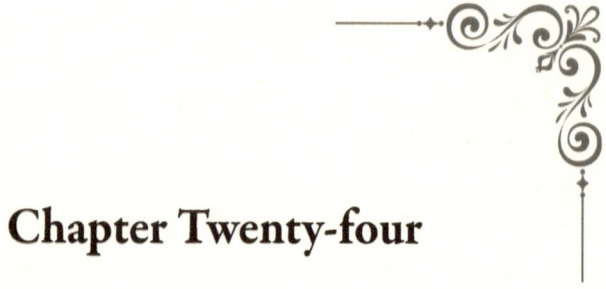

Chapter Twenty-four

Barrett stared at Timothy with indignation rising inside him like magma in a volcano. "Someone painted a bullseye on the goose's back?"

Maybe the bird attacked someone who, rather than talk to the owner, decided to give fair warning of the consequences of it happening again.

"Grandfather says it was a prank." Sarah Jane swiped at her wet face.

Barrett fumbled for a response. When the little girl's tears continued, he pulled her to his side in an awkward side-arm hug that relaxed as her sobs resided. "It'll be all right." But who would deliberately upset a child like that?

Barrett glanced at Andy. The boy sat on the bank with his back to them as if he hadn't heard the conversation. His bobber disappeared under the water and the pole bent, but he did nothing to reel in whatever he'd hooked on the line. "You have a fish, Andy."

He jumped and cranked the reel, bringing in a small carp that fought like one twice its size.

Andy's catch failed to provide the excitement Barrett expected from the boy. He gave his pole to Timmy. "Watch this for me, will you?"

After congratulating Andy on the catch, Barrett pulled the boy aside and lowered his voice. "What do you know about what happened to Sarah Jane's goose?"

"Why does everyone think I know anything?"

"Because guilt is written all over your face." Andy tried to walk away, but Barrett stopped him. Somehow, he had to get through to the boy, even if it took blunt words. "Either someone has a nasty sense of humor or he sent a message. What if it's the latter and he tries something worse next time? Maybe against your mother or siblings?" Barrett didn't add the judge. He figured there was no point, given the strained relationship between grandfather and grandson.

Andy's eyes narrowed. "Don't say that."

"Then tell me what you know now, son. Maybe I can help."

The boy hung his head. A moment later he lifted it. His jaw tightened. "I think it was the Larson brothers. Probably Tad."

"Those are the boys I saw on the other side of the river the first time we met?" The same ones who had watched from the back of the Danby property.

"Yes, sir."

"What makes you think it was them? Why paint a target on Snowman's back?" Barrett waited, but Andy said nothing. "Were they warning you about something?"

A quick bob of the boy's head confirmed Barrett's suspicions.

He dug deeper with no basis for his thoughts other than common sense. "Does this have anything to do with the incident at the Stark place?"

The boy's bony shoulder rose and fell in answer.

"I can see you're afraid of them—"

"I am not!" Andy frowned and lowered his voice. "I'm not afraid for me."

"For your family?"

Andy turned toward his sister. "Sarah Jane is just a little girl."

Barrett could remind the eleven-year-old he wasn't much older than his siblings. "Why would they want to frighten you and threaten your sister?"

Andy studied the ground and toed the mud, which stuck to the tip of his shoe.

Barrett scrounged for anything to get through to the boy. "You helped the Larson brothers start the fire."

"No. I told you I had nothing to do with it."

"Then why?"

"They made me promise I wouldn't say they were there."

"And if you did?"

Andy turned sad eyes to Sarah Jane. "Somebody would pay."

This was too much like the conversation with Tanner.

After taking a moment to gain hold of his outrage, Barrett crouched to the boy's eye level. "Andy, those kinds of promises have no honor. By protecting one who commits a crime, you're considered no better than they are. Your silence tells that person that he's free to do it again, or to do something even more vile. Don't you think it's time that the police knew the truth...if not for your sake, for that of your family and others they might hurt in the future?"

Andy raised his chin in a show of defiance. "I hadn't thought of it that way."

Once they had gone over the incident and Barrett asked various questions to clarify the details, he pointed to the boy's fishing pole. "Get your things together. We'll take Timmy and Sarah Jane home, then talk to your mother and—"

"Mother went to her Widow's Might meeting and won't be back until four o'clock."

Barrett pulled out his pocket watch. That was close to an hour. "Then we'll wait. In the meantime, you might as well go ahead and fish." He patted the boy on the back. "You'll be doing the right thing by talking to the police."

"Will I go to that reform school?"

Based on the boy's reaction to the threat against Sarah Jane,

Barrett believed Andy's story and vowed to fight hard to see that he was deemed a hero and not a villain. "We'll explain that you had nothing to do with the fire but wanted to protect your family and so kept quiet about what really happened."

EDYTHE RETURNED HOME to find Barrett sitting in a chair on the front porch with Andy occupying the one beside him. Her steps stuttered at the grave expressions on their faces. She climbed the steps. "What's going on?"

Barrett looked at Andy and tipped his head. "You tell her."

"Tell me what?" She gripped the porch post, preparing herself for more bad news. She should have known better than to let Andrew leave the property today. "What is it?"

Her son stood before her. "I know who started the fire."

Edythe fought to calm her racing heart. She had been wrong. This was good news, wasn't it? "Who?"

He told her about two boys named Larson—the youngest around Andrew's age and the older boy about thirteen.

Larson? Edythe searched her memory but couldn't recall having heard the name among her son's friends.

After describing what happened to Mr. Stark and the probability that the boys marked Snowman's back, he said, "Mr. B. J. says I need to tell the police."

"Yes, you must. This is wonderful, Andy." Only after hugging her son did she realize she'd called him Andy. From now on, she would return to calling him the more familiar name, the one *he* wanted to be called, not the formal name her father insisted upon. She turned to Barrett, who now stood beside her, and threw her arms around him, not caring if the neighbors saw. "Thank you."

"Don't thank me yet."

She drew back. "But surely, this means we no longer have

anything to worry about."

"Let's see what the police say."

Edythe's elation withered at the uncertainty in his response.

When they reached the police station, Barrett asked for Officer Brennan. A few minutes later, the policeman escorted them to a private room barely large enough for the four of them to crowd around the table.

"Now,"—the officer addressed her son—"I understand you have something to tell me."

"Yes, sir." Andy's voice was little more than a whisper.

"Speak up."

"Yes, sir." Encouraged by Barrett's nod, Andy sat straight in his chair and faced Brennan. "I know who set the fire to Mr. Stark's shed."

Officer Brennan stared at Andy, a stare that caused Edythe's nerves to jump. "Go ahead."

"It was one of the Larson brothers."

Brennan wrote the name in a notebook. "How do you know this?"

"I saw it."

"You were with them?"

"Not with them...exactly. I started to cut through the property and saw them."

The officer nodded. "Tell me what happened."

Captivated by Andy's account, Edythe listened to every word, her anger against the Larson boys growing stronger with each mention of their names.

The moment Andy saw the two boys near the shed on the Stark property, smoke curling from their cigarettes, he'd turned to leave. Unfortunately, they caught sight of him.

"Tad tried to get me to smoke one of his cigarettes, but I told him no, that it made me sick the last time. Mr. Stark came out of the house. Then, the shed was burning, so I started to run off. I looked back and saw Mr. Stark on the ground and the Larson boys running away."

"You were caught on the property. Why didn't you run off too?"

Andy told Officer Brennan the same thing he'd told Edythe when proclaiming innocence weeks ago—he'd wanted to check on Mr. Stark but fear held him back. Before he could convince himself to move, others exited the house, so he hid among the bushes.

Edythe shook her head. If she'd been a better mother, more concerned about her children than her father, this situation might never have happened. Andy would not have sought company with two such cruel ruffians who showed no guilt in injuring a man. Mr. Stark might never have been hurt. All this was her fault.

Evidently, Barrett sensed her self-recrimination, because he squeezed her fisted hand. Physically, she relaxed under the affection and strength of his touch, but regret still swirled inside her.

Once her son finished speaking and Officer Brennan ran out of questions, the policeman closed his notebook. "I'll pay a visit to these Larson boys and talk to Mr. Stark again. Perhaps he's gained a better recollection of the incident."

"There's something else you should know," said Barrett. "Andy fears the boys painted a bullseye on his sister's pet goose as a warning for him to keep quiet."

Edythe's hand—the hand he still held—curled once more. Were her children not safe until those miniature criminals received their punishment?

"I witnessed them watching the house."

She glanced at Barrett. "When?"

"The day you and your father argued."

Officer Brennan eyed Andy. "Is that true?"

"They were there. I saw them from my bedroom window."

She spun in her seat toward her son. "You never said anything.

Do you realize the seriousness of your silence?"

Andy hung his head.

"He realizes it, Edy." Barrett pulled her to her feet. "Thank you for your time, Officer Brennan. We'll look forward to hearing the result of your inquiry."

Edythe thanked the officer, rested a hand on Andy's shoulder, and guided him from the room. Once they stepped onto the sidewalk, she tugged on Barrett's sleeve, stopping him. "What do you think?"

"I think we should wait until Brennan investigates. He took good notes and didn't reject Andy's story. I believe he'll be fair." He glanced at Andy, who walked several feet ahead of them, before he slipped her arm through his. He edged closer and lowered his voice to a near whisper. "What did your father say?"

"I..." She really must speak with the judge—if necessary, tie him down when he returned.

"He still doesn't know." Barrett's tone confirmed his disappointment.

"He's been gone for days, and I don't know when he'll return."

A grunt, better described as a growl, emanated from Barrett's throat.

"We were about to discuss it on Friday when we heard Sarah Jane's screams over what happened to Snowman. Afterward, he disappeared again. I haven't seen him since." Edythe paused to let the reminder of the incident with the goose sink in, hoping he would understand. "I'll speak to him as soon as he returns." If not before the reception to announce the promotion of Ansel to the presidency of the bank, then immediately afterward.

Her father had sprung Tuesday night's event on her in a scribbled note he'd slipped under her bedroom door before disappearing. It meant another night in Ansel's company.

He was an additional problem demanding her attention.

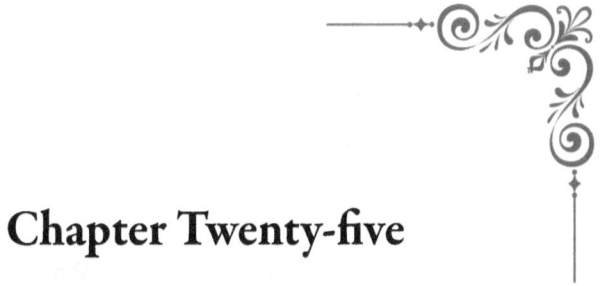

Chapter Twenty-five

Tuesday afternoon, Barrett entered Newland's Department Store and stopped near the door to look around. Mark had told him Roslyn Malone worked behind the perfume counter on the first floor.

A young man with the air of importance looked up and smiled. "Welcome to Newland's, sir. My name is Mr. Pittman. What may I help you with today?"

The young man's grin infected Barrett and wiped away the frown he'd worn since learning the judge still knew nothing of Edy's relationship with him.

Barrett glanced around. "Nice store."

"Yes, sir. It's the best outside of Chicago." The smile broadened.

"I'm sure it is." Barrett got down to business. "I was told Mrs. Roslyn Malone worked here."

Pittman pointed toward the front corner of the building. "Yes, sir. You'll find her in the perfume department."

Barrett had no idea what Mrs. Malone looked like. "Is she the only employee selling perfume today?"

"Yes, sir. She'll be happy to help you with a purchase."

"Thank you." Barrett hadn't come to make a purchase, but he kept that to himself. He found the woman he sought rearranging ornate bottles inside a glass case. "Mrs. Malone?"

She looked up from her task. Not much older than Mr. Pittman, her smile shone as bright. If all the salespeople who worked here were as congenial as the ones he'd met so far, it was no wonder the store did such brisk business. "May I help you, sir?"

He introduced himself as an attorney. "I'm aware this isn't a proper place for a conversation, but I'd like to ask you some questions about your husband."

Her smile fell. "Gil? Have the police found him?"

"No, ma'am." Barrett looked around. "Would it be possible to meet with you after your shift?"

Mrs. Malone stretched her neck as though looking for someone, then gestured to a woman a few yards away. "Muriel, would you mind watching my counter for a few minutes? It's important."

Muriel sauntered toward them, gave Barrett the once over, and moved behind the counter. "Take your time."

Fortitude and, perhaps, the wrath of a deserted wife fueled Mrs. Malone's footsteps as she marched to his side. "I could use a cup of coffee, Mr. Seaton."

After being seated in a restaurant in the next block, Barrett ordered two coffees and waited until the waitress brought them before stating his business. "I'm a friend of Mark Gregory's and am representing Jeremiah Quincy."

"Yes, Claire mentioned you and Mark traveled to Peru looking for Mr. Olesky." Mrs. Malone rushed to say, "I don't want you to think Claire spreads tales, and I don't know anything else."

He grinned to put her at ease. "Don't worry. Actually, I'm hoping you can provide a little more information about the man."

She stopped in the midst of raising her cup to her lips. "Me? I never met him."

"Are you sure?" He stirred a little cream into his coffee. "To be more accurate, Mrs. Malone, I'm hoping to be able to tie him to your husband and his crime."

Barrett had expected to see her jaw drop, her face to lose color—anything but the sparkle of elation in her deep blue eyes.

"You think he was Gil's partner."

Perceptive, though he wished she'd have kept her voice down. Only a few people occupied tables in the café at this hour, granting those who sat within earshot better ability to hear a conversation he wasn't ready to make public. "Not exactly a partner, though at this point, I'm not sure. It's why I've come to you."

"The night Gil ran off, he argued with a man at our house."

"Who?"

"I wish I'd seen him. I heard the voices but couldn't make out the words. Then the man left. I asked Gil about it, but he wouldn't tell me anything. We quarreled and I went to my parents' farm for the night. The next morning, he was gone." Her nails tapped the side of her coffee cup. "What makes you think Mr. Olesky—"

"I believe his real name is Asa Osbourne."

"What makes you think Osbourne is the same man?" She lowered her voice this time, giving Barrett the notion she'd hoped others in the café heard the story of her quarrel with her husband. Perhaps it was her way of assuring them she hadn't agreed with or supported Gil Malone's crime.

"Your husband was an accountant with Newland's, correct?"

"Yes. He managed the department, which gave him access to the books and accounts. That's how he was able to steal the money without others knowing."

Barrett wondered about her ease in believing the worst of the man she'd married. "You're certain he's guilty of the embezzlement?"

"Yes."

The force of the statement left no doubt in Barrett's mind as to her anger toward Gil Malone. "Are you aware of anything else in your husband's past that might have left him susceptible to blackmail?"

This time, her jaw slipped. "Blackmail?"

"I'm simply trying to establish or rule out possibilities. Was he ever accused of a crime or had he spent time in prison?"

"Not that I'm aware of. It wasn't my intention to marry a former convict."

He clenched his jaw to keep from mentioning that innocent men went to prison and, upon release, were worthy of happiness. But he wasn't here to defend Wynn. "You know of nothing in his past that someone might have used to force him into the theft?"

Her mouth twisted as she considered the question, and Barrett gave her time to present him with a well-thought-out answer. "Gil avoided talking about the past and became angry when I pushed for information. I suppose that was my first hint that he wasn't the man I'd imagined him to be." She swirled a spoon through her coffee cup, though she'd added nothing to the drink. It rattled against the sides, her only sign of emotion. "After the first few months, Mr. Seaton, our marriage was little more than a notation written in a Bible."

"I'm sorry." He hated to ask but it might prove the reason for blackmail. "Was your husband seeing someone else?"

"If so, he kept me in the dark about it." A droll chuckle escaped. "Then again, he kept me in the dark about the embezzlement."

The rest of their discussion provided no new helpful details. After walking Roslyn Malone back to Newland's, Barrett let her talk him into purchasing a lily of the valley perfume that reminded him of Edy—gentle, yet with more resilience than she believed. The sale hadn't taken much persuasion, since one whiff had him imagining her wearing it on their wedding day.

A day only in his imagination if she didn't use that resilience to tell her father about them.

DURING THE RECEPTION, Edythe stood at one end of her father's drawing room and sipped Mrs. Cameron's punch, her stomach still in knots over Andy's visit to the police on Sunday. They hadn't heard anything from Officer Brennan, but she had prayed without ceasing, as she'd read in her Bible. Would it help?

Since speaking with Verbenia, Edythe had devoted time each day to reading scripture. She prayed for a closer relationship with God and proof of his loving care. In the gospels, Jesus performed miracle upon miracle, showing His love and drawing people closer to the Father.

Jesus wept. Reading those two words had produced an ache inside her. Then He had brought Lazarus back to life. Another miracle.

Was having Barrett back in her life her own special miracle, proof of God's favor?

Her attention had strayed from the conversation between Ansel and the two couples who stood alongside them, laughing at something one of their group had said. She should join the others in their laughter but had no idea what they found funny. Instead, the smile she had planted on her face an hour ago—fake and frozen—caused her cheeks to ache.

How she despised these gatherings. Men who did little more than drink and talk business until the alcohol wrested crass words and actions from them.

Women who had nothing better to do than congregate in small groups and gossip about the latest poor soul unworthy of an invitation to whatever event they deemed important. She would be one of those poor souls talked about if not for her father's standing in the community. On the other hand, they probably talked about her anyway.

The only bright spot in the evening was the presence of Phoebe Crain and Spence Newland. However, she hadn't had much time to converse with them.

Ansel stuck to her side as if they had just finished a three-legged race and forgot to untie the rope lashing them together. She must take him aside after the party and make it clear she had no interest in him beyond friendship.

How could she when every time she looked at him, she thought of Barrett leaning in to kiss her? Every time he smiled at her, she heard Barrett's laughter. His every touch to her hand made her long for Barrett's arms around her.

Barrett Seaton was the only man she wished to have at her side for a lifetime, but could she really trust that he felt the same for her? What would she do if he abandoned her a second time?

Edythe glanced at her father standing across the room and shook off the old, unwarranted thoughts. The judge had remained missing from the house until this afternoon. She had enjoyed the peace his absence provided. Unfortunately, his late arrival hadn't afforded her an opportunity to sit him down to talk about Barrett.

He crooked his finger and gestured for her to come to him. His mood blazed a bit too cheerful this evening for her comfort, but she did as he bid with Ansel acting as her shadow.

Her father clasped her arm and drew her alongside him. He cast a smile, first at her, then Ansel. "Ladies and gentlemen, I have an important announcement to make." The room quieted, allowing him to announce his big news. "Many of you know that Mr. Sinclair, president of the First National Bank of the Wabash, has tendered his resignation due to poor health. Of course, that came as a shock to all of us on First National's Board of Directors. However, we have voted and are of one mind." He turned toward Ansel. "We have offered the position to Mr. Ansel Treadway, and he has accepted."

Edythe followed the lead of her father and others in the room in applauding Ansel's good fortune. She leaned closer to Ansel. "Congratulations. I know this is something you sought."

Ansel's features twisted. She had expected him to be grinning from ear to ear, not looking as though he'd lost the position.

When the applause died down, she turned back to her father. His attention had snagged on something—or someone—at the entrance to the room. A few others noticed and turned to see.

She followed their glances and her gaze lit on Barrett. He smiled at her from the drawing room doorway, but it was overshadowed by the distrust in his eyes when his gaze shifted to her father.

The judge never mentioned inviting Barrett. How long had he been here? She took a step forward to greet him, but her father grasped her arm and pulled her back to his side.

"As happy as that news is for Mr. Treadway, I have even greater news. It's been several years since my dear daughter Edythe suffered the loss of her beloved husband, Lamar."

Edythe's stomach churned. What was he up to?

"Until recently, she has dedicated her life to raising her three children."

"Father—"

"I have gathered you here tonight to announce that she has found a man to share that duty, that privilege."

Her gaze darted to Barrett, who remained across the room, his mouth tight and body rigid.

"Please congratulate my daughter on her engagement"—the judge sneered in Barrett's direction—"to Mr. Ansel Treadway."

Edythe almost choked on the sudden intake of air. Had she truly heard her father proclaim her engagement? To Ansel? She wanted nothing more than to shout a denial, but it was as though her father had snatched her voice as well as her right to decide her future. Again.

Her glance shot toward the place where Barrett stood. He stared at her. All she could do was stare back. Ordering her feet to move and her mouth to open ended in disappointment.

A few moments later, Barrett spun on his heel, and even over the noise of their guests, she heard the front door slam.

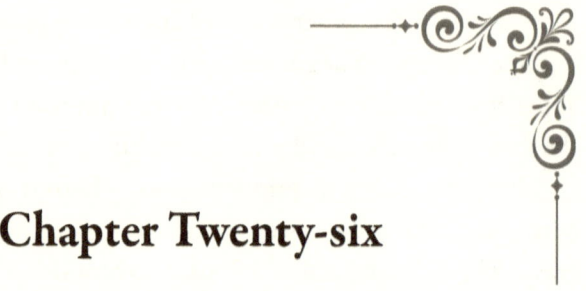

Chapter Twenty-six

The slam of the door propelled Edythe's feet into motion. She pushed through the crowd in her father's house to get to the foyer.

While those around her offered their congratulations, her gaze dropped to the two pieces of paper on the floor where Barrett had stood. She picked them up and pressed the halves together. An invitation to the reception. She read the handwritten note on the back.

How could her father have done this to Barrett? How could he lie to her, then publicly announce a forthcoming marriage without even asking if it was what she wanted?

Oh, Barrett.

Edythe glanced at Ansel, her so-called fiancé. He'd shown no surprise at the time of her father's announcement. Now she understood the guilt she thought she'd imagined on his face earlier. His chin sank with his inability to withstand the glare she sent him.

The crowd parted as Edythe stalked back to him and whispered, "You were promised the presidency in exchange for this?"

"It wasn't like that, not really."

But it was. She could see it in the red creeping up Ansel's face from under his collar. It advanced like an army to capture his ears and seize the skin running all the way to his hairline. His jaw tightened and his nostrils flared. "May we discuss this later? We don't want to embarrass your father."

"No, we wouldn't want that would we? We will discuss this sooner than later." The words cracked like a whip, but she couldn't dredge up an apology for their sting. Right now, she had something more urgent to do.

Without looking at either man, she rushed out of the room before they could stop her. Let the two of them come up with an excuse for her absence.

Upstairs, Edythe blocked out the sounds of laughter from below. She was a fool! A fool to let down her guard against the judge. A fool to have kept her mouth shut after his announcement. She should have shouted the truth from the rooftops, despite the impropriety of humiliating her father and Ansel in public. Was that what Barrett had waited for while his stare bore into hers—a denial?

This would not happen. She would not be forced into another marriage to a man she didn't love. Unlike last time, she'd grown strong enough to defy her father's plan. No matter what he did—castigate her, bruise her, toss her and her children to the street—his heavy-handed days of ruling over her life were finished.

Yes, she could confront the judge and Ansel, but it was Barrett who worried her most. Her father knew full well how his adversary would react to his announcement and had timed it for the moment Barrett arrived.

Please, Father God, if you don't care for me, at least show compassion for Barrett.

She couldn't help it. Her recent yearning for a closer relationship—a desire for a Fatherly love—prompted her to add another plea. *Please don't doom us to repeat the past.*

Was she also a fool to believe God warranted her trust when He seemed to turn away whenever she needed Him most?

Edythe grabbed a cloak to ward off the night air, knowing nothing would ease the chill of apprehension over what she must do. After wrapping it around her and raising the hood, she tiptoed down the back stairs into the kitchen, startling Mrs. Cameron. "Do you need something, Mrs. Westin?"

"*Shh.*" Edythe pressed a finger to her lips, trotted past the woman and out the back door into the darkness. Yes, she needed something. She needed Barrett's understanding.

She ran down the quiet streets of Riverport, nothing but the barking of dogs trailing her. At one point, the dark figure of a cat shot across her path, but she hadn't the breath to scream.

Once she reached Barrett's street, her pace slowed until she stood at the end of his walkway. Her chest heaved as she stared at the house she'd always admired, a house she had begun to hope might one day be her residence. Now it stood before her, huge and menacing, a shadowy symbol of the ire she was sure to face from its owner.

Second thoughts nudged her to turn around and wait to talk to Barrett until he'd had time to calm down. That was the logical thing to do.

That was the weak thing to do, and she was so very tired of weakness.

Edythe climbed the steps of the porch and rapped on the door. With no answer, she beat harder, insistent that he open up to her, for all that the dark house stood as proof he probably hadn't come straight home.

Finally, the door opened. Even while holding an oil lamp with the reflection of a flame that danced happily across his face, Barrett stared at her with a look as dark and formidable as the house. "Go home, Edythe. We have nothing to say to one another."

"We have much to say. I didn't know, Barrett. Believe me."

"You didn't know your father would announce an engagement, or you didn't know I'd be there to witness it?"

"Both." Her voice came out as little more than a squeak.

He eyed her a long, agonizing moment. He shook his head. "What difference does it make whether you knew? You said nothing.

Not one word of denial."

"I was in shock."

"You let the judge steer your future without a fight, and that peacock next to you grinned as though he had won some valuable prize." He set the lamp on a hall table, then leaned against the door frame and crossed his arms. "And after I left? Did you deny your engagement to those in attendance?"

What was she to say?

"I thought not." His prolonged sigh did nothing to ease the fierceness in his expression. He held out a small paper box for her to take. "My wedding gift to you."

Her hand quivered as she took hold of the box. She knew the label. "Oh, Barrett, I—"

"Goodnight, Mrs. Westin." He shut the door with a firm click.

Edythe remained on the porch for untold minutes, staring at the wooden panel and seeing only Barrett's furious face swimming before her.

After pulling a handkerchief from a pocket in her cloak, she twisted it in her hand, twisting and twisting until the wrinkles might never iron out. She should open that door, march inside, and demand he hear her out. A strong woman would do that—a woman of determination and courage.

She turned and lumbered down the porch steps, her strength and courage dispersing like the smoke from the neighboring chimneys.

BARRETT HAD LEFT THE department store after his conversation with Roslyn Malone, confident he was on the right trail and that Osbourne blackmailed Tanner, Gil Malone, and Dulong with the intention of pressuring them to commit a crime. How many others could be added to that list?

He knocked several times on the door to the Dulong house and waited...as he'd made Edy wait outside his door last night.

Barrett couldn't remember a time when he hadn't believed in or relied on God. What he'd yet to understand was why God often stood aside while the innocent suffered. Where was justice when sinful people thrived at the detriment of others? People like Hayden Danby.

As memory of the reception roared back with full force, once more Barrett's temper raged as hot as it had last night.

He had suspected the judge was up to no good in sending him the invitation. As Mark had said, the man possessed a record of deviousness. It hadn't stopped after ruining Edy and Barrett's future twelve years ago.

He'd considered declining the invitation to the reception but hadn't wanted to chance that the judge was on the up-and-up and, therefore, run the risk of hurting Edy's feelings. In not listening to the inner voice that told him differently, he was to blame for the man's enjoyment of his pain.

Although he'd prepared himself to be ambushed by some sort of ruse from Danby, he hadn't expected Edy's participation in that ambush. What did it matter whether she'd known about her father's plan? From where he'd stood at the entrance to the room, she made no effort to set anyone straight.

Why had he let her do this to him again?

He couldn't allow his personal troubles to interfere with Jeremiah's defense, so he pushed the anger aside to concentrate on his work.

Thinking no one was home at the Dulong residence *again*, he turned to go. Then, behind him, he heard the front door open. Changing course, he saw a wispy middle-aged woman half-hidden by the door, her expression guarded.

"Mrs. Dulong?"

"Yes."

"My name is Barrett Seaton. I'm Jeremiah Quincy's attorney."

"I don't want to talk to you."

She started to shut the door, so he thrust a hand out to prevent it. "Please, ma'am. This is important. I've tried to visit you a couple of times in the past two weeks and was told you were out of town."

"I said I don't want to speak with you. Leave me alone."

Before she could push the door closed, he rushed to say, "I believe your husband was being blackmailed to commit a crime."

Panic outshone the outrage he'd expected from a loyal wife. She searched the street in both directions.

"My client didn't kill your husband, Mrs. Dulong, but he might be punished for it unless you speak up. I don't think you want an innocent man to pay for something he didn't do." Barrett waited, giving her a chance to mull over what he'd said.

Without a word, she opened the door and stood aside to let him into the house, then peeked outside again before closing the door. Once they entered a modest parlor, she sat on the edge of the sofa, her hands knotted on her lap.

Barrett took a seat in a nearby chair. "I'm sorry for your loss, Mrs. Dulong, and for catching you by surprise with that news."

"I don't know why you think my husband was blackmailed. Claude did nothing wrong."

"But you do know someone put pressure on Mr. Dulong for a particular reason?"

She nodded. "I only saw him once, but I know who you mean." Her fingers picked at the material of her plain, black dress with a mechanical motion. "My husband never told me his name. Claude refused to talk about him."

"Can you describe him? What did he look like?"

Hers was a vacant stare much like Harold Tanner's when he recalled his experience with Osbourne. "Maybe fifty or so and dressed like a gentleman."

"Did he have any distinguishing physical characteristics? A beard? A—"

"His hair."

Barrett's heart raced. "What about it?"

"It was mostly dark but had a white streak running through it about here." With her finger, she drew a line down the front of her head. "I was standing at the top of the stairs when he walked to the front door to leave. As he prepared to put on his hat, somehow, he sensed me there and looked up." Her body shivered. "Cold. That man had the coldest smile I've ever seen."

"What did he want your husband to do?"

"I told you, Claude wouldn't discuss it. But the man scared him."

"Mrs. Dulong, I think he wanted your husband to embezzle money from the brewery. Do you have any idea why he would believe Mr. Dulong would agree to do such a thing?"

She scowled. "I told you he did nothing wrong."

"Yet the man with the cold smile threatened your husband in some way, hoping to force him into the theft. There must be something he held over Mr. Dulong."

She stared at her lap. "I don't know."

Barrett decided to let it drop for now. Jeremiah said Dulong entered the tavern looking for someone. If he was right about Asa Osbourne, chances were good the men were to meet at Swain's. With Dulong being thrown out of the tavern, perhaps they met up afterward in the shack. Dulong told Osbourne no and, without the mercy he showed toward Tanner, Osbourne killed him.

"What was your husband's state of mind that afternoon?"

She shrugged. "He'd received a telegram and was furious. He left the house shortly after."

"To go to Swain's?"

"Claude hated the use of alcohol."

Yet he worked in a brewery.

Barrett studied a photograph in a frame sitting on a nearby table. "Is that your husband and son?"

She picked up the frame. Judging by the mixture of pain and pride etched in the lines around her eyes, she was a woman devoted to her family. "My Claude and our Vincent." She touched the face of the young man dressed in the uniform.

"Your son is a soldier?"

"He was."

"Ah. Does he live around here?" Something about the photograph nagged at Barrett, so he kept asking questions, hoping for a revelation to break loose.

Her face grew pale.

"Where does he live, Mrs. Dulong?"

Her cooperation changed, replaced by the firm set of her jaw. She set the photograph back on the table. "I'm tired and have nothing more to say to you, Mr. Seaton."

He stood on the porch after being shown out of the house, his mind replaying the conversation. All of a sudden, that revelation he'd hoped for resounded like cannon fire.

He'd received a telegram and was furious. He left the house shortly after.

Words danced across his vision—words like "Major" and "U. S. Army." The words on the scrap of paper he'd picked up in the shack where Dulong died.

Mrs. Dulong's information wasn't enough to connect the telegram her husband received to the torn paper, but if they were connected, it was possible Osbourne's blackmail involved Vincent Dulong.

Then again, maybe Barrett grasped at straws.

Rather than turn around and confront the widow, Barrett decided to take the paper and his theory to the police and insist they investigate. Hopefully, they would connect those pieces and give him something to present a jury as reasonable doubt.

EDYTHE OPENED THE BANK'S door to let an elderly woman exit before she entered the building. She'd waited for Ansel to pay her a call, preferring he come to her rather than her being forced to visit his home and set neighboring tongues wagging or interrupt his work. But he never did, which left her with no choice but to disturb his business day.

Regardless of whether she and Barrett ever found a future together, she would not continue to allow Ansel to count on their engagement ending in wedded bliss.

The lovely scent of lilies of the valley behind her ears gave her added incentive.

If only her father had stayed put long enough this week for her to inform him of his plan's failure. Instead, he'd chosen to leave town after the reception with only another message delivered by Mrs. Cameron. The coward.

Edythe scanned the employees and patrons coming and going in the busy bank until she located her "fiancé" sitting in a tiny office in a far corner. After crossing the room, she stopped in front of his desk. "May I speak with you, Ansel?"

He looked up from the book he'd been writing in and winced. "I've been expecting you." He closed the account book and nodded toward the doorway. "Until Mr. Sinclair leaves and I move into the president's office, I'm stuck in this little space with no door. There's a meeting room upstairs. I believe it will be quieter and a less public place for our talk."

The less public, the better.

Ansel led her to a room off the hallway on the second floor. Leather chairs surrounded a long table with an inlaid design. The furniture occupied the center of the space and left little room to move around. He shut the door and invited her to take a seat at the table but he stood near a window, looking out on the town, his profile set in stone. "I trust you're feeling better."

They must have excused her absence from the reception as sudden illness. "I'm in perfect health."

"I'm glad to hear it. I know you've been burdened by your son's situation."

Was he delusional? Yes, Andrew's problem weighed heavily on her, especially since she hadn't heard anything from Officer Brennan, but did Ansel think he bore no responsibility for her distress?

"I should have paid you a call. After all, it's something one would expect a fiancé to do. But..."

"But knowing the engagement was a mockery, you didn't want to damage your new position by admitting to it?"

A muscle jumped in his cheek. "Your father discussed it with me shortly before the guests arrived. It wasn't how I wished things to progress between us."

"Then you understand that we cannot continue with this sham."

His shoulders slumped. "Frankly, Edythe, I'm relieved."

"Relieved?"

"I want the position of president of this bank."

"And my father promised it to you if you married me."

"It's true, but the timing of the engagement announcement was not my idea." He turned to face her. "Please, don't misunderstand. I looked forward to our union. Although we haven't known one another long, you're one of the finest women I've ever met. It would be an honor to marry you."

Edythe didn't bother with an "If things were different..." excuse when her lack of affection toward Ansel would not change.

"That first night, the night I noticed Mr. Seaton standing at the street, watching your father's house, I suspected your feelings for me would never be the same as mine for you."

"Mr. Seaton has little to do with my opposition to a marriage between us."

"I almost wish he did. I have no qualms about fighting for something important. I fought hard for the position of president of this bank and won it."

Edythe could have reminded Ansel that he got the position through accepting a role in the judge's underhanded scheme. If he were already married, would he still have been considered for the presidency? Hopefully, her father had the decency to see that Ansel kept the position.

She moved to his side at the window and laid a hand on his arm. "I don't approve of your part in this farce, but my father had no right to do what he did without consulting either of us. I had no right to go to supper with you when I knew nothing could come of it. I'm sorry you were caught between us."

"You have nothing to apologize for. I'm the one to blame. I let my ambition go to my head." He rested a hand on hers. "Have you and Seaton worked things out?"

The memory of Barrett's anger weighed on her. "At this point, I'm not sure it's possible."

"It's a pity and his loss."

Unfortunately, it was also a loss for her children. They admired Barrett.

BARRETT TREKKED THROUGH the sanitarium's yard toward Wynn. He stopped at the side of the wicker chair that accentuated his brother's shrunken frame.

Wynn's Bible sat on his lap as he read out loud. He had entered prison an agnostic and walked out a believer. At least something good had come from his years behind bars.

"'Thou shalt guide me with thy counsel, and afterward receive me to glory. Whom have I in heaven but thee? And there is none upon earth that I desire beside thee. My flesh and my heart faileth: but God is the strength of my heart, and my portion forever.'"

Barrett blinked over and over, trying to clear his vision. Wynn's voice was stronger than the last time they had talked, and he spoke the words with the fervency of a prayer—the prayer of a dying man. When Barrett's swallow caught on a moan, he covered the emotion with a slight cough.

Wynn looked up. "Don't be sad for me, little brother. God gave me a life I nearly squandered. Soon, He'll give me a new one, one where I'll be healthy and happy for eternity."

Barrett cringed at hearing his brother speak of his death. The loss of the years they might have spent together grieved him and reminded him of why the end would come so early in Wynn's earthly existence. "You didn't squander your life. Too much of it was taken from you."

With a faint nod to the chair a few feet away, Wynn said, "Sit down. There's something for us to discuss." The statement sounded like an order, but his brother's downcast features and quiet voice said he wasn't looking forward to whatever he had to say.

Barrett dropped into the chair and crossed one leg over the other, propping his hat on his knee. He sought a relaxed stance to cloak the tension and grief running through his body. He breathed in fresh, cool air tinged with a hint that autumn waited around the corner. Would Wynn see the harvest of the corn or the fall of colorful leaves?

"It's long past time we discussed what happened the night they arrested me."

"Wynn—"

"Don't interrupt." His brother spit out the words with more force and volume than Barrett had heard from him in weeks. "It's long past time I was honest with you, so let me talk."

Honest? "About what?"

"I've confessed to Edy and asked her forgiveness, but confessing to you is a lot harder." Wynn exhaled. "I suppose you could call this my deathbed confession."

Deathbed? His brother's hoarse chuckle chafed Barrett's nerves.

"There's no easy way to say it, so I'll be blunt. I was guilty that night I was arrested. I robbed that drugstore."

The landscape spun as Barrett tried to grasp his brother's words.

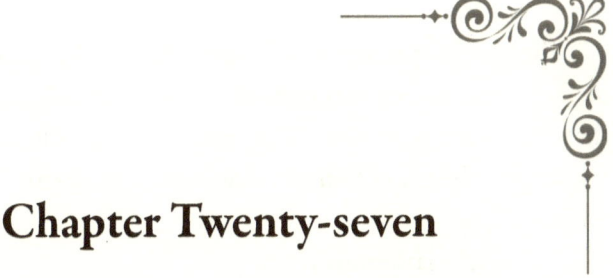

Chapter Twenty-seven

Throughout the years, Barrett had believed in Wynn's innocence. He'd believed because his brother denied any guilt—the brother he'd revered. "But you told me you didn't do it."

"I told you a lie."

Barrett jumped to his feet, ignoring the hat that fell to the ground. "That can't be true. They found no money on you, no proof."

Wynn's mouth twisted into a smirk. "I was robbed."

"That's not funny."

"No, but it's true. If I hadn't been so drunk, I might have prevented the deed and certainly wouldn't have taken part. I can't tell you how sorry I am to disappoint you. I suppose not possessing the money should have worked in my favor."

"The jury assumed you'd hidden it before you were found."

"Yes."

He tried to wrap his mind around the gravity of his brother's words. "You injured a man, Wynn."

"No." He shook his head. "No, I didn't, and that's one thing I won't have you thinking of me."

Barrett opened his mouth to argue until the truth flashed in his mind. His brother had never been a violent man, which was one of the reasons Barrett had always believed him innocent. He couldn't imagine Wynn hurting someone. So, if he didn't hit the druggist, who did? "You weren't alone that night."

"I'll tell you the same thing I told Edy. There's no point in going down that road, because I won't talk of it. It's done."

The shock of his brother's confession had wiped from Barrett's memory the earlier mention of Edy's knowledge. The realization that she'd been privy to this information and hadn't told him added kindling to the fire of betrayal that burned in his gut. "When did you tell her?"

"We spoke last month."

"A month ago?" Why hadn't Edy told him during their time in the country, a time when they had cleared the air about their past? His reawakened feelings had rekindled his trust in her and set them on the path toward a future together...before she'd pushed him off it and over a cliff. "You told her and not me? Didn't I deserve to know?"

"Don't blame her. I asked her not to say anything to you. I wanted to tell you myself."

"Yet you've waited a full month. You waited *twelve years*." With fingers interlocked, his hands pressed down on his head as though the force would contain his frustration. With Wynn. With Edy. With everything he'd believed until this moment. "All this time, I've defended you. I accused Judge Danby of sentencing you to prison as punishment for my relationship with his daughter. I let the incident ruin a future for Edy and me."

"I know. I'm sorry. I never had the courage to admit my guilt to you."

Barrett's arms dropped to his side. "Am I that much of an ogre?"

"You're that much of a loyal brother. For some reason I never understood, you looked up to me." Wynn raised his head, sorrow darkening his eyes. "How could I bear to fail you?"

"Perhaps you should have thought of that before you robbed the drugstore."

Wynn nodded. "You're right, and I have no excuse for what I did."

Barrett struggled to gain control of his anger, his disappointment. For years, he'd blamed himself. He'd blamed Edy's father. And all along, Wynn was guilty of the crime for which he'd been charged.

Had Barrett known the truth from the beginning, how would it have changed his life, his relationship with Edy? Would he have left Riverport without her, giving her the opportunity to marry someone else, or fought all who stood in their way, including Lamar Westin and the judge?

He couldn't say. Because he still blamed himself for Wynn's plight. "Keeping my word to you would have given you no chance to commit a crime that night. Instead, I stole away to meet Edy, leaving you alone to—"

"To get drunk and rob a man." Wynn's mouth twitched with a grimace. "Your staying around the house that night would not have stopped me. I'd already determined my plans for the evening and sought an excuse to get away from you. To be honest, I rejoiced when you took that lie—that extra sin—away from me."

Barrett studied his brother, trying to ascertain the veracity of his words. Wynn's gaze was steady, intense, unwavering. Did he hope to drill the truth into Barrett through eye contact?

"My time is short, but the one thing I want you to know is that I don't regret going to prison, because that's where God reached me. That's where all the Bible teaching Grandpa drummed into us paid off. It's where I found peace. I'm not afraid of the grave. It's then I'll stand in the presence of a merciful Father who loves me and has forgiven me. God is just but forgiving, and He expects the same from us."

Just but forgiving.

"I deserve your scorn as much as I deserved my sentence."

"I don't hold ill-will toward you, Wynn. I wish you'd told me sooner." Before he'd ever made a fool of himself in front of the judge.

Wynn turned the pages of the Bible, going forward into the New Testament. "It says right here in Philippians, the fourth chapter, 'Be careful for nothing; but in everything by prayer and supplication with thanksgiving let your requests be made known unto God. And the peace of God, which passeth all understanding, shall keep your hearts and minds through Christ Jesus.'"

He shut the Bible but continued to quote its message with his eyes closed and his head pressed against the back of the wicker chair. "'I've learned, in whatever state I am, therewith to be content. I can do all things through Christ which strengtheneth me.' I am content, Barrett. I have that peace only God can give a person, more peace than I ever had in my whole life."

"I'm happy for you." Happy and yet brokenhearted. While his brother had found the answer to the turbulence in his life, death loomed over him.

Wynn grabbed Barrett's arm, his hold as weak as it was determined. "For a while, I convinced myself that your relationship with Edy cost me more years than I would have otherwise spent in that prison. Don't be like me. Don't continue to hold on to your anger with Judge Danby and Edy. You're the one it hurts in the end."

Given what happened at the reception and the recent repetition of history, Barrett couldn't promise to change. He placed his hand over his brother's. "I'm proud of you, Wynn"—his voice cracked—"and I've always been proud to be your little brother."

AFTER HAVING HER RUBY ring assessed by a jeweler in the next town, Edythe returned to her father's house, dragging with exhaustion, a consequence of the past week—the past two months, really.

As she climbed the porch stairs, she no longer thought of the residence as home. At least, it wouldn't be once she decided to sell her mother's ring. She should have sold it to the jeweler this afternoon and been done with it, but something held her back. Possibly, she was more sentimental than she'd thought. If so, she must get over it.

Andy entered the foyer and blocked her way to the stairs. "Grandfather's home."

A tremble flitted through Edythe's fingers, adding difficulty to the removal of her hat and gloves. The time had arrived to tell her father his plan had failed. "Where is he?"

"He went out back with Sarah Jane and Timothy." Andy stood straight—his feet apart, his arms crossed. "Should my name be Andrew Seaton?"

Edythe ran the odd question through her mind three times before the words struck a blow that staggered her. "What on earth makes you ask that question?"

"Grandfather looked at me, said I was like my father, and cursed Mr. B. J."

Edythe massaged her forehead. "I'm sure you misunderstood. Your name is Westin, because you are a Westin. Mr. Seaton is not your father." And she shouldn't need to reassure her son of it.

Andy's eyes shone with unshed tears that brought dampness to her own while her blood boiled over her father's irresponsible and vulgar behavior. "Then why does he hate me?"

"He doesn't hate you." The words rolled off her tongue as though she had confidence in them. "You go on up to your room. I'll handle this. And Andy..."

"Yes, ma'am?"

"This isn't a proper conversation to bring up to anyone, not even your brother and sister. Do you understand?"

"I didn't think it was." He stepped away from her. When he reached the top of the stairs, he spun on the balls of his feet. "You and Mr. B. J. were friends a long time ago, though, right?"

"Yes. At one time, we were good friends."

"He likes you as more than a friend, Mama, and I think you like him."

Her son's perception went beyond his years. Unfortunately, he hadn't seen her with Barrett since the fiasco of the engagement announcement. He wasn't aware that Barrett refused to even speak to her.

"You won't marry that banker, will you?"

"No."

"I think you should marry Mr. B. J."

She squeezed the gloves in her hand, stunned that this boy who had adored his father would suggest she marry anyone. "You like Mr. Seaton?"

A quiet smile crept onto Andy's face. "Sure. He's nice and not a bad fisherman."

After he ran down the hall, Edythe walked into the drawing room. The memory of the conversation with her son chilled her. How much more of her father's destructive behavior must she tolerate?

Tomorrow, she would take the ring back to the jeweler and leave it there. Afterward, somehow, she would find work to support her children, even if it were something as lowly as sweeping the streets.

Because despite her child's approval of Barrett as a father, it wasn't meant to be.

Edythe cranked the phonograph and shut her eyes. As she swayed to the music, allowing the piano strains to calm her, she rehearsed what she'd say to her father.

Perhaps it wasn't the words she must rehearse but the tone in which she said them. If he sensed hesitation or fear, he would gore her like a bull in the ring.

She opened her eyes. Hesitation? Fear? No such emotions brewed inside Edythe. She whipped around, ready to find and confront the man who had wreaked havoc on her life and the lives of her children.

She needn't go far. He stood in the doorway to the drawing room, his shoulders limp. Lines defined the space between his eyes. For the first time in her life, she saw him as old.

Chapter Twenty-eight

The judge dropped his suit coat on the back of the sofa. "I want to talk to you."

"I want to talk to you, too, Father." *Good.* She'd hit the right tenor, somewhere between respect and resolve.

Edythe let the music from the phonograph fade into silence. The sudden quiet emphasized her father's groan as he dropped into a chair by the fireplace. "I heard you broke your engagement to Ansel."

Was that the reason he'd cursed Barrett and upset her son? "Since it was something I never agreed to, I didn't consider myself engaged. As for Ansel, I hope you will follow through with his promotion."

He waved the statement away. "It wasn't his fault."

She had expected agitation, a raised voice and argument, not this quiet apathy. She'd prepared herself for standing her ground, but he retreated without a shot fired.

"I suppose you've already worked things out with Seaton."

He didn't deserve to see the pain Barrett's rejection caused her, but she was tired of secrets. "He thinks I betrayed him and wants nothing to do with me."

"He was never good enough for you, Edythe."

"That's not been your decision to make."

"It's every father's duty to strive for the best for his child."

"In doing so, you paid no mind to what I wanted in your determination to break us apart." Edythe let the words roll out, no longer fatigued and no longer caring to mind her tone. "You stole

Barrett's letters thinking that was for my good?"

"Yes."

The quiet admission knocked her off balance. "Do you still have them?"

"I burned them as soon as they arrived...unread."

"How could you do that, Father?"

"I wanted to shelter you and keep you from making the same mistakes as your mother."

"For the last time, I am not my mother."

"You're more like her than you wish to think—both in positive and negative ways. When Seaton ran out on you, Edythe, I did what I had to do to protect you."

"There's a difference between proper protection and unreasonable control. You've crossed that line too many times, Father. Even worse, I've let you do it. No more. And while we're on the subject of Barrett Seaton, never again upset my child with disgusting and false allegations."

His brows dipped. "What false allegations?"

"You led Andy to think Barrett is his father."

"I said nothing of the kind to the boy."

"How did you think he would interpret your claim that he was like his father when, in the same breath, you cursed Barrett?"

"I was upset and didn't mean for Andrew to hear my...opinion of Seaton."

"Well, he did."

"In truth, Edythe, I've had no will to be a grandfather to the boy."

"That *boy* understands how far down your nose you look at him."

"I've my reasons. After finding you'd met with Seaton behind my back, I saw a dreadful future for you. Then when he left town, I knew he wouldn't do the right thing by you."

"The right thing?"

He went on as though he hadn't heard her. "Soon after your

marriage, you announced you were expecting a child, and I realized I'd been right to insist you marry someone else."

"But you weren't." Should she judge him too harshly when the timing had surprised her, too? Still, the insinuation hurt. "For your information, Barrett and I never..." Her skin warmed. "Andrew is Lamar's son."

The judge stared at her—searched her—in a way that left her feeling exposed.

"Why do you think Barrett wrote those letters you stole? If you had read them,"—the idea of it caused her to cringe—"you would have changed your mind about him. Instead, you believed the worst and thought to save yourself the humiliation of having an unwed mother in your house." She stopped pacing and stared at her father. "How could you imagine that of me?"

Rather than answer outright, he said, "Andrew looks nothing like the twins."

"No, he doesn't. Are you so blinded by your hostility toward Barrett, that you can't see Andy looks like me? Same hair and eyes. Same facial features." Edythe paced back and forth in front of the sofa. "That's why you've always treated Andy like some poor relation. You despised Barrett so much you couldn't stand to look at your grandson."

He pressed a hand to his forehead in defeat and moments passed before he spoke. "When I learned you kept your relationship with Barrett secret, all I saw was the man who took Mary Ellen from me. All I saw was how I'd failed you both."

Edythe wished to continue to rail against him in retaliation for almost thirty years of manipulation, but too much blame rested on her. If she'd let Barrett court her properly years ago, as he'd wanted to do, and been honest with her father, her life and the lives of those she loved might have turned out differently.

"I suppose I let my feelings for Seaton control my reaction to

Andrew. I will apologize to my grandson." Her father sank farther into the seat of the chair, leaned his head against the back, and stared at the drawing room ceiling. "Your mother died."

The announcement, so random and unexpected, weakened her knees and forced her onto the sofa. "I always wondered if I might meet her one day." She had her answer. "When? How did you learn about it?"

"She didn't die alone, Edythe. I've been with her these last weeks."

A brick to the head couldn't have stunned her more. "You knew her whereabouts?"

"The day Mary Ellen left Riverport, I hired someone to find her. His agency has kept me informed ever since."

Would her father never cease to cause her anguish? "You were aware of her location all these years and chose not to tell me?" She shook her head. "Wait. You said 'these last weeks.' Her death was recent?"

"She passed today."

The muscles in Edythe's throat throbbed with the desire to release a sob, to mourn all she had missed by not having her mother in her life. "Why didn't you tell me she was ill? Why didn't you take me with you and let me say goodbye?"

He raised his head and leaned forward in the chair, his arms on his knees. "She refused to see you. I tried to convince her. She'd have none of it."

Her mother hadn't wanted to see her. "Why?"

"The man she ran off with left her years ago. Ever since, she's lived a hard life. She couldn't bear for you to see her shame."

Edythe covered her mouth and drew in a breath before she dropped her hand to verbally attack her father. "You were aware of my mother's situation and did nothing to help her? You're nothing but a selfish, bitter man!"

Each wrinkled eye released a tear that rolled down his face to hide in his mustache, shredding Edythe's heart despite her anger with him. "For years, I couldn't forgive her for leaving us."

"It's too late now."

His expression pleaded for understanding, maybe for her pardon. "No. I was given the time and opportunity to assure her of my regret, to ask her for forgiveness."

Some of the heat of Edythe's fury cooled.

He sighed. "I should have insisted she see you one last time."

In all honesty, if presented with the opportunity, would Edythe really have wanted to see a woman who permitted pride to keep her from her child?

Yes. Yes, she would. Because Mary Ellen Danby was her mother.

"That was her decision, Father. You need to let others make their choices no matter the result."

Her father rose and approached with guarded steps, looking down on her, his face twisted into sorrow. "I have many wrongs to atone for, my dear, but I hope it isn't too late for you to forgive me and forgive your mother."

Not long ago, Edythe had fully realized the breadth of God's love for His creation. The sacrifice Jesus paid offered generations of people the opportunity to receive mercy for the sins they'd committed, including her mother and father. How could Edythe accept God's gracious and merciful forgiveness, yet deny her parents her own mercy?

"I will try, Father." She shuddered at the insufficient answer, but right now, that was all she could promise.

EVEN DURING THESE LAST weeks of Wynn's illness, Barrett had refused to give more than a glancing blow's consideration to this day. He'd lived a dream of a happy ending for himself and for his brother. Now he was numb—unable to move, unable to feel.

The coffee Mrs. Quincy had brought to his office had lost its steam, leaving only a slight scent to linger in the air, along with the stink of Barrett's remorse and grief.

He sat pressed against the back of his office chair, staring at the paper on the desk. It had arrived fifteen minutes ago and remained where he'd tossed it, as far away from him as possible, but within reading distance. Short and to the point, with an expressed message of sympathy, Dr. Ellis informed him of Wynn Seaton's death.

In the early hours of this morning, Barrett became the last Seaton. Betrayed a second time by the only woman he'd ever wanted to carry his name, he would likely remain so.

He'd failed to save Wynn. He'd failed to keep his distance from Edy. And he'd failed to save himself a second round of pain.

Then again, maybe failure wasn't his problem. Maybe it was naivety. He was naive to expect everyone to receive fair treatment in life. He expected wrong to be made right and the guilty to have their sins revealed. He expected the punishment to fit the crime and the innocent to be exonerated. Well, he'd learned his lesson—once with Wynn, twice with Edy.

The doctor called Wynn's passing a peaceful transition to eternity. Peaceful or not, it didn't take away from the fact that Wynn died for a mere fifty dollars—money he lost in a matter of moments. At least his brother had ended the Ned Flannigan farce.

Now that Barrett had been informed of the truth about the robbery, what was he to do with it? It only deepened his guilt over not remaining at home that night.

And yet...

Prison had saved Wynn's soul. It brought him into eternity with God in a way that all the Sundays spent in church had never done. Wynn did die in peace. He had received the earthly justice due him as a criminal, but God's grace and mercy saved him from receiving the justice due him as a sinner.

God is just but forgiving.

Barrett gripped the arms of his chair. Jesus paid the price that allowed Wynn to be forgiven by God. It was the ultimate injustice, because it was a debt He hadn't owed.

He expects the same from us.

God expected Barrett to treat others in a just manner and forgive the wrongs done to him.

Don't continue to hold on to your anger with Judge Danby and Edy. You're the one it hurts in the end.

He did hold onto his anger, and it did hurt him. It hurt others.

Since the night of the reception, Barrett had considered dismissing Edy as his client. But she wasn't his client. Not really. His responsibility was to her son. How just was a decision like that when it came to the boy? How merciful was it to let Andy face an uncertain future without the experience of someone who might help prepare him should the worst happen?

Barrett might never understand why good people suffered—sometimes, unfairly—but that didn't excuse him from his responsibility to show mercy and forgiveness to others.

ONCE THE FEW MOURNERS had walked away—mainly staff from the sanitarium—Edythe remained, unsure what to do or say.

Clothed in fine dark wool, Barrett stood still and solid as granite in front of the precipice of the empty hole, the final resting place of Wynn's body. He stared at the casket being lowered into the ground by the men the cemetery employed for the task.

Edythe fought tears, not so much for Wynn but for his brother. Maybe a few were for herself, for the fact that Barrett never glanced at her during the burial service, yet she was certain he had been aware of her presence. She'd stood behind him, and when Dr. Ellis greeted her by name, Barrett's body grew rigid.

Would he resist her effort to provide comfort, if but for a moment?

Stepping forward, she reached out to touch Barrett's shoulder but pulled her hand back.

With another delivery of books to the sanitarium, she had learned of Wynn's death and wanted to say her goodbye. Maybe coming had been a mistake, but despite Wynn's flaws, she wanted to honor his memory.

Besides, she owed Barrett evidence of her love whether he accepted it or not.

The day of Lamar's funeral, she'd spoken to mourners gathered in her home after the service. Few people touched her. Few hugs. Little physical contact from anyone but her children. Only rote expressions of sympathy from people with whom she had nothing in common. Words she couldn't even remember now. Despite the fact that she and her husband were little more than good friends, how she had longed for the arms of comfort.

Lips quivering, Edythe ventured a fingertip touch. His muscles tightened, and then relaxed. The fact that he didn't pull away emboldened her. She slid her hand over the material of his black coat until her palm rested on the top of his shoulder. It was all she dared do.

As they stood, unmoving, her throat raged with fire, leaving words of sympathy to burn up before they reached her mouth. Honestly, what could be said at this moment that might make a difference for him?

Nothing. Not now. Not here.

They endured the silence side by side for what seemed an endless time but was more like a couple of minutes. Neither of them twitched a muscle as her black attire absorbed the warmth of an Indian summer sun. Dampness formed along her hairline and up and down her spine.

With a final squeeze of his shoulder, she turned and walked away.

When she reached her carriage, Edythe twisted to glance behind her. Barrett remained in the same spot, still unmoving...except for the hand that wiped each side of his face.

Chapter Twenty-nine

Two days after Wynn's funeral, Barrett stood outside Judge Danby's front door, his emotions as raw as the skin on a scraped knee. It was time to lay aside the past, to apologize to the judge for Barrett's own failing—his resentment and anger. The thought of it was like swallowing castor oil, so maybe he had a little more internal work to do.

The judge opened the front door and stared at Barrett. He expected the man to demand he get off his porch, off his property. If so, Barrett would obey, content to tell himself he had tried.

Fine. That was the quitter's way out.

He'd speak his piece, or as much of it as Edy's father would listen to before slamming the door in Barrett's face.

His expectations changed with the defeat written in the older man's demeanor. "Come in, Barrett. We have things to discuss."

Barrett? Not Seaton? Not boy?

He stepped inside and removed his hat. From his spot in the foyer, he looked around the vacant area—for Edy.

He hadn't known how to handle her presence at Wynn's funeral and the soft, sympathetic touch that reminded him of all he had lost in less than two weeks. So, he'd said nothing. After she walked away, he'd battled the temptation to call her back. Grovel at her feet if necessary, or act like her father and order her to break her engagement to the banker.

What good was it to want someone who didn't want him

enough to make her own decision about their relationship? But he was working to forgive her—he was bound and determined to do so.

Barrett followed the judge into the drawing room. This wasn't his first glimpse of the inside of the house. Twelve years ago, he'd walked into this very room, pleading with the man to let Wynn go free. It was the last time he'd begged for something from Hayden Danby.

Now he'd returned to beg for forgiveness.

"Have a seat."

Not much in the room had changed. It was the judge's attitude that struck a foreign note.

Barrett waited until the older man flopped into a chair by the fireplace as though he hadn't the energy to sit properly. "I'll stand if you don't mind." He came for a purpose and when that purpose was achieved, he would leave.

"Suit yourself. I can say what I have to say no matter where you are." He caught Barrett's gaze. "I owe you an apology."

"You owe *me* an apology?"

"Yes, and you'll get it once. Don't make me repeat myself."

Barrett controlled the urge to grin at the growled declaration. "No, sir. I'm listening."

"Years ago, I let my personal experience cloud my judgment when it came to my daughter and her wishes. I told her I only wanted to protect her, but I've done a good deal of soul-searching lately and realized that bitterness and fear drove my actions. Learning Edythe had fallen in love with a man destined to be an attorney brought back all I'd gone through with her mother. Finding out you'd returned to town set those feelings off again, so I arranged for Ansel to court Edythe."

And break Edy and Barrett apart.

"In exchange, I promised him the presidency at the bank." The judge eyed him. "She knew nothing of the engagement until I announced it at the reception last week. It wasn't something she sought or welcomed."

"Or something she turned down. I was there, remember? You saw to that." Barrett's body warmed with a renewed anger and disappointment that he beat back.

A hint of a smile appeared on Danby's face. "Yes, I remember. At the time, it gave me great pleasure to watch you stalk off." He grew sober. "Then Edythe's mother died, and I mistakenly suggested to my eldest grandson that he was your child."

Barrett sank into the nearest chair. Andy his child? An impossibility but a fact that continued to sting. How he would have enjoyed being the father of all three of Edy's children.

Ignorant of the way Barrett's mind whirled with the revelations, the judge said, "I spent my wife's last days with her. She was buried yesterday."

That explained their absence when he paid a call here last evening. "I'm sorry, but let's go back to your telling Andy I was his father."

"Edythe wasted no time in taking me to task for all my mistakes, including that one. Lately, my daughter has acquired more mettle than I credited her with. She also made certain Ansel knew there was no engagement between them."

A flutter in his gut took Barrett by surprise. Flutters weren't something a man readily admitted to. "I didn't know."

"My daughter didn't love him any more than she loved Lamar. Her sights were set no higher than you, in the past and the present."

Were? That flutter turned into a hefty cannonball. If he and Edy had lost another chance at a future together, the blame rested with Barrett. Rather than give her time to deal with her father's deception and lie, he'd assumed—a second time—that she wasn't strong enough, setting his pride free to ruin everything between them.

Was it too late to bow and scrape at her feet?

First...

"Judge, I came to tell you I was wrong. Before he died, my brother admitted to committing the robbery at the drugstore."

Danby nodded. "Sometimes, we choose not to see the truth about others...or ourselves. It brought me no pleasure to send anyone to prison, not even your brother."

Yet he'd been willing to send Edy into another marital prison.

At a knock on the door, the judge left the room. A moment later, Barrett heard Officer Brennan's voice and stepped into the foyer to greet the policeman.

Upon seeing Brennan's frown, Barrett's heart skipped.

MASCULINE VOICES IN the otherwise tranquil house disturbed Edythe's embroidery of a tablecloth, her wedding gift for Claire and Mark.

She poked the needle into the linen, set the gift on the sitting room sofa, and walked into the foyer. A policeman stood near the door, talking to her father.

"Officer Brennan?" When his attention shifted to her, Edythe froze. Rather than the expected smile on his face—confirmation that the Larson boys had confessed—his grim expression spoke of bad news. She clasped her hands together in a tight hold. "What is it?"

"I spoke to Tad and Hollis Larson. They denied the story your son told but admitted being at the Stark place when Andrew started the fire."

"They lied to you."

He moved a few steps closer, his expression one of pity. "I'm afraid that's not all. Mr. Stark has regained bits of his memory. He thinks he remembers a boy with dark hair."

"He thinks? He isn't positive?"

"His mind's still cloudy."

"What about the other boys? Does he remember them?"

His cap spun in his hands. "No, ma'am."

"That doesn't prove my son was to blame."

"The Larson boys have dark hair."

Edythe whirled at the statement from the oh-so-familiar voice. "Barrett." She hadn't noticed him standing near the staircase. Why was he here?

Barrett stepped forward. "What's next for Andy?"

"I'm afraid he'll need to report to a judge in the morning, Mr. Seaton."

Edythe's gaze locked on the police officer. "Reform school?"

"That will be up to the judge, Mrs. Westin."

She marched to her father. "Do something before my son is sent away for no reason. Talk to the judge."

"I know Judge Griffin. If I try to intervene, it could worsen Andrew's situation."

"What could be worse than sending a child away from his family? To lock him up?"

Barrett moved closer. "We'll think of something, Edy."

Edythe took a step toward him with an impulse to close the gap between them and fall into his embrace, to let him comfort her. But she stopped, determined to stand on her own, to face this situation with the type of gumption none of the men here had ever credited her with possessing. "We? It's my understanding there is no *we*."

EDY AIMED A SCORCHING glare at Barrett and brushed past all three men on the way to the staircase. "If you will excuse me, I need to see my son."

Barrett stood by as she ascended the stairs with quiet footsteps and a graceful motion that never failed to mesmerize him.

He should not have left it to the police to look into Andy's accusation against the Larsons. He shouldn't have allowed his difficulty with Edy to get in the way of his duties as Andy's lawyer.

She was right on another point. Those boys lied.

Officer Brennan cleared his throat. "Judge Danby, please have young Mr. Westin at the police station by nine o'clock tomorrow morning."

"He'll be there." The judge saw the policeman out and turned to Barrett, his lips set in a firm line. "Obviously, both of us have fences to mend."

Barrett's upward gaze landed on the empty hallway at the top of the stairs. He relived the feeling of Edy's hand on his shoulder as they stood near Wynn's grave. After she'd left, he stayed there for more than hour, grieving and praying for wisdom.

Today, he hadn't the time to lament the situation. Somehow, he had to figure out a way to prove the Larson brothers lied and free Andy from the threat of reform school. And he must do so before tomorrow morning.

"Mr. B. J." Timmy tugged on Barrett's coat. "Come see my experiment."

"I'm afraid I don't have time right now, son. I have work to do."

"Well, when you come back, maybe you can help me like you did with the fingerprints."

"Sure. I'll see you—" An idea halted Barrett halfway to the front door. He spun. "Timmy, did you get Andy's fingerprints?"

"Yes, sir."

"May I see them?"

The eight-year-old ran upstairs and returned with a sheet of paper bearing his brother's name. He handed it to Barrett. "See that scar on his thumb? He cut himself on barbed wire one day, so his are easy to identify."

Barrett had seen the scar the day Andy cleaned the fish. He'd counted on it marring the thumbprint and studied the interruption in the inked swirls. "Good work, Timmy. May I borrow this?"

"Don't lose it."

"I won't."

If all went well, the Trouble Brothers would soon sing to the police of their guilt.

Chapter Thirty

Edythe knocked on her son's bedroom door. She'd left him an hour ago after drying his tears and drying her own. Telling him of the Larson brothers' lies and the possible consequence for his life was the hardest thing she had ever done. His little body quaked with fear when she held him in her arms, never wanting to let go.

"Andy, it's time for supper. Wash up and come downstairs."

No doubt the whole family would waste Mrs. Cameron's good meal. Word traveled through the house in a matter of minutes after the officer departed, and it left them all without appetites, even her father. But they might think better with at least something in their stomachs.

With no response, she knocked a second time and turned the knob. "Andy?"

Edythe scanned every empty corner, then knelt and looked under the bed. "Andy, where are you?"

She searched every bedroom, calling his name, to no avail. Where had he gone?

Finding her father in the drawing room, words rushed from her mouth in a panic. "Andy is gone."

The judge dropped the newspaper he'd been reading and looked at her. "Gone where?"

"I don't know. He isn't in his room or anywhere in the house."

"Well, he must be somewhere close. Did you look in the yard?"

After the two of them and the twins scoured every room in the house and every foot of Danby property, including the small stable, Edythe gripped the kitchen counter, using it to hold herself up. "He's run away."

"Now, you don't know that for a fact." Her father laid a hand on the wrist he'd once bruised and gave it a gentle squeeze, his flesh warm and comforting. "Even if he did, he can't have gone far. I'll search the neighborhood."

While he was gone, Edythe paced the kitchen floor and peered out the window. If only she would see Andy hiking through the backyard, but the encroaching darkness enabled her to see little more than shadows. Thinking of her baby wandering alone in the dark of an autumn night—upset, fearful, and probably chilled—a powerful sense of the old helplessness washed over her.

Helpless?

No. She couldn't remain in this state. She must do something. Pressing her fingers to her temples, she mumbled, "Think, Edythe. Where would Andy have gone?"

She straightened. Had he gone to Barrett for counsel or comfort?

She called to the twins and instructed them to tell their grandfather she'd gone to Barrett's house to look for Andy, then dashed for the door, pausing to grab a cloak and a lantern.

Within minutes she'd hitched Jester to the gig. As she drove the horse toward the street, Mr. Peters chased the vehicle and jumped onto the seat next to her, rocking the body of the conveyance and looking entirely too joyful at the prospect of a ride.

She urged the horse into a trot. "I don't have time to convince you to stay here, Mr. Peters, so hold on."

BARRETT SAT ACROSS the table from Officer Brennan, pulled from his pocket the sheet of paper he'd gotten from Timothy, and placed it on the table inside the familiar small room of the police station.

"Unless you have evidence to prove the Westin boy didn't set that fire, there's not much I can do for you, Mr. Seaton."

"I think I have a way of getting that evidence but will need your help." Barrett pushed the paper with Andy's fingerprint across the table. "This has Andy's thumbprint. He said he never touched the board. I'm asking you to examine it for that print. I think you can agree that it would have been impossible for him to hit Mr. Stark hard enough to knock him out without using both hands, including his thumbs."

The man's eyes narrowed as though he tried to see the impossibility in his mind. "I expect so."

"If I'm right, you won't find that print on the board."

"You know fingerprints aren't admissible in court cases."

"You and I know that, but do the Larson brothers? I doubt it. A little pressure while telling them there's proof Andy never touched that wood might convince them to tell the truth."

The officer scratched the back of his head. "I don't know, Mr. Seaton."

"If we don't try, we'll send an innocent child to a reform school." Barrett raised the paper in his hand. "I'm not advocating for a lie. What I hope is that being faced with an impossibility, those boys will confess on their own."

"That's only if we don't find Andrew Westin's fingerprints on the board."

"Understood." It was a gamble, one that might prove to be Andy's undoing, but it also might prove he didn't injure Mr. Stark.

"Wait here. I'll see what I can do."

Officer Brennan walked out of the room, leaving the door open. While Barrett waited, sudden, commanding shouts and heavy footfalls drew him into the main room of the police station.

Two officers scuffled with a man who attempted to break free of their hold and run for the exit. The officers spun the man around, giving Barrett a good view of his face.

Vincent Dulong.

Barrett walked up to the front counter. "What's going on?"

The officer behind the counter glared at Claude Dulong's son. "The idiot thought that as long as he confessed to the murder of his father, we would say all is forgiven."

Barrett jerked his gaze back to the young man. So far, the officers maintained their hold. "He confessed to the Dulong murder?"

"With a little persuasion from his mother."

Barrett studied the swollen bruise on the man's face. "Her work?"

"Seems she did a little investigating of her own after your visit and found the rest of that telegram in her son's room. The young man was known to be spoiled, mostly by her, but she gave him what for when she learned the truth of how and why her husband died."

As soon as he'd connected Vincent Dulong with the paper he'd found in the shack, Barrett had given Officer Souter his suspicions involving Asa Osbourne. He'd insisted they look for both men but only anticipated Dulong's son to be questioned about the embezzlement, not the murder. He'd credited Osbourne with that crime. "Is his confession trustworthy?"

"We think so. Evidently, Claude Dulong contacted an Army friend of his, some muckety-muck, and learned his son had been caught drunk on guard duty. The Army gave him six months hard labor, but when Vincent got out, he told everyone he'd earned an honorable discharge. Somehow, the other man we're looking for discovered the truth and tried to blackmail the elder Dulong into embezzling from the brewery."

So Barrett was right about Osbourne but wrong about the role of Vincent Dulong. He'd looked at the murder as one of rage, yet imagined Osbourne as cold and calculating. He should have seen the two didn't go together. "What set off Vincent to kill his father?"

"The old man said no to the embezzlement. He'd had enough of the son's antics. When Vincent learned he would sink or swim on his own, he became furious. He figured hearing of his bad behavior wouldn't have set well with his fiancée's respectable family, and she might call off the wedding."

High-pitched screams and screeches came from the young Dulong as he continued to struggle for freedom. The policeman grimaced at the sound but remained behind the counter, appearing confident in the skill of his fellow officers to bring their prisoner under submission.

The officer shook his head. "What a sad state."

Sad, indeed. "Have you found Osbourne?"

"Not yet."

Tanner had called him a ghost. He'd certainly disappeared.

With a violent yank, Dulong wrenched free. His feet stuttered back, sending him into Barrett who, for a moment, was knocked off-balance too. Before Dulong could lurch away, Barrett leaned forward and grabbed the man, encompassing the flailing arms with his own.

Dulong tried to drive an elbow into Barrett's ribs, giving them a glancing blow. Using his greater height and strength, Barrett hung on, restraining him until the policemen managed to cuff their prisoner. With nods of thanks, they ushered the now-sobbing Dulong toward the cells at the back of the police station.

Barrett turned back to the officer behind the counter, breathing hard. His spirits soared with both satisfaction and exhilaration. He couldn't wait to reunite Jeremiah and Mary Quincy. "I'd like my client discharged."

"I've already started the paperwork, Mr. Seaton."

"Thank you."

Barrett sobered. Osbourne hadn't done the stabbing, but the mysterious man embodied a danger that must be stopped before someone else was hurt.

EDYTHE TUGGED THE REINS, halting Jester in front of Barrett's house. She turned to the dog. "Stay!" Not that she expected the order to be obeyed.

By now, complete darkness had fallen, yet no light shown through the front windows. Perhaps they were in the kitchen. She beat on the front door and called Barrett's name, waited a few seconds, and beat again. With no answer, the hope of finding her son here plummeted along with the evening's temperature.

Now what? She spun toward the street and rubbed her forehead as if rubbing an answer into her brain. Where else would Andy have gone?

She should have seen something like this coming. When she told him the Larson boys blamed him, red mottled his face and his eyes darkened. No, he'd said. They were to blame for everything.

Could he have gone to the boys' house to confront them?

Edythe trotted to the street and started at the dark figure on the seat of the gig. She had forgotten Mr. Peters. "Good boy for obeying."

The day Andy told Officer Brennan what happened at the Stark place, he also told the policeman where to find the Larson brothers, so she turned Jester in that direction.

A few minutes later, she pulled up in front of a small house, its yard hemmed in by a horseshoe-shaped clump of trees. Blackness surrounded the ramshackle structure like an ominous prophecy, but a dim light glowed inside. Oddly, it gave that portion of the house an even more tumbledown and eerie appearance.

If she were sensible, she'd drive on. But Andy could be inside.

When it came to her child, she'd risk her welfare in a moment to see that he was safe.

She glanced at her shaggy companion. While not known for his competence as a guard dog, Mr. Peters' sheer size might deter any threats. The dog stared at the house. A low growl emanated from his throat, encouraging Edythe. He might be reacting to her apprehension, or he could have hidden talents none of them realized.

"Let's go, Mr. Peters." The dog jumped to the ground and followed her to the house.

After several knocks, the door opened and a boy a few years older than Andy glared at her. "What do you want?"

A younger child—presumably Hollis—joined his brother. With enlarged eyes, he struck Edythe as terrified. She would blame his fear on Mr. Peters, but the boy hadn't given the dog a second glance.

She drew in a breath of courage. Heavens, the bulky Tad Larson was intimidating for someone so young. "I'm Mrs. Westin. I'm looking for Andy."

"He ain't here."

A short, simple, and unsatisfactory response. "Have you seen him in the last few hours?"

The dog growled again as though warning the boy to tell the truth.

"I told you he ain't here."

Edythe used the little light available to examine an ugly mark on Tad's cheek. Someone had hit the boy recently. She couldn't imagine him permitting Hollis to do such damage without taking his revenge, but the younger child displayed no visible marks.

Where were their parents? "I'd like to speak with your mother and father."

"They ain't here either."

Mr. Peters sniffed the ground around the wooden steps and skimmed his nose along what seemed to be a trail that rounded the corner of the house.

The younger boy gripped the arm of his brother. "Tad."

Tad grimaced at the animal. "We don't like dogs on our property, lady. Get him off."

Sarah Jane's dog barked, eager for her attention. "I'd say there's something about you or your property *he* doesn't like."

Rather than call Mr. Peters back, she tracked him to the rear of the yard where he stopped near the door of a shed and whined. The sound of footfalls shuffling through grass and fallen leaves told her the Larsons kept pace behind her.

"What's in this building?"

"None of your business." Tad picked up a stick and threw it at Mr. Peters, striking him on the hindquarters. The dog yelped and ran to the safety of the trees.

Edythe had held to her waning patience by a thread. She wheeled on the boys. "Stop that!"

Mr. Peters had run off, but he'd led her here for a reason.

"Mama?"

She almost missed the faint voice coming from inside the building. "Andy?"

"Mama, in here."

Tad Larson edged between Edythe and the door. After shoving the teen aside with a physical strength that surprised her, she raised the thick and solid board laid across the door. Yanking the wooden handle, she entered the small space. Her nose wrinkled at the smell of oil and the accumulated dust that threatened a sneeze. "Where are you, Andy?"

He rose from a corner of the murky interior and crossed the space, a large pail in his hand. Behind them, the door slammed shut and the board on the outside fell into place with a loud and menacing thud.

Outside, Hollis shouted, "What are you doing, Tad?"

Then nothing.

Left in blackness as intense as the despised cellar of her childhood, Edythe clutched her son and struggled not to scream.

Chapter Thirty-one

Once Dulong was escorted to a cell, Barrett returned to the room where Officer Brennan had left him.

Time ticked by. The officer finally reappeared, carrying the board and the sheet of paper Barrett had borrowed from Timmy. "We found nothing to match the thumb print you gave us. You realize, of course, we can't take your word for it that this print belongs to Andrew Westin. We'll need to get our own sample."

"I'm hoping you won't need it. Will you go with me to the Larson house?"

"Now?"

"Now."

The officer released a heavy breath. "I suppose it won't hurt to ask the boys a few more questions."

Minutes later, Barrett stopped the carriage in front of a place as daunting as the older boy's glower. "What are the parents like?"

"Can't say."

He eyed Brennan. "You didn't meet them when you questioned the boys?"

"The children were home alone at the time."

Children had few enough rights in society. They should at least enjoy the right to have their parents present when speaking with the police.

Noticing a faint light in the broken-down house, the two men approached the door and Barrett knocked. On the other side of the wood, the hiss of an argument ensued. Though he couldn't understand all that was said, he recognized the voices as belonging to two young males.

Brennan called out, "Open up to the police."

One of the voices, perhaps the younger boy, squealed and the pitch grew higher. A few seconds later, everything quieted and the door opened, revealing a portion of the oldest Larson boy's scowling face. "They ain't here."

Barrett cocked his head at the statement. "Who isn't here?"

He glanced behind him. "Uh...our folks. Yeah. They ain't here."

"When will they return?"

"Don't know."

The answer left Barrett with a dilemma. Time dwindled for Andy. Did they question the boys as planned or wait until the parents returned?

Brennan showed no such quandary and pushed the door open, shoving Tad a few steps back. "We want some answers, boys. Why did you assault Mr. Stark and burn his shed?"

Barrett walked into the two-room house after the officer. Although he wasn't above using a little intimidation when warranted, he hadn't intended to browbeat the children. He'd hoped to present them with the facts in a more subtle manner and see where it led. At least, at first.

The smell of burned beans—the most pleasant of the odors hanging about the house—reminded Barrett he hadn't had his supper. Not that the boys' meal tempted him.

A few faded clothes were strewn over worn furniture that hadn't seen a dusting in ages. Trash littered the floors, and a draft from a broken window chilled the room. In a far corner, a half-drawn curtain hid a portion of an unmade bed, and a half-filled burlap sack lay on the floor beside it.

The younger boy's quick breaths and contorted face continued to reflect his fear. He—Hollis was it?—ducked behind his brother. "You ain't gonna hit us, are you?"

"No, boy, I won't hit you." The officer's tone softened—some. "But I want the truth."

Barrett peered closer at the mark on Tad's cheek. "Looks as though someone's already hit you. Who?"

The boy's hand sprang to cover the reddish mark. "Nobody. I tripped."

In the past, Barrett had seen the faces of women who had "tripped" and come away with skin that turned black and blue.

His gaze drifted to the clothes. Something about them, other than their shabby condition, intrigued him. "Where are your parents?"

Hollis gulped, and Tad said, "I told you. They ain't here."

"They 'ain't here' now or not at all?"

The policeman studied the room, his frown revealing he'd come to the same conclusion as Barrett. These children lived alone. "Sit down boys."

"You can't—"

"I said sit down."

Hollis obeyed immediately, Tad with reluctance. Both sat on the edge of the tattered old davenport planted in front of a wall covered in yellowed newspaper.

"Now answer Mr. Seaton's question. Where are your parents?"

"Ma's dead."

Tad glared at his brother. "I told you to keep your mouth shut."

Barrett knelt in front of Hollis. If either of them told the truth, it would come from the youngest and most frightened. Time to divide and conquer. "And your father?"

The boy glanced at his brother, then his gaze stuck to the badge on Officer Brennan's uniform coat. "He left a month ago and ain't come back."

Tad snorted. "No loss for us."

What had these boys suffered in their young lives?

Barrett arrived at the house wanting nothing more than to see them punished for their lies and violent deeds...for justice to prevail and Andy freed from blame. At the same time, he wished to find the man who'd ducked out on his responsibility to care for his children, to raise them to become moral, decent human beings.

Brennan whipped out a notebook and ink pad from a pocket of his uniform. "You boys place your fingers on this pad one at a time, ink them up, and then press them to the paper."

Hollis began to shake. "W-why?"

"We already know the fingerprints we found on the board don't belong to Andrew Westin, so that leads me to conclude one of you struck Mr. Stark." The officer provided the explanation with the ease of ordering a sandwich for his lunch. He held out the ink pad, but the boys merely stared at it. "Come on, now."

Tad sat back and crossed his arms. "We don't have to do that."

Barrett laid his hand on Hollis' arm. "When a man does something wrong, he needs to take responsibility. He doesn't compound it by blaming someone else. This is your opportunity to be a man and tell the truth of what happened that night."

Tad grabbed his brother's other arm. "Don't do it, Hollis. They're trying to trick you."

Tears filled Hollis' eyes. "B-but, Tad, they'll see. They'll know."

"I said shut up." Tad's command lacked harshness, and Barrett waited for the facts he'd come to hear.

EDYTHE'S EYES STRAINED to adjust to the darkness inside the windowless building, just as her nerves strained against the temptation to panic.

Her breathing quickened and her head grew light. She fought

the memories the entrapment raised, the bone-shaking terror over the possibility of never being found. In the quiet, she heard the cackle of her grandfather and his taunts about graves. He'd claimed to be teasing her, but as far as Edythe was concerned, the man had been insane.

Beating back the impulse to slide into a state of hysteria, she employed her role as a mother—the protector of her son—and dwelled on the fury she felt toward the Larson boys and herself. How reckless of her to turn her back on them as she had done with her grandfather. She supposed she should consider herself fortunate they hadn't knocked her or Andy unconscious as they'd done to poor Mr. Stark.

She swallowed. What if they set the shed on fire?

The darkness closed in again and the air became damp and musty. *Stop it, Edythe.*

Rather than focusing on the fear from having once been buried in a cellar, Edythe focused on the moment her father found her—his gentle hold, the reassuring murmurings in her ear, the outrage over the situation.

For too many years, she had assigned her father's harsh character to God. Until recently, she hadn't recognized that her heavenly Father waited for her to turn to Him, to trust Him, to realize He couldn't abide the wickedness of sinful people. And it was the sins of people that made life difficult.

As she'd recently chosen to trust that God loved her, she also accepted that the judge did, too, even during times when his actions contradicted that love.

"I'm sorry, Mama." Her son's soft voice suited the quiet inside the shed. "I tried to get them to admit they lied."

How he thought to accomplish something like that, she couldn't... Her eyes widened. "Did you hit Tad?"

"Yes, ma'am, and I told him I'd give him another punch and

another until he told the truth." Rather than shame, his voice projected pride. "That's when they dragged me in here and locked the door."

While disapproving of Andy's method, Edythe marveled at her son's courage in taking on a bigger boy. It encouraged her to fight harder against *her* fear.

After closing her eyes to pray, she suppressed a desire to laugh. What difference was there in whether her eyes were opened or closed when she couldn't see much anyway? But it was the stance one took when praying, wasn't it?

Lord, in these past weeks I've accepted that You are more than a disciplinarian, more than a puppet master seeking to control every aspect of Your children's lives, and that You love me because I am Your child. God, You know where we are and our circumstances. Grant us both calm and a way to freedom.

A peace she'd rarely known overcame her, and she knew the truth. In her ignorance, she had placed the control of her life in the wrong hands.

"What if they never admit to what they did, Mama? I don't want to go away to that place."

Edythe pulled him closer, both of them needing each other's warmth to combat the growing chill of the night. Besides, unable to see more than a dark outline of his frame, she hadn't let go of her son since finding him in the shed.

The two of them stood by the door, ready to escape whenever the boys returned. Surely, they planned to return.

"There's nothing to fear, because I love you, Andy, and God loves you. As long as we believe that, we're as free as if we could walk right out that door, because it's fear that holds us captive."

Her son drew in a breath and grew taller in her hold. "Don't worry, we'll get out of here."

"Yes, we will."

The spacing of the homes along the road meant that the neighbors likely hadn't heard her previous cries for help. Certainly no one had come to rescue them. But one more attempt wouldn't hurt.

Edythe beat on the door again and called out. She pressed her ear to the wood but heard nothing except the eerie hoot of an owl somewhere in the woods.

This building was solid compared to the ramshackle condition of the house. "Did you notice anything that might help us get out of here, Andy?"

"I didn't see much before they shut the door, but I found this pail." He slapped the metal and the tinny sound rang out. "I figured I'd hit them with it."

She winced. "Let's try not to strike anyone again if we can help it."

Edythe reached out and felt around the area near the door, searching for anything to help her break through to the outside. Perhaps something to loosen the hinges? Her fingers touched the silky threads of a spider's web along the frame. She yanked her hand away and shivered as she dusted off the sticky strands.

No fear, remember?

She extended her arm. Ordering Andy to stay with her, she used her hands to walk around the walls of the shed. She shuffled her feet, careful not to trip over something unseen on the floor. Her hands explored shelves holding cans, some empty, some containing a liquid she couldn't identify in the dark. She grabbed the heaviest one and pushed it at her son. "Hold this."

Edythe investigated the rest of the shelves and walls until her hand landed on something metal—a pipe, maybe. She raised the item, slid her hand from one end to the other, and laughed. "Now *this* I know how to use." She gripped the body of the crowbar and held it against her.

A rustling under the shed caught her attention. She halted and cocked her head to listen.

Andy whispered, "What's that?"

"I don't know. A raccoon?" *Oh, please, not a skunk.*

The rustling stopped under their feet and a whine took its place, followed by sniffing evident through the spacing of the shed's floorboards.

Edythe laughed with relief. "I think it's Mr. Peters."

"You brought him?"

"He invited himself, but without him I wouldn't have found you." She crouched and placed her palm over a slight gap between two boards. Another whine rolled from the dog's throat. "I wonder how he fit under the shed. I doubt there's much room between the floor and the ground."

"But he did it."

"Yes, and if that colossal dog could do it, you can too."

Edythe inserted the claw of the crowbar into the gap.

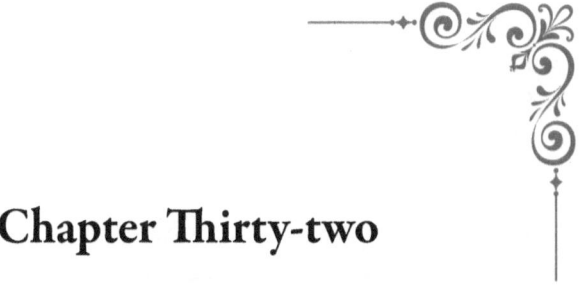

Chapter Thirty-two

A sob broke from Hollis Larson's throat. "I didn't mean to. It was an accident."

Barrett turned his head to see Brennan's eyebrows arched, evidence they both had expected to hear Hollis blame his brother for hurting Mr. Stark. "What happened?"

"He was gonna catch us."

"Mr. Stark?"

The boy nodded. "While Tad and Andy yelled at each other, I was smoking inside the shed and dropped my matchstick into a bunch of old rags. Before I knew it, the shed caught fire and—"

"Hollis, no."

The boy ignored his brother's warning. "The man grabbed Tad by the hair and hurt him. I didn't know what to do, so I hit him with the board."

Barrett's pity for Hollis swelled with each word of the boy's quiet confession.

"I didn't mean to hurt him. I just wanted him to let go of my brother."

Officer Brennan drew in an audible breath and released it in a slow exhale. "All right, boys. Come with me." He grasped the arm of each defeated brother and led them to the door.

Barrett extinguished the lamp in the house and walked outside. A bark drew his attention to the back and the large, shadowed shape of a dog standing by an outbuilding. The animal loped toward them and jumped up on Barrett with a familiar, exuberant friendliness. "Mr. Peters? What are you doing here?"

"You know the dog?"

He turned to the officer. "He belongs to Sarah Jane Westin."

Mr. Peters ran back to the shed and jumped on the door.

Barrett ran to the building, dislodged the bar across the door, and tossed it into the grass, then he flung open the door. Seeing raised arms wielding a large paint can—he jerked back. "Whoa! Edy, it's me."

"Barrett?" She dropped the can and rushed into his arms.

The blood pounding in Barrett's eardrums had almost drowned out the voice he knew better than anyone else's, the one he wanted to hear for the rest of his life. "Are you all right?"

Any compassion he'd felt for the Larson boys dissolved. Aware of Edy's fear of dark places, he had in mind to shake each brother until his teeth rattled. The Trouble Brothers, indeed. What she must have endured in the pitch blackness.

"Yes." She gasped. "Andy."

When she turned around and faded into the darkness of the shed, he went after her.

"Watch where you step, Barrett."

With the door open, moonlight illuminated the interior. He saw a large hole in the floor and a few boards thrown to the side. Andy popped up from the hole, only his head and shoulders showing.

Barrett helped the boy onto solid flooring. "What's going on?"

"Mama found a crowbar and pried up the floorboards so I could escape and open the door."

Amazing. "Mark told me you employed a mean crowbar."

Edy laughed. "I've discovered it's one of my talents." She wrapped her arms around Barrett's neck and pressed her cold cheek against his. "I prayed someone would come. I'm so glad He sent my knight."

"From what I can see, I rode in too late. You, my former damsel in distress, had everything under control."

Officer Brennan dragged the Larsons with him to the door of the shed. "What's this all about?"

Edy nodded to the boys. "They locked us inside."

The policeman frowned at Tad. "You just keep making more problems for yourselves, don't you? Come on." The three of them tromped through the grass and leaves toward the carriage.

"I had no idea you were here." Barrett led the two of them from the shed and scanned the area, seeing no horse and buggy but his. "Surely you didn't walk."

"Andy did. I drove here looking for him." She turned toward the boys. "Where is my horse and gig?"

Tad jerked to a stop and glanced over his shoulder. "In the woods."

The scattered clothes. The burlap sack. Barrett ventured a question. "Were you planning to steal the vehicle and leave town?"

"No. We figured to *borrow* it to look for our pa."

Edy caught Barrett's arm. "Let's leave it be for now. I want to get Andy home before..." Her voice faded.

"Don't worry about Andy." Barrett scuffed the boy's hair. "The Larson brothers admitted everything. We'll talk to the judge tomorrow. I have a feeling you won't be going anywhere, son." *Son.* He wanted to spend the rest of his life saying it.

Andy let out a *whoop*.

Edy's hold on Barrett's arm tightened. "How did you get them to tell the truth?"

"Timmy gets the credit for taking Andy's fingerprints. I remembered the scar I saw on Andy's thumb and knew that if his prints weren't on that board it would give Officer Brennan reason to doubt the Larson boys' story."

"You took a chance that Andy hadn't touched it."

"I believed him when he said he hadn't. Compared to the alternative, it didn't seem much of a risk."

"Thank you for not walking out on us. I'm sorry for implying we didn't need you."

"You were worried about your son, and I deserved it, because I did walk out on you for a time—emotionally. But I'm back, Edy. I'm back to stay."

EDYTHE STRETCHED HER legs, relaxing on the blanket she'd spread over the grass a few yards from their spot on the river. Childhood laughter rang out, a carefree laughter she'd missed for too long. Finally, her children experienced the freedom due their younger years—the freedom to be children.

As she'd done often since leaving that horrid shed, she shut her eyes and praised her merciful heavenly Father, who had worked everything out for the good of her family.

Barrett sat on the blanket next to her. He stared off across the river. "How are things going with your father?"

"He rules the roost as always, but life is better—more peaceful." She smiled. "He tries to be less demanding, and I try to be respectful but firm. So far, we've done well to meet in the middle."

Barrett pointed to Andy and her father fishing side by side from the riverbank. "That looks promising."

"It's a fragile truce. Andy hasn't completely forgiven him for the years of callousness, and I'm not sure the judge knows how to fully atone for what he's done."

"Change takes time. What he's doing now will go a long way in bringing them back together."

Hope sprang up inside at Barrett's mention of change. "You and my father are on pleasanter terms."

"As with Andy, it's a fragile truce, but I think we understand one another better."

"I'm glad." With time, they might all understand one another better. "How are the Quincys?"

"Happy to have the ordeal over. Hopefully, the police find Osbourne soon. He's wreaked too much havoc in this town and on the people he's come in contact with. I'll be looking for him, along with the police."

Edythe stared out over the water, accepting his need to bring the guilty to justice. "Even with all the anger my family has experienced, it's hard to imagine a child murdering a parent. I feel sorry for Mrs. Dulong. She's lost both a husband and a son." Edythe thanked God she hadn't found herself in the same situation.

"Unfortunately, she'd spoiled him. It's now a case of reaping what's been sown."

"Parents walk a fine line between too much and not enough discipline. It's hard to determine when to constrain a child's activities and when to turn him loose to discover his own path." Mrs. Dulong was too lenient with her son. The Larson boys' father both abusive and neglectful. Edythe's father? He meant well...much of the time. And her? She was learning to discipline her children with resolve while tempering it with love and grace. "What will happen to Tad and Hollis?"

"I'm afraid their ending won't be as happy as Jeremiah and Mary's. Like Osbourne, they've done a lot of damage to themselves and others."

Andy's repentance before the judge earned him a lecture for not telling the truth earlier. He was sent home with the instruction to mind his p's and q's. The Larson boys still had to learn their fate. "Do you think they will go to the reform school?"

"It's almost certain, especially since the police haven't located their father." Barrett grasped her hand, his gaze uncertain. "Would it upset you if I helped them?"

SANDRA ARDOIN

Edythe explored her feelings on the matter. "While part of me remains angry over what they did to my children, I pity them for their upbringing. I'm sure it wasn't easy and contributed to their cruelty toward others."

"No one could claim they're angels, but if it makes you feel better, I believe Tad's painting the bullseye on Snowman and locking you and Andy in the shed were meant to protect his brother, who struck Mr. Stark out of panic."

"Hollis also set fire to the Starks' shed."

"With the help of oily rags and a dropped matchstick. An accident. Hollis isn't a bad child. I think the smoking was a way to please Tad. I know what it's like to look up to an older brother."

Barrett had told her of Wynn's confession and that he understood her promise to keep it to herself. Together, they mourned his brother's loss.

Edythe was struck by both the beauty and risk involved in relationships. None were perfect. Some were destructive. Others suffered from misunderstandings. Those worthy of fighting for required the courage and determination to do so.

"In answer to your question, no, it won't upset me. Do your best for those boys."

He clasped her hand. "You are one of the kindest people I've ever met. I admire you for it."

"Only admiration?" She waited to see if he'd recognize the question he'd asked her the day of the bicycle-riding lesson.

His lips twitched, telling her he had made the connection. "It was never only admiration, Edy."

He left off the part that told her it would never be only admiration, but she had to know. "Do you love me in the same way you did years ago?"

He drew back in feigned shock. "This newfound boldness is quite staggering, Mrs. Westin. At the same time, it's charming."

"Learning my boldness charms you doesn't answer my question." She held her breath, longing for him to acknowledge the rekindling of the trust between them—the foundation for a solid love.

Barrett's grin slipped into a frown. "The truth is I'm no longer the same young man, Edy."

His response squeezed her insides until they ached. Her head dipped. "I see."

He caught her chin and tilted her head upward until she was forced to look into those beautiful umber eyes. Their gaze bore into hers with a passion and earnestness he'd never shown her in their younger years. "See this, Mrs. Westin. See the depth of my feelings for you. I don't want to love you the way I did then. I want to love you better. I want to love you as a grown man—a man of maturity. A man of forgiveness. Time and experience have taught me the fragility of the bonds that tie two people together and the dedication and communication it takes to keep those bonds from breaking. I want to love you for as long as we live. I do, and I will."

Her spirit soared. "I've changed, too, Barrett. I don't love you as someone who needs a protector or a refuge. I love you as a woman seeking to be a helpmeet, a partner in life...if you'll have me."

Her father paused in passing them on his way from the riverbank. "Oh, for crying out loud, Seaton. Kiss my daughter and get it over with."

Edythe grinned when her father winked at her and hiked away. He might often be irascible, but at this moment she appreciated his peevishness.

Barrett grimaced. "As I said, a fragile truce. I don't think the judge and I will ever see eye to eye on most things." He leaned closer. "But I'll admit, in this instance, we're in agreement."

With a slight tilt of his head, his lips touched hers with restrained tenderness, as though he waited for her to pull away. She gripped the front of his shirt and urged him closer, issuing her own demand—one he met until her head swam with giddiness.

A wet tongue slurped over her ear and temple. To the hoots and claps of three children, she wrenched away from Mr. Peters' effort to join in on the kiss.

Barrett laughed and handed her a handkerchief, then he jumped up and chased both squealing boys into the water, shouting merry claims to dunk them.

Edythe's father stood off to the side, his mouth puckered but unable to hide the hint of a grin peeking from within his mustache.

This was the future. Through good times and bad, this was family. This was love.

A Word to Readers

I tend to complain about the length of time it takes me to complete a book. Months. And months.

But, you know, I find the Lord teaches me things as I write. One of the things I was reminded of while writing *Rekindling Trust* was that God has His timing, so there's no choice but to hang on for the ride. Sure, I've known that for a long time, yet sometimes I need to see things in action for those lessons to sink in.

In my desire to get a book written, I inevitably find out that some of the best ideas pop into my head late in the process. I'll think things are done, the story is told and everyone lives happily ever after. Then, all of a sudden, God inserts an idea into my head that's perfect for the story. He reminds me that I need time for those ideas to percolate to the surface like the rocks in my yard. If I'm in too big a hurry, I'm not only shortchanging the story, I'm shortchanging you. I don't want to do either one.

So I'm not one of those writers who is capable of putting out numerous books a year, but as long as I'm putting out stories you enjoy reading, that's what matters, right?

Please consider leaving a short, honest review on a retail site that carries *Rekindling Trust* and/or Goodreads. No need to get fancy. A couple of sentences without spoilers will do, or a star rating. Both will be greatly appreciated!

Don't forget to look for the third and final novel in the Widow's Might Series. To learn of its release or about upcoming specials, subscribe to my Love and Faith in Fiction newsletter and get *Unwrapping Hope*, the prequel novella to the series, as my thank you.

Happy reading!

Sandra

Acknowledgments

People can tell you, but until you've tried it, you won't understand how hard it is to write a book. At least, I didn't before I started on this journey years ago. But we writers can't take more than a few steps without the help of others.

As always, I'm so grateful to you, Heidi Chiavaroli. You have my back and tell me when certain things aren't working—in this case, my weak-willed heroine—so I can fix them.

To my brainstormers—Jerusha Agen, Angie Arndt, Marie Coutu: Thank you for your insight. I enjoy batting ideas back and forth with you all.

To those of you in the Corner Room: You bless me with your support and the way you share word of my stories with others. You are a joy and an encouragement!

My editor, Lynne Tagawa, is a brave woman to tackle my manuscript. Seriously.

And a mighty thank you to the Lord, whose child I am.

Historical Romances by
Sandra Ardoin

About the Author

AS AN AUTHOR OF HEARTWARMING and award-winning historical romance, Sandra Ardoin engages readers with page-turning stories of love and faith. Rarely out of reach of a book, she's also an armchair sports enthusiast, country music listener, and seldom says no to eating out. Visit her at www.sandraardoin.com. Connect with her on BookBub, Facebook, Twitter, and Goodreads.